AN English BOY IN NEW YORK

AN ENGLISH BOY IN NEW YORK

T.S. EASTON

HOT
KEY
BOOKS

First published in Great Britain in 2014 by Hot Key Books
Northburgh House, 10 Northburgh Street, London EC1V 0AT

A CIP catalogue record for this book is available from the British Library.

ISBN: 978-1-4714-0149-7

1

This book is typeset in 10.5 Berling LT Std using Atomik ePublisher

Printed and bound by Clays Ltd, St Ives Plc

Hot Key Books supports the Forest Stewardship Council (FSC),
the leading international forest certification organisation, and is
committed to printing only on Greenpeace-approved FSC-certified paper.

www.hotkeybooks.com

Hot Key Books is part of the Bonnier Publishing Group
www.bonnierpublishing.com

For Tilly

Tuesday 16th April

Haven't been able to write for a while. After the excitement of the Knitting Championships, I've been spending the last few weeks trying to catch up with my studies. I've also had a number of orders for the Hoopie off the internet and been spending a lot of time with my girlfriend, Megan. Or trying to. In fact, we're currently struggling with some serious scheduling issues. A week ago I forced her to spend an hour or so sitting opposite me so that we could coordinate our movements.

'Right, let's get our diaries out,' I said.

Megan looked blank. 'Who has a diary these days?' she said. 'I just use my phone for that kind of thing.'

'But what if your phone runs out of battery?' I asked, shaking my head in disapproval.

'I'll charge it.'

'What if Lloyd Manning throws it in Hampton reservoir?'

'He only does that to *your* phone,' she pointed out.

Eventually we managed to sort out some dates to see each other. After some heavy compromise on my part, mind. I'll tell you what, Megan's a tough negotiator. It's like the Americans and the Iranians discussing the decommissioning of chemical weapons.

And being of the female species, she reserves the right to completely ignore all arrangements and just do what the hell she likes. As I found out a couple of days later.

'I thought we were seeing each other tomorrow?' I said as she kissed me on the cheek.

'I wanted to see you today,' she replied, smiling sweetly. 'Don't you want to see me?'

'It's not that,' I said. 'I like seeing you very much. Just . . . I prefer having an arrangement in place first.'

She gives me a look at that point and I have to pretend like I'm joking. But I am deadly serious. Nothing is more unsettling to me than spontaneity.

Plus, it is playing havoc with my knitting. How am I supposed to fill my Hoopie orders when young girls are floating around my room looking pretty and opening drawers and finding magazines and accidentally breaking bits off the ziggurat?

So. It's a work in progress. The relationship, I mean. The ziggurat's finished.

In other news, Mum's in trouble with the Magic Circle. They sent her a stern letter which I said they should have sent by owl if they're serious about the whole magic thing. She's under investigation for allegedly revealing details of a magic trick on Twitter. They reprinted the offending tweet.

@dcopperfield Thanks for wonderful new show last night. Amazing spectacle all thanks to mirror.

Which, admittedly, reads like she's suggesting that @dcopperfield was using a mirror to trick people rather than using actual magic. In reality Mum just forgot to type an @. She meant to write . . . *all thanks to @mirror* because she won the tickets through a competition in the *Daily Mirror*. Clear misunderstanding but it's started a bit of a Twitter storm, at least within the stage magician community.

Dad, meanwhile, is bereft at Frank Lampard's retirement from Chelsea.

'He's still in the England squad,' I pointed out.

'He never scores for England,' Dad said miserably.

I resisted stating the obvious, because ever since since I came out as a knitter, Dad's been making a real effort to be more supportive and embrace me as his only son. This means bonding activities such as marathon DVD evenings. My fault really, I made the mistake of telling Dad I'd hadn't completely hated watching *Band of Brothers* with him. So now he's bought the first two series of *Homeland*, which quite honestly might as well be the same three episodes playing over and over again as far as I'm concerned. I tend to switch off after the fifteen-minute opening credits with extended trumpet solo.

Spies, soldiers and trumpet music leave me cold. Surprisingly, I'd rather watch programmes about gangsters with saxophones. How's that for subverting the male knitter stereotype? But Dad's just not interested. It's hard to find common ground with a man who didn't like *The Sopranos*.

Wednesday 17th April

Just had the most boring discussion about the family holiday this year. But since neither I nor my sister Molly have any say whatsoever in what we do or where we go, I don't see why my parents even bother pretending to 'discuss' it with us.

The upshot of this 'discussion' is that we can't afford a proper holiday, so we're going hiking in Snowdonia next week with Dad's friends from the Camper Van Society. Yep. That's pretty much as dire as it sounds. I don't mind group holidays when we go camping in the summer, with Mum's friends. They're all lovely and put up bunting and know how to cook and the dads are funny and patient and Mum's friend Gina's daughter Pippa is rather pretty and wears tiny bikinis.

But we're not going camping with Mum's friends in July, we're hiking with Dad's friends in April. Dad's friends smoke cigars and drink cheap Pilsner lager and his friend Pete, who works for Royal Mail, is way too shouty and tells dodgy Islamophobic jokes. But the worst thing is that they all have sons around my age who do nothing but play aggressive games of football around the campsite and knock down other people's washing lines. Not my style, but I can hardly just sit in the van and knit. Can I?

Things could be better round here.

18th April

Things are looking up.

A huge parcel arrived today from KnitFair USA, which is

only the biggest and best knitting fair on the PLANET. And
with it, a letter from someone named Brandi.

Dear Ben,

*Congratulations on winning the English Knitting
Competition. We're so excited to be welcoming you to
this year's KnitFair USA.*

*My name is Brandi DeLacourt and I am a PR
executive for the Knitting Guild Association of
America. We're handling the PR for this year's
KnitFair USA and I'm thrilled that you'll be one of my
clients. There's already a lot of interest in you because
it's quite unusual for young men to be involved in
knitting. I've seen the articles in the UK press about
your amazing success. If it's OK with you, I'll be
arranging some interviews with interested media here
in NYC. Please sign the release form and send it back if
you're happy about doing a few interviews and events.*

*Please find enclosed two Executive Club class tickets
to New York. You'll be landing at JFK Airport. JFK
are the initials of John Fitzgerald Kennedy, one of our
famous presidents from history. I've arranged hotel
accommodation for you for a week. Please email to
let me know whether you want a twin, double or two
singles for you and your companion. The fair itself runs*

from Friday 17th May to Sun 19th May so you and your friend have a few days beforehand for sightseeing and hopefully some interviews.

New York can be an intimidating place for visitors but don't worry, I will meet you at the airport and take you to your hotel. I've enclosed a programme guide for the fair so you can plan which demonstrations, lectures, forums and so on you'd like to attend. We're proud to be unveiling the new KnitMaster 3000 knitting machine on the 19th, so that demonstration should definitely be in your schedule!

Please find enclosed tickets for you and your companion as well as four extra tickets you can give away on your blog.

I'm really looking forward to meeting you, Ben. Please do email me at the address below if you have any questions.

Yours,
  Brandi DeLacourt
  Knitting Guild Association of America
  4th Floor
  1276 5th Avenue
  New York, NY
  delacourtb@knitfair.com

Oh no. What a *disaster*! I won't be able to go hiking with Dad's friends, after all! No charred sausages. No stand-up rows between Mum and Pete, the Islamophobic postman. No bruised shins from pretending to enjoy playing football. No having to hide knitting in my sleeping bag.

Instead, I'll have to fly Executive Club class to New York with Megan Hooper, be forced to shop for wool in Bloomingdale's, be press-ganged into romantic walks through Central Park, and get force-fed Philly cheesesteak sandwiches and veal Parmesan. What a terrible, terrible blow.

6.34pm

'But we've had this trip booked for months!' Dad said, looking so desolate I nearly felt bad.

'It's SUCH terrible timing,' I agreed, shaking my head sadly.

'I'm really pleased for you,' Mum said. 'You'll have a great time. I'm a bit gutted you're going to leave me to face Islamophobic Pete on my own . . .'

'Shouty Pete, you mean,' Dad said. 'He's not Islamophobic. Not since the post office made him go on that awareness course.'

'Whatever,' Mum said. 'Frankly, I'm not sure I want to go hiking at all now. I was relying on Ben as my one source of intelligent company.'

'Thanks very much,' said Dad.

'Are you taking Megan with you?' Mum went on, regardless.

I nodded. 'That's the idea.'

She raised an eyebrow.

'You two haven't been . . . alone together . . . much,' she said slowly.

8

'We've been alone together,' I said.

'Not . . . *properly* alone, is what I mean,' she said. 'Have you?'

Oh. My. God.

'We've been alone together plenty, thank you very much,' I said quickly. 'I haven't had any complaints about our alone-time frequency. Or length.'

'OK. But you've never . . . flown all the way across the Atlantic with a girl before, have you?'

'No.'

'I thought not,' she said, nodding.

'Hang on,' I said. 'What do you mean?'

'I just want you to know, that if you have any questions about anything . . . in that area, then you can come to me any time.'

I was so horrified I forgot how to speak. I just shook my head vigorously.

'Or you could talk to your father, if you'd be more comfortable doing that?'

'No,' I said, finding a small voice. 'I don't think I would. I'll handle it on my own. Thanks.'

'Pleased to hear it,' she said. 'Just, take things easy, won't you? It takes a while to get the hang of . . . long-haul flights.'

I smiled weakly and fled. She is so embarrassing.

Friday 19th April

10.00am

I just got off the phone with Joz. The electricity in his house keeps going off for no reason, which means he keeps missing the end of programmes. He missed the last ten minutes of the new series of *Homeland* last night which he knows I am obliged to watch with Dad. Joz had phoned to see if I could fill him in. I don't think I was much help. I knitted through the last episode and may have missed some crucial plot twists. Also, I can never remember the names of the characters, or the names of the actors for that matter, just the films they used to be in.

'So the guy from *The Princess Bride* . . .' I began.

'Who?'

'The guy with the beard.'

'Saul?'

'Yeah, I think so. Anyway, he's talking to the girl from *Romeo and Juliet*.'

'What? Who?'

'You know. Her from *My So-Called Life*. Except now she's really old.'

'You mean Carrie?'

'Yeah. That's it, Carrie. So she's talking to the guy from *The Princess Bride*, when the bloke from *Band of Brothers* comes in.'

'Eh?'

'You know, Major Thingie, the ginger bloke.'

'Brodie?'

'Is that his name? Except now he's bald. The guy who was blown up by an IUD.'

'You mean an IED?'

'Is there a difference?' I asked impatiently.

'One's a bomb,' he said. 'And the other is a contraceptive

device.'

'Sorry, I get confused by military terms. And contraceptive terms, for that matter.'

'Quite an important difference though.'

'Yeah.'

'Oh, look, forget it,' he said. 'I'll just look it up online.'

'But what if the power goes off again?'

'Dammit!' he said.

'Maybe you should get an electrician around,' I suggested.

'Southerly Electricity have been around three times but can't find anything wrong,' he said. 'I reckon they think we're making it up.'

'Why would you make up something like that?'

'I know! Anyway, whenever they come around everything's working fine. But this morning it went off again and we couldn't make toast and the power shower wouldn't work, and Dad couldn't iron his shirt. We've got an electric loo upstairs and that wouldn't flush.'

'What about keeping a log?' I said.

'It was the log I needed to flush,' he replied. 'Why would I want to keep it?'

'I mean keep a diary, you knobber, detailing what times it goes off. Then you can compare it to your electricity usage and prove there's a problem.'

'You're a genius, Ben,' he said.

'It's been said before,' I admitted.

Saturday 20th April

12.54pm

So I prepared it all so carefully. I wore a fedora and Dad's braces over a white singlet. I stuck a toothpick in my mouth and waited for Megan to arrive.

'Hey, doll,' I said when she finally turned up, late. She was looking hot in her green Waitrose uniform. I offered her an opened pack of Oreos.

'Hello,' she replied, eyeing me and the Oreos suspiciously.

'You and me, doll,' I said. 'Walking by the Hudson. Taking in a Broadway show. Drinking a highball at Joe's Bar, riding the B train home afterwards, handing a greenback to a kindly bum. How about it?'

'What on earth are you talking about?' she asked, sitting down at the kitchen table. She looked a bit dark under the eyes.

I slapped the tickets down on the table. 'We're going to New York, baby. That's what I'm talking about.'

Megan opened the ticket and stared at it. She didn't look quite as excited as I'd expected.

'Executive Club class,' I pointed out. 'Extra leg room. Real metal cutlery. Attentive flight attendants.'

'Wow, Ben,' she said. 'This is amazing.'

'And of course there's free entry to the KnitFair for all three days,' I pointed out eagerly.

'Mmmm,' she said. 'Brilliant.'

'You don't sound as enthusiastic as I'd hoped,' I said.

She paused for a moment.

'It's just that things are tough at the moment. At home,' she

12

said. 'Gran's really not well and Mum needs me . . .'

'It's only a week,' I said gently. 'Your mum would understand that, wouldn't she?'

Megan looked up at me and forced a smile. 'It's not that simple, but thank you for asking me, Ben. It's amazingly generous.'

'But . . .'

She shrugged. 'I'm not sure I'd be very good company anyway. I'd be worrying about Gran, and Mum.'

My heart sank. Was she saying no? How could she say no to this?

'Look, don't say no just now,' I said quickly. 'See how things go over the next few days. Talk to your mum about it. Think things over. Please?'

I must have sounded a bit desperate, because she nodded and said she'd think about it. I've felt a bit flat since then. I'm torn between sympathising with Megan about her gran, but at the same time I can't help wondering if she's using this as an excuse. Maybe she just doesn't want to go away with me?

Sunday 21st April

Megan texted me this morning and said she won't be coming to New York. I'm too bummed to write about it just now. I'm focusing on possible replacements instead. Here's the list so far, in order of preference.

Jessica Swallow
Joz

13

Freddie
Mum
Mrs Frensham
Joe Boyle
Natasha
Gex

Feel a bit bad about Gex but can you imagine him being let loose in New York? Guns are practically compulsory there. Gex is obsessed with guns. He's taken to carrying around a replica Browning 45mm (which is actually a water pistol. He has loads of water pistols). I had a bad dream last night, in which I was driving over the Brooklyn Bridge pursued by a thousand cop cars, sirens ablaze, with Gex in the passenger seat, hanging out of the window and firing at the cop convoy with his Super-Sopper Aqua Blaster.

So, all things considered, Gex is bottom of the list.

But I can't *really* ask Jessica Swallow to go with me, can I?

Then again, it would solve the issue around taking another student with me. I could tell her I need to be accompanied by a responsible adult and that my parents are unavailable, or dead, or something, and that she's my only option and did I mention Executive Club? Hang on. What am I thinking? I have a girlfriend who, even though she's let me down, is a bit miserable at the mo. Also Jessica Swallow is happily back together with Hampton FC legend Joe Boyle. If I tear their relationship apart, then Joe's form on the pitch will suffer again and Hampton FC will definitely be relegated this year. I can't have that on my conscience.

I crossed Jessica Swallow firmly off the list with a marker pen. I'll talk to Joz tomorrow.

9.13pm
I caught Mum and Dad playing Rude Scrabble on the iPad this evening. They denied it but I know what they're up to. They've adjusted the settings so they get fifty bonus points by putting down swear words. I won't go into details because this is a diary that will be read by my probation officer, but needless to say Dad was delighted when mum put *SHAFT* near a triple-word score because he happened to have two *C*s, a *K* and a blank.

I've made them delete all the rude words they added to the dictionary.

'I play Scrabble with Molly sometimes,' I pointed out to Mum. 'I don't want her pressing the Hint button and having it suggest she adds *J-O-B* to the word *HAND*.'

Mum looked a bit sheepish then, and she promised she wouldn't do it again, but Dad was cracking up in the kitchen, so I don't trust them one iota.

'It looks like Megan can't come to New York,' I said as Dad came back in, breathing weirdly and with a red face.

'Have you broken up already?' Mum asked, a bit too quickly. I looked at her in hurt surprise.

'No,' I said. 'But thanks for immediately jumping to that conclusion. '

'So why isn't she going?' Dad asked.

I explained about her gran, that she hadn't been well for a while and in any case thought my name was Simon. I didn't

15

say that I thought it was a poor excuse but maybe they picked it up from my tone.

'When I get old,' Dad said. 'Put me on a flight to Switzerland. I don't want to be a burden to anyone.' He says things like this a lot. But I suspect when it comes to the crunch Molly and I won't be able to prise his fingers away from the boarding gate at Heathrow.

'I've changed my mind,' he'll squeal. 'I don't want to go with dignity.'

I'll have to get something in writing.

I'm joking.

Monday 22nd April

You know how in fly-on-the-wall documentaries the producers often have to inject some artificial tension into the story? They might be filming some B-list celeb learning how to do something for the first time, like baking a cake, or recording a song, or performing open-heart surgery and there'll be a phone call they're nervously waiting for where they find out if the cake rose, or the song got to number one, or the patient survived.

'This is the big moment,' the voice-over person (usually Dermot O'Leary) will say. 'If things have gone badly, it could mean the end of (insert B-list celeb's name here)'s career in baking/singing/cardio surgery.'

Well, my whole life is like that. A series of moderately dramatic episodes and a constant, low-level anxiety. There's the occasional properly exciting moment, of course, like when I won at the All-UK Knitting Championship. But mostly it's minor triumphs or, more often, slight disappointments.

I popped into the school office at break today.

Lloyd Manning was sitting outside Mrs Tyler's office looking thunderous.

'What have you done this time?' I asked. I was full of courage knowing that he couldn't very well start gouging my eyes out here in the office.

He ignored me.

'Don't talk to him,' called Miss Lucie the receptionist. 'What do you want here, anyway?'

'Is Mrs Tyler free?' I asked.

She was, as it happened, and Miss Lucie told me to go straight in.

'Hi, Ben,' she said brightly. 'What can I do for you?' Mrs Tyler's been a lot happier since I won the knitting competition. I'm not saying it was entirely down to me, but a week after the win, Virilia announced a new three-year sponsorship for the school. We're now the Virilia Academy of Excellence in Mathematics and Agriculture. The sports hall is getting a new roof and has now been renamed the Virilia Academy Stadium of Dreams.

'You know how I won that knitting competition,' I began.

'Yes. Thank you,' she said.

'Well, I've been given two tickets to go to KnitFair USA.

17

In New York.'

'How wonderful.'

'But it's in term time. In a couple of weeks, as it happens.'
She frowned and paused.

Dermot O'Leary popped up in my head and started
speaking in a quiet, concerned voice. 'Will Mrs Tyler
allow Ben to travel to the US? If she doesn't, it could
mean the end of Ben's hopes.'

'How long would you be going for?'

'A week, just a week,' I said. 'And a day, because I'd fly back
on the Monday.'

'And you said you had two tickets? Will your mother be
going with you?'

'Er . . .'

'Another student?'

'Possibly . . .' I said slowly, trying to gauge her reaction.

'Who?'

'I'm not sure yet,' I replied. 'I have a few options.'

'I'm happy for you to go, Ben,' she said. 'Mr Hollis from
Virilia will be delighted to hear you are pursuing your knitting
interests. You know they are very keen for us to develop our
entrepreneurial focus. I am however less sure about allowing
two students to go. I'd have to be reassured that it would be in
the long-term interests of the other student as well.'

Oh God. Looks like it might have to be my mother after
all, if I don't think of something quick.

* * *

Dear Ms Gunter,

*Thank you for your letter dated 19ʰ April,
requesting my attendance at a Waypoint Assessment
Conversation on the 4ᵗʰ May. I am emailing you today
to ask if it would be possible to re-arrange the date for
that appointment as I will be in New York at that time
attending KnitFair USA.*

*Sorry about this. I am free the week before, or the week
after. Or indeed any other week. My calendar is almost
entirely empty right up until the SuperStitch Eisteddfod
in Wokingham on the 24ᵗʰ June.*

*Best wishes,
Ben*

So about five seconds after sending that email I get a call from
Ms Gunter.

'Hello, Ben? It's Claudia Gunter here from West Meon
Probation Services.'

'Hi, Ms Gunter, I just sent you an email!'

'I know you did, Ben. That's why I'm calling.'

'Good news about KnitFair, isn't it?'

'Well . . .'

'Top male knitter Fabrice Gentile is going to be there. And
there's a demonstration of a new system for shearing a sheep,
treating and dying the wool and knitting it into a jumper all
in a hundred and twenty minutes.'

'I'm sure it's going to be a blast, Ben,' she said. 'The problem is that you can't go.'

The incidental music swelled and Dermot piped up again. 'It's a crushing blow for Ben. And completely out of the blue.'

'What?' I spluttered. 'Why not?'

'You're on probation, Ben! One of the terms of your probation is that you don't leave the country.'

The room swam and I felt a bit sick.

'But you were there when I won the prize,' I protested. 'Why didn't you tell me then?'

'I thought it was next year's KnitFair they were talking about.'

'I was just getting back on the straight and narrow,' I said. 'A disappointing setback like this could force me back into a life of crime.'

'You shoplifted a bottle of Tia Maria from Tesco,' Ms Gunter said in a withering tone. 'You're not Tony Soprano.'

'It was Martini Rosso, actually,' I reminded her. 'From *Waitrose*.'

'Couldn't you phone them up and ask if you can attend next year's show?' she said.

'I've already got e-tickets!' I said. 'They're not going to want me next year. Especially if I have to tell them I'm a hoodlum.'

'You're hardly a hoodlum, Ben,' she said patiently.

'So why can't I go to America?'

Ms Gunter sighed. 'I'll make some calls. See what I can do.'

'Thanks, Ms Gunter,' I said, hope surging again.

'I'm not promising anything, Ben. The Home Office doesn't tend to make exceptions.'

I was so wound up after that roller coaster of a phone call that I couldn't even concentrate on my knitting. The Hoopie I was working on now has a noticeable sag to the left. I'm not even sure how I did it but the hem on the left is two to three inches lower than the right.

I've decided not to tell anyone I might not be going to America. This is the New Ben. Positive Ben. Focused Fletcher. If I pretend everything's OK, maybe it will be.

Tuesday 23rd April

I'm a little concerned about Molly. She came home from school on Friday to tell us she has a boyfriend named Finlay. I was alarmed to hear they'd had what Molly called 'a romantic moment' on the buddy bench. This turned out to be nothing more worrying than a quiet chat and an exchange of Moshi Monsters which isn't as disturbing as it sounds. Mum and Dad just laughed at the whole thing but I don't think it's right that children of seven should be having relationships. More to the point, what if Finlay and Molly outlast me and Megan?

I caught up with Joz at lunch today and asked him about New York. '*Another* knitting fair?' he asked, looking pained. 'I thought you were over the knitting thing.'

'I'm not,' I replied. 'Look, the fair itself is only on the

weekend, the week before is just sightseeing and . . .'

'. . . and what?'

'And the occasional knitting-related media event.'

'So I'd be like your assistant?'

'Yeah, like in the Tour de France. My support team.'

'I drive after you in a car with spare needles on the roof rack?'

'Yes, and inject me with performance-enhancing potions in the team bus.'

'Potions?'

'Tea,' I said. 'And Hobnobs.'

'And will we get the chance to go to a bar?'

'Mmm, not sure about that. You have to be twenty-one to drink in the US.'

'You're not selling this to me.'

'I can't believe you're considering turning down the chance to go to KnitFair USA,' I said, agog. 'They have a monkey there who can crochet. A crocheting monkey!'

He shrugged. 'Also I don't really want to leave Amelia just at the moment. She's pretty vulnerable.'

'I can't believe I'm hearing this,' I said. 'Don Joz the ladykiller. Author of *Fifty Shades of Graham*. International playboy, turns down a chance to go to the US because of some *girl*.'

'She's not just some girl,' he said. 'What we have is special.' He underlined this point by hawking a huge, phlegm-filled lugie onto a tree stump a few feet away.

'She's one lucky little lady,' I said, trying not to be sick and wondering how to change the subject. 'Any luck with the manuscript?' I asked after some thought. Joz has finished *Fifty Shades of Graham* and has sent it off to a few publishers in London.

'Couple more rejections,' he muttered.

'Sorry to hear that,' I said. 'Maybe erotica is dead.'

'No chance. Erotica has been around for centuries. I've been researching it.'

'I bet you have.'

'I mean literary erotica. Anaïs Nin, Marquis de Sade. It's all free on Kobo.'

'Wait a minute. *You've* been reading Marquis de Sade?'

'Well, dipping in.' He leaned towards me and whispered. 'Did you know he used to eat people's poo?'

'Really?' I cried. 'That's disgusting.'

'He used to make his lovers eat marzipan so the poo wouldn't taste so bad.'

'If he doesn't like the taste, then why's he eating it?'

'I know. He should just eat the marzipan,' Joz said. 'Cut out the middle man.'

'I'm having a horrible flashback to that night at your place when you made me watch *The Human Caterpillar*,' I said, shuddering and laughing at the same time.

It's a shame Joz can't come to America. He's revolting, and a bit weird, but he's funny.

Well, that's three people off the list. Who's next? Oh yeah. Freddie. Sigh. At least he won't turn me down. He has no girlfriend, no job, no literary pretensions and, as luck would have it, all his grandparents are already dead.

23

Saturday 27th April

I've actually been spending a bit more time with Freddie recently. Today I rode my bike out to Hampton FC's ground for my guilty displeasure. I may have mentioned this before but I hate football. Dad calls it the beautiful game, but sitting in an ice storm watching twenty-two badly tattooed smokers run through heavy mud and failing to score is not the classic definition of beauty, as described by the poets.

So why am I still going to watch Hampton FC even though Dad isn't there? I think there's possibly been some behind-the-scenes discussions between my subconscious and my psyche that acknowledges that although the whole knitting thing is completely cool and we're all fine with my sexual identity and my being able to flange my selvages in a delightfully cheeky way doesn't mean that I'm effeminate, nonetheless it's important not only to remember my masculine side but also to exhibit it in public from time to time. Hence, the odd appearance at a manly football match.

So there I was, sitting between Freddie, wearing a huge Puffa jacket, and Gordon McGavin from McGavin's Electrical Solutions, who was wearing a Russian hat and a sheepskin coat. I had a 4-ply merino wool tank top under my roll-top cable-knit sweater plus a beanie I'd knitted over the weekend and I was still colder than I'd ever been in my life.

'They say they're building a new stand next season,' Mr McGavin grunted. 'Hopefully it'll be made of concrete. Cut out some of this sodding wind.'

'They could build it out of ice,' I suggested. 'Like that

hotel in the Arctic.'

Hampton were playing Liss and neither team had much zip about them. It was heavy going in the mud, the weather was freezing and with no exciting Joe Boyle, there was also no ravishing Jessica Swallow sitting in the stands, so no one to show off to.

At half-time I staved off boredom by reading Freddie's dad's copy of the *Daily Mail*. There was an article about deep vein thrombosis which you get if you sit still on a plane for too long. Apparently this granny had to have her leg amputated after a flight to, you guessed it, New York. She then had to sell her house to pay the medical bills.

So that's something else to worry about. Yippee.

'So, Freddie,' I began, as Milford kicked off the second half. Hampton's left back slipped in the mud and lay helplessly, watching the ball trickle over the line.

'Corner!' someone shouted.

'How would you like to go to America?'

'Eh?'

'America. New York. Remember I won those tickets?'

'No.'

'Remember at the Knitting Show in London?'

'Oh right. You won?'

I paused. Had he really forgotten already?

A Liss centre-half booted the ball randomly into the melee before the goalmouth. The exhausted players watched it plop into the churned mud and sit there. For a moment, nobody moved. Then the goalie stepped forward in a manner which said, 'Well, if no one else can be bothered, I suppose it's up to me,' and banged it back down the pitch. The rest of the players set off after it with a collective sigh.

'Yes. I won. Famously,' I reminded him. 'I got a trophy. Joz broke his arm. Gex disguised himself as a sheep and had to go into hospital with blood poisoning from the dye. Remember?'

'Oh yeah,' Freddie laughed.

'So I won some tickets to go to another knitting show in New York,' I went on patiently. 'And there are two tickets. So I wondered if you wanted to go with me?'

'To New York?'

'Yes.'

'On a plane?'

'Or we could walk?' I suggested.

'I can't walk. I have an infected verruca.'

'OK, let's fly, then.'

'Well . . .' Freddie seemed to be thinking about it.

'I'll come if he doesn't want to,' said Gordon McGavin. 'Always wanted to go to New York.'

'Thanks, Mr McGavin,' I said. 'I'll put you on the reserve bench.'

He took me at my word and made me punch his number and email into my phone.

The ball had become bogged down in the far corner of the pitch. The players huddled around it, seemingly in no hurry to bring it back. Possibly they'd realised we couldn't see what they were up to over there and were having a quick smoke break.

'So you'll come?' I asked.

'Yeah, s'pose,' Freddie said.

'Don't get too excited, will you.' I slumped back in my seat.

Why do I bother? I should have just sold the bloody thing on eBay.

Monday 29th April

Ran into Ms Swallow at school today. She was struggling with some boxes of essays for marking and I offered to help carry them to her car. She was wearing her hair up in a ponytail and I was so busy watching the smooth skin on the back of her neck that I forgot to listen to what she was saying.

'. . . Ben?'

'What? Sorry.'

She'd stopped to turn around and had a half-smile.

'I said, I hear you're off to New York next week?'

'Oh yeah. Did Miss Tyler tell you? She gave me permission to miss the classes as long as I take some work with me.'

'Yes. It sounds amazing. You're so lucky. You don't happen to have a spare ticket, do you?' she laughed and carried on towards the car.

I laughed too. In a slightly strained way.

'Are you taking Megan?' she asked.

I shook my head. 'She can't go.'

'Oh, shame,' she said. 'It would have been fun to take a transatlantic flight with her.'

'Totally.'

'So who are you taking?'

'Not sure yet. There are a few people interested; someone's going to be disappointed.'

'I know, I could go as your chaperone,' she said. We both laughed again at the thought.

'I'll add you to the list,' I said weakly. Then I nearly collapsed as she bent over to rest her box on the ground.

She's so beautiful. Imagine if she did come to New York with me. She might drink a little too much champagne on the flight over and fall asleep on my shoulder. Or maybe she'd be scared of flying and I'd have to put my arm around her in a comforting manner.

And once there, maybe the man from Priapia would offer me a top job thinking up knitting patterns and I'd turn it down and Ms Swallow would ask me why and I'd say, 'Because you're my muse, Jessica Swallow, and I couldn't design so much as a table mat without you by my side.' And she'd say, 'Why have you never told me this before?' And I'd say, 'It was my secret. But I can't lie to you any more.'

Then she'd kiss me in the Bronx. As it were. We'd move into a nice brownstone apartment on the Upper West Side and I'd turn into a beardie hippy type and she'd do charity work and have an affair but own up to it and we'd get through it together and I'm going to stop because this whole thing is just turning into a John Irving novel and I don't even like John Irving.

I've got to stop obsessing over Jessica Swallow. I have a girlfriend!

5.47pm
I had a call from Mr Hollis just now. The neat man from Virilia who has taken such an interest in my entrepreneurials.

28

'Hello, Ben,' he said. 'I hear you're off to New York.'

'That's right,' I said. 'I'm going to the KnitFair USA.'

'There might be some fantastic business opportunities there for you, Ben.'

I hadn't really thought too much about that, to be honest.

'Our parent company in the US is called Priapia,' he went on. 'Now, they have a clothing and textiles arm. It would be useful for you to meet with them.'

'Would it?' I asked. I felt tendrils of anxiety suddenly creep down my spine. 'What would I say?'

'Oh, it would be very informal,' Mr Hollis said. 'They're all very friendly. Just a chat, really.'

'What about?' I pressed.

'I think you should show them your clever design. The thing is, Ben, you are quite marketable. A young, male knitter, engaging, good-looking, if you don't mind me saying . . .'

Was he coming on to me?

'Textiles and clothing is a crowded market, Ben,' he said. 'It's hard to get a product to stand out. Your cardigan design, and your story, might just be able to do it.'

'Really? I'm just a kid from Hampton.'

'Sometimes that's all that people are looking for.'

Tuesday 30th April

4.33pm
So I get a call today.

   'Ben?'

29

'Yes, Ben speaking.'

'It's Freddie.'

'Hi, Freddie, how's the verruca?'

'Hurts,' he said. 'I talked to Mum, about going to New Orleans?'

'New York?'

'Yeah, that's what I meant. She says I can't go.'

'So now she's being all maternal, is she?' I said, a bit annoyed. 'I mean, who was it who left you and your nine-year-old sister home alone for an entire weekend with nothing more than a multipack of Walkers crisps.'

'And some custard creams,' he reminded me.

'Yeah, all right, but the point remains –'

'I don't have a passport,' Freddie interrupted me calmly. 'She says I can't go because I don't have a passport.'

'Oh,' I said. 'Fair enough.'

Another one bites the dust. Who's next?

Oh, that's right.

My mother.

7.52pm

Don't get me wrong. I love my mum. And we get on very well most of the time, when she's around. But when I heard I'd won a week in New York for two my first thought was not, 'Ooh, I hope Mum's free!'

But I'm desperate now.

'Do you fancy coming to New York with me, Mum?'

Mum and Dad glanced at each other in surprise.

'It's just that Megan can't come, and I know you love the

30

US. I have a spare ticket. It means missing out on climbing Mount Snowdon, of course . . . ha ha . . .' but I tailed off at the sight of her embarrassed face.

'Ah. The thing is, Ben . . .' she began.

'Oh God, Mum,' I said shaking my head slowly. 'You're not going to turn me down as well?' I'm such a loser, I can't even get my mum to go to New York with me.

'Well, not exactly,' she said. 'The thing is, your father and I are coming anyway.'

I paused. 'What?'

'We're coming with you, anyway,' she repeated.

'Try stopping us!' Dad said.

'No Snowdonia?'

'Snowdonia will still be there when we get back,' Dad said.

'What about Molly?'

'She's going to stay with Auntie Angela.'

'And school?'

'She's seven. She can miss a week.'

'Can you afford to fly to America?'

'It's all right,' Dad said. 'I've been getting loads of work lately. And your mum's been turning tricks.'

My eyes bulged.

'I've *sold* one of my tricks,' she corrected him.

'Which one?' I asked.

'The Corpse Bride.'

'Is that the one where you murder someone in the audience?'

'I don't murder them, I accidentally kill them and it's not real,' Mum said impatiently. 'Anyway. Now I'm suspended by the Magic Circle, and your father has his bad knee, we thought it might be a good time to get away.'

'Well, that's . . . a big surprise,' I said. I wasn't really sure how I felt about both of them being there, to be honest. I'd been looking forward to getting away from Dad for a while, but if I wasn't going to be going with Megan, then it wasn't as if they'd be cramping my style. And since I couldn't find anyone else to go with me, then at least I'd have some company.

'I won't be able to do sightseeing with you,' I said. 'At least not every day.'

'I'm sure we'll keep ourselves busy,' Mum said, winking at Dad.

'Your mum's going to look up an old flame,' Dad said.

'What?' I said. 'What old flame?'

'His name's Diablo,' Dad said archly.

'Diablo is not an old flame,' Mum said to me, blushing. 'We were in the same class at Magic School. We practised our prestidigitation together.'

'I'll bet you did,' Dad said.

'If you'd rather I didn't see him . . .' Mum began.

'I don't mind,' Dad said. 'But if he tries to stick his sword into your magic box I'll . . .'

'I'm going to my bedroom,' I said hurriedly, darting for the door.

I spent the rest of the evening knitting a pair of orthopaedic compression stockings to combat DVT on the plane. I tried them on and they're a snug fit all right. Not particularly attractive, but very definitely orthopaedic.

Dear Ben,

*It was good to talk to you the other day. I just wanted
to pass on the details of our parent company in the
States.*

Priapia
175 5th Avenue
New York, New York
*I've taken the liberty of contacting one of my associates,
Robert D'Angelo. He has asked if you could pop in to
see him at 10.00am on Wednesday 15th May. He'd
love to see a sample of the Hoopie and chat to you
about your interest in knitting. It will be a casual,
informal meeting, but please note that punctuality is
very important in US business.*

*Please don't hesitate to contact me if you have any
questions.*

Yours sincerely,
James Hollis
Virilia Investments

Wednesday 1st May

I went to visit Mrs Frensham today. Considering the
circumstance under which we met – me knocking her over with
a stolen bottle of Martini Rosso – we've become quite good
friends. You might say it's odd: a teenage boy being buddies with

a pensioner, but she's good company now that she's stopped trying to decapitate me with giant lollipops, and we share a mutual interest in the craft of knitting.

It was too cold to sit in the Knitshed, so Mrs Frensham and I sat around her gas fire instead chatting and stitching. Jasper, her dog, lay between us, farting occasionally. The outdoor work I was doing for Mrs Frensham as part of my community service (following aforementioned Martini Rosso incident) is pretty much all finished, but our Monday night sessions have become an institution and I couldn't possibly stop visiting now. She usually finds a few jobs for me to do around the house before we get down to the serious business of knitting.

Mrs Frensham is working on a pair of hand warmers at the moment, which I'm actually a bit jels about. I don't have time for little luxuries such as hand warmers. It's all big-scale Hoopies and tank tops for me. I'm also doing a Hampton FC scarf for Dad's birthday. It's a double-knit using extra warm 4-ply. Scientifically designed to withstand the absolute zero temperatures at the ground.

Mrs Frensham was on the NY hitlist but when it came to it I had my doubts about actually asking a sixty-four-year old woman to come on holiday with me. I'd only put her down in the first place because I wanted to reassure myself that I had lots of friends. In fairness, she does love knitting and I always feel comfortable and relaxed in her presence, but I'm not sure that necessarily would carry us through a flight to New York and a week in a three-star Manhattan hotel. Our odd friendship works because we have a comfortable routine, in a familiar, safe environment and I probably shouldn't mess with that.

'How's that girl of yours?' Mrs Frensham asked.

'Megan? She's OK.'

'Introduced you to her parents yet?'

'Oh yes. I get on well with her mum, she has fantastic Tupperware.'

'Fantastic what?'

'Tupperware. All the lids fit all the boxes. You get shallow boxes, middle-sized boxes and deep boxes. But the lids are interchangeable.'

'Oh, when you said "Tupperware",' said Mrs Frensham, 'I thought you were meaning something else.'

'Funny you should say, but last week I did see a bit of Mrs Hooper's *Tupperware*,' I told her. 'When she left her bedroom door open a bit. I caught a glimpse in the mirror as I walked past. She has a very impressive collection,' I added. 'Of *actual* Tupperware, I mean.'

'I'm sure she does,' Mrs Frensham said.

I've got to watch myself on the double entendres, or else I'll turn into my parents. Damn them!

We paused for a while to concentrate on our respective knitting, the only sounds the pleasant click of the needles, the hiss of the gas fire and the quiet gurgle of Jasper's digestive tract.

'I hope you haven't told Megan how much you admire her mother's Tupperware,' Mrs Frensham said after a while, as though reading my thoughts.

'I might have mentioned it,' I said. 'Why?'

'Good-looking woman that Naomi Hooper,' said Mrs Frensham.

'That's true,' I said. 'Anyway, Megan's refusing to come to New York with me.'

'I'm sure she has her reasons.'

'Yeah, like she's gone off me.'

'Maybe,' Mrs Frensham said absently.

'Do you think she's gone off me?'

'She might.'

Mrs Frensham's honesty was in some ways refreshing but at the same time completely unwelcome.

'Actually,' I said defensively, 'it's to do with her gran being ill.'

Mrs Frensham looked up sharply. 'Lottie? Lottie's ill, is she?'

'Do you know her?'

'Yeah. She's a Portsmouth girl like me.'

'Were you in the same class at school, then?'

Mrs Frensham threw a pincushion at me.

'She's twenty years older than me, you little twerp!'

'Oh sorry.'

'Do I look the same age as her, is that what you're saying?'

'No,' I said.

Yes, I thought. They were both white-haired and wrinkly. They dressed the same. How was I to know?'She was my teacher,' Mrs Frensham. 'Lovely lady.'

'Yes,' I said. 'Though she can't remember my name. She calls me Simon.'

'She used to know a lad called Simon,' Mrs Frensham said, a faint smile came over her face. 'Handsome bloke.'

'Really?' I asked, feeling pleased with myself. 'I suppose that's why she thinks I'm him.'

'Maybe.' Mrs Frensham looked at me doubtfully. 'So you

think Lottie being ill is the reason she's not coming with you?'

'That's what she said.' I shrugged. Who knew what the truth was.

Dammit! I've just looked closely at the Hampton FC scarf I've been knitting for Dad and have realised I've misspelled Hampton as Hamton throughout. His birthday is tomorrow, I've no time to knit another.

Hamton FC. Twelve times.

What can I do?

10.15pm

I emailed Marie from the *Knitwits!* podcast and she got back to me straight away, asking if I'd like to meet up and record an interview while I'm over in New York. This is a big deal. I have no idea how many people listen to that podcast but there must be loads. Everything about it is proper quality, except for Marie's sidekick, Alanna, who's slightly irritating. And also they're going through a phase of knitting mainly animal-shaped cushions at the moment which doesn't interest me so much, frankly. But apart from that, it's the best knitting podcast I've found. She's going to contact me again while I'm in New York to arrange the exact time and place.

So who's next on the list after Mrs Frensham? Joe Boyle, who I put on as a joke. Hampton FC's star forward is not going to want to spend a week with a knitting weed in New York, even flying Executive Club. And anyway, what would we talk about? We don't have anything in common except that we both fancy his girlfriend and it might make things awkward if that came up.

So after Joe is Natasha. The full-figured girl who runs Pullinger's, where I get my wool. She's an interesting possibility. Three things in favour:

1) She has a genuine interest in knitting.
2) We get on well.
3) Megan might be jealous.

Three things against:

1) I suspect that Natasha secretly fancies me, which could make things difficult.
2) She talks ALL THE TIME.
3) Megan might be so jealous she dumps me.

Thursday 2nd May

Popped into Pullinger's after school to pick up more Hoopie wool. Natasha was working. She was wearing a low-cut top and kept leaning over the counter blinking at me.

'So, I'm going to New York next week . . .' I began.

'I LOVE New York,' she said. 'So romantic.'

'Well, it's only to KnitFair USA,' I said, playing things down.

'God, I wish I was going to KnitFair USA,' she sighed. 'I'd give anything.'

'Mum and Dad are tagging along,' I said, rolling my eyes. 'How sad is that?'

'Brilliant!' she said. 'Your dad is so funny.'

'Is he?'

'And your mum's magic tricks! So clever.' She blinked quickly again.

Having trouble with your contact lenses?' I asked.

'No,' she said, looking puzzled. 'I've not got them in today.'

'Anyway,' I said. 'I'm going to be pretty busy in New York . . . Media commitments and so on.'

She gazed at me like I was Harry Styles. 'Wow. You're going to be on the telly?'

'Probably not. Newspapers, maybe. I have my own PR person. Her name is Brandi, would you believe?'

'Brandi?' She interrupted the blinking for a moment so she could raise an eyebrow.

'She works for the Knitting Guild Association of America, or something,' I explained.

'People in PR can be a little false, don't you think?' Natasha suggested.

'I'm sure she's not like that.'

'Just be careful, Ben.'

'I will,' I said, hurriedly paying for my purchases and heading for the door.

I mentally crossed off the one person on my list who would have bitten my arm off for the ticket if offered. I felt a bit bad about not asking her. But some people just want it too much.

Who's next on the list?

Oh God.

6.45pm

Gave Dad his Hamton FC scarf just as he was about to head out on a twenty-mile bike ride. This is how middle-aged men like to spend their birthdays, apparently.

He held the scarf like it was the Turin Shroud.

'It's beautiful, Ben,' he said quietly.

'It's just a scarf,' I replied, embarrassed by his reaction. 'And I spelled Hampton wrong.' He looked up at me, his eyes slightly moist.

'That just makes it even more special,' he said. 'No one else will have a scarf quite like this.'

'That's true.'

'Thanks, Ben,' he said. 'I'll wear it on Saturday. In fact I'm going to wear it now.' And then he went off on his bike, wearing brightly coloured Lycra, the scarf wrapped three times around his neck. Dad's obviously at that age where he's quite comfortable being a figure of fun. He honestly doesn't care what he looks like. Both he and Mum are either completely unaware of how embarrassing they are in public or else they like it. I think parents get off on embarrassing their children. How else to explain the ridiculous clothes, the awful music, the kaleidoscopic outdoor Christmas decorations?

Friday 3rd May

4.12pm

'You should have come to the party, innit?'

'Yes, I heard about the party,' I said. 'It sounded grim.'

I'd caught up with Gex in the park, and we sat around there for a while, wasting time watching the younger kids from Gex's estate throw bricks at passing trains on the Portsmouth line. Now we'd come back to his little house on Ratchett Street (or Ratshit Street as Gex calls it) with the mattress in the front garden. I like to think that if I'm ever down on my luck and reduced to sleeping rough, I know there'll always be a bed for me in Gex's front yard. It's a bit rough round here. If Hampton were New York, Gex would live downtown. Very downtown. Possibly under the town. Today he was dressed as a gangsta-rapper, with shades, a singlet and a huge gold watch. We were eating cheese toasties in his kitchen.

'It was the nuts, man,' he said. 'It really kicked off.'

'I heard the police were called.'

'Yeah! They didn't do nothing,' Gex said, shrugging. 'Just took a couple of lads off and then we got back to it.'

'What did your neighbours say?'

'They didn't mind, because we planned ahead and invited them too.'

'You invited Mrs Gupta?'

'Yeah.'

'Did she come?'

'No.'

'No,' I said. 'I didn't think so.'

'Point is, she was invited,' he said.

'Also, I heard from Joz there was puke everywhere.'

Gex shrugged. 'That was no problem. I just let the Staffies in the next morning and they licked it all up.'

'OK. I take it back, Pippa Middleton,' I said once I'd stopped

41

retching. 'You are the host with the most.'

There was a knock at the door. It was the TV licensing people.

'You guys again!' Gex said.

'We still haven't received your licence fee,' the man said. 'We know you have a telly.'

'Yeah, we got a telly,' Gex said. 'But like I told you, it don't work, innit.'

'Can you prove that, sir?'

'Not personally,' Gex said. 'But, tell you what. If you can make the telly work. I'll give you the cash.'

So the man came in and discovered that Gex was telling the truth. His telly hasn't worked for ages. The man went back out to his van and came back with his toolkit. We carried on chatting while the man took the back off Gex's telly. It's the largest telly I've ever seen and completely obscures the window in Gex's front room. Gex's dad bought it off a Polish truck driver, who said it came from Russia. It worked for a couple of weeks, giving off a bit of blue smoke, and then it stopped.

'Do you wanna come to Wicked wiv me and Joz and Freddie on Saturday?' Gex asked me.

'No, I'll be in New York on Saturday.'

'In Basingstoke?'

'What? No. Not New York Nite Club! I mean the real New York. In America.'

His mouth dropped. 'Sick, man. Like with gangs and drugs and drive-by shootings?'

'Well, I think they've cleaned up most of the crime problem . . . '

'Like in *The Wire*?'

'That was Baltimore. I'll be in New York.'

'Like *The Sopranos*?'

'That was New Jersey, I'll be in Manhattan.'

'Like in *Gangs of New York*?'

'Um, or maybe like a less violent film set in Manhattan?'

'Like what – *Kick Ass*?' Gex suggested.

'More like *Maid in Manhattan*,' I said wearily.

'You watch way too many chick flicks, dude,' Gex said.

'How many is too many?'

'One.'

'Look, do you want to come or not? I asked, a bit narked.

Gex stood and held out a grimy hand which I took, not entirely without hesitation.

'I'm there, blud,' he said.

'Awesome.' I tried to feel happy that I'd finally found someone to take to New York.

I tried really hard.

Sunday 5th May

8.11am

I emailed Ms Tyler this morning to let her know I'd asked Gex to come with me to New York and would it be all right if he missed a week of school. I remembered she'd told me there had to be a beneficial reason for the student to attend and I couldn't think of one, so was a bit worried she might say no. But as it happens she replied very quickly with a yes.

Perhaps she was thinking Gex's absence might be beneficial to the rest of the school.

Tuesday 7ᵗʰ May

6.57pm
So Ms Gunter phoned this evening. 'You owe me,' she said, sounding a bit grumpy.

'You've sorted it?'

'I've sorted it. I've arranged for a temporary relaxation on your travel ban on the proviso that you place a Skype call to me, personally, once every twenty-four hours while you are away.'

'That's brilliant,' I said. 'Thanks.'

'This is a huge relief for Ben,' Dermot O'Leary said. 'Failure to get Home Office approval would have been a major setback.' Dermot does like to state the bleeding obvious.

'Ben,' she went on. 'I had to use a lot of professional credit to arrange this. If you screw up, even once, then I am going to be in big trouble. I will probably be shuffled out of my job and end up working in the ASBO team, or in a maximum-security prison, or even worse, I could end up working in the Home Secretary's office.'

'What's wrong with the Home Secretary's office?'

'My ex-husband works there.'

'I didn't know you'd been married!'

'Look, this isn't about me,' she said impatiently.

'Everything will be fine,' I said confidently. 'When have I ever let you down?'

'You need to call every day, Ben,' she repeated. 'They will be monitoring.'

'Like *Enemy of the State*?' I said, impressed.

'And it needs to be a Skype call, with video. It may be recorded. You can't call from a payphone outside a strip club at four in the morning. Nor do I want to be called in the middle of the night,' she said. 'New York is four hours ahead. You need to call me by midnight US time, but that is 4am here. So you need to be calling me by 2pm every day. That way you'll be calling me by 6pm UK time. Do you understand?'

'Of course,' I said, scribbling this down. 'I'll put it in my phone, AND my diary.'

'Ben,' Ms Gunter said. 'I'm doing this as a favour to you. Because you helped me out of a sticky spot earlier this year when you won the knitting thing.'

'Thanks, Ms Gunter,' I said. 'I really appreciate it.'

'OK, but after this, we're square.'

Sheesh, I thought as I put the phone down, trying to quell the shiver of anxiety that ran through me. All I have to do is skype the woman every day.

What could possibly go wrong?

Wednesday 8th May

7.12pm

I've invested in a new phone. If I'm going to be doing all this skyping I need a big screen and a powerful battery. I've gone for the SBC Stiletto. Very thin and murderous. I'm not normally a big gadget freak but I do love this phone. It has some pretty cool games on it too. I've also discovered a knitting app which is amazing. You can use 3D graphics to design your own virtual garments and mess about with the colours, the weaves, the wool thickness and so on. It is totes.

I gave my old phone to Mrs Frensham, as she is the only person I know who doesn't have a smartphone. I tried to explain pay-as-you-go to her but I don't think she got it.

Gex came over today to discuss the trip. He also reported that the TV licensing man had managed to fix the giant telly.

'So did you pay the licence fee?' I asked.

'Nah, we don't have to cos of Gramps living with us.'

'That can't have gone down well,' I said. 'That guy was working on that telly for ages.'

'He was cool about it.' Gex shrugged. 'I made him a cheese toastie.'

'Yes, I can see how that would compensate,' I said.

Gex was looking very chipper. Dare I say, almost excited?

'You looking forward to taking a bite out of the Big Apple?' I asked him.

'Oh yeah, man,' he said. 'Those New York girls are going to go mental for us.'

'Really?' I asked. 'What makes you think that?'

'The thing about American girls, right,' he said, coming closer to me and speaking in a low voice, 'is that they love our English accents, innit?'

'You don't really have an English accent though,' I pointed out. 'You have a sort of Jamaican–Pakistani thing going on most of the time.'

'I can do English,' he said, sniffing.

'You mean, that accent you do that sounds like the Queen in drag?' I said. 'Best not to try too hard, mate. You know, don't overdo it.'

Nothing it seemed was going to dampen Gex's spirits today, though.

'Hey, I have a second cousin in Brooklyn!' he said. 'I'm going to go and visit him.'

'You have an American relative?'

'Yeah, Dad's sister's kid, innit.'

'So this guy in Brooklyn is your father's sister's son?'

Gex nodded.

'So, he's actually your cousin. Not your second cousin. Your second cousin would be your –'

'Yeah, whatever.' Gex looked impatient now. 'Don't go off on one, you're harshing my vibe, blud.'

'OK. Anyway . . . I'll probably be busy for a day or two with PR stuff, so that would be a good opportunity for you to catch up with your family.'

Gex grinned. 'He has a "Family" all right.'

'What do you mean?'

'He's in a gang, innit.'

'How do you know that?'

'Everyone in the family knows.'

'You mean the family, or the Family?'

'The FAMILY,' he said, tapping the side of his nose. '*Capiche?*'

I regarded him dubiously. 'Gex, maybe it's not such a good idea for you to get involved with organised crime.'

'I can handle myself,' he said.

'I don't care. I'm still on probation, remember,' I said. 'Ms Gunter had to pull a lot of strings to get me permission to go. You can't screw up, you'll bring me down as well.'

'Look, man, be cool. I'm not going to get involved. It takes years to get accepted into a gang, anyways.'

'Glad to hear it.'

'And you have to cap three people before they let you in.'

'And we're only there a week,' I reminded him.

'Though, a lot can happen in a week.' Gex nodded sagely. 'Know what I mean?'

'Unfortunately, Gex,' I said despairingly, 'I know exactly what you mean.'

Thursday 9ᵗʰ May

7.38pm

So I saw Megan at college today, in the common room, for the last time before I leave for New York. It didn't go quite as I'd anticipated. Megan seemed disappointingly cheerful.

'You're going to have such a great time,' she said. 'I'm so jealous.'

'Well, you could have come,' I reminded her. 'I'd rather be

sat next to you than Gex.'

'I'm glad to hear it,' she said. 'But you know why I couldn't come.'

I wasn't sure I did, really.

'I'll miss you,' I said.

'It's only a week.'

'So you won't miss me?'

'Of course. But we can skype?'

I nodded. Another person to remember to skype.

'Central Park should be pretty this time of year,' Megan went on brightly.

'Goodbye, Megan,' I said.

'Why are you saying goodbye?' she asked. 'We're going to the same class.'

I'd forgotten that.

'Yes but . . . I have to go to the toilet,' I said.

'OK, knock yourself out,' she said, raising an eyebrow.

I could have handled that better.

Friday 10th May

10.34pm

My anxiety/mild OCD issues have kicked in big time. Can't sleep, so I did a dummy pack, made a list, unpacked in order to check everything off against the said list, then repacked. I keep getting up and staring at my luggage – and wondering if I've missed anything . . .

This is proper girl behaviour. It has to stop.

The other thing I am worrying about is obviously Gex. Not

just because he is Gex, and that means all manner of ill-advised, uncouth and possibly illegal scenarios could happen over the next week, but because he is pathologically unreliable and I have had to resort to devious lies to ensure he gets on the same plane as me.

Normally, the advice is to get to the airport two hours before your flight leaves, which seems to me to be cutting it awfully fine. What if the coach is delayed? What if your watch battery runs out? What if Gex tries to smuggle his replica water pistol onto the plane and anti-terror police pump bullets into his brain? I want to get there three hours before the plane leaves. At least then I'll have time to wash Gex's brain matter off my Converse before boarding.

So, this is where the devious plan kicks in. As Gex is never on time for anything and I'm predicting he will resist strongly if I try to get him to the airport three hours before the flight is due to leave, I've told him the plane leaves TWO hours before it actually does. That way even if he's an hour late we'll still get there when I want to get there.

Genius. What could possibly go wrong?

Mum and Dad are dropping my sister at Auntie Angela's, who lives close to Heathrow, so they'll take a cab. I'm glad I'm not travelling to the airport with them. If I know my parents they'll be late and hold everyone up. They are on the same flight as us but in (*snort*) economy.

My packing earlier was interrupted by a call from Mr McGavin, rather surprisingly.

'Is that ticket still going for New York?' he asked.

'Er, no,' I said.

'Just kidding,' he said. 'I actually was phoning to ask if you could knit me one of those Hampton scarves. I'll pay of course.'

'I'd like to,' I said slowly. 'It's just Dad likes the fact that his is the only one . . .'

'Oh, come on, Ben,' Mr McGavin said. 'No one's a bigger Hampton FC fan than me.'

'Can I get back to you?' I asked. 'I'm off to New York tomorrow and have a lot to do.'

'Take your time, Ben,' Mr McGavin said. 'I'd really love one of those scarves, but I understand if you can't.'

I don't like turning down work, I thought as I put down the phone, but Dad had been so delighted by the scarf. It was unique, and there's something wonderful about unique. I'd have to give it some thought.

Have I mentioned that I think I'm allergic to the colour cerise? I've tried to knit using cerise-coloured wool twice and each time I've ended up with a blinding headache and red blotches on my fingers. I'm going to have to google this. It's a shame, because I like the colour cerise and there's a lovely pattern which cries out for such a warm tone in the latest issue of *Knit!* magazine.

Maybe antihistamines might help.

Saturday 11th May

8.14pm

Megan further undermined the dramatic goodbye scene by popping around earlier to wish me *bon voyage*. She gave me some Union Jack boxer shorts and a kiss and told me to watch out for American girls who have great teeth but are often emotionally unstable.

Is that a hint of jealousy I detect in her?

'Are you going to be OK?' she asked.

'Of course. Why wouldn't I be?'

'Well. It's just you're not always the best at dealing with . . . stress.'

'Stress? I'm going on holiday.'

'Hmm,' she said. It was as if she wanted to say something else but was holding back.

'Now you come to mention it, though,' I said, 'I am a bit worried that I don't know how much to tip anyone. What if I get it wrong?'

'Try not to worry about it.'

'For example,' I said. 'If you stop someone on the street and ask for directions, do you tip them?'

'I don't think so.'

'What about the hotel receptionist?'

'I'm not sure.'

'That's the thing!' I cried. 'There are no rules. I looked this up on the internet and everyone says something different. You're supposed to tip taxi drivers, but not if they take you on a roundabout route. How will I know? I don't know the routes.'

'I'm sure you'll figure it out,' she sighed.

'I wish you were coming,' I said. She frowned and for the briefest moment I thought I saw her lip quiver slightly. But then she was just normal old Megan, all bustly and down-to-earth.

'It's not the right time,' she said. 'Do you know what I mean?'

'Yes.'

But I don't think I really do know what she means. Is she talking about her gran being sick? Or does she mean it's not the right time in our fledgling relationship? After all, we haven't actually taken a proper 'transatlantic flight' yet, as Mum might have put it. A few jaunts in a single-engined plane, yes. One quick helicopter flight to the Isle of Wight one night at her place when her parents were out, maybe. But that was all. It's a long way to New York.

Ben's Note: For Future Historians and Interested Parties at West Meon Probation Services. Since returning to the UK I have re-written and expanded on all diary entries I made while in New York or while travelling there and back. Though I made frequent diary entries I often found myself without the time to do justice to what was one of the most extraordinary weeks of my life. I tended to scribble notes and made a few voice memos and recordings which I have added to the narrative along with newspaper cuttings. I have not changed the order of anything, though some names may have been changed and I may have slightly altered my own dialogue to better reflect what I meant to say rather than what I managed to stammer out. Please note that I have not exaggerated Brandi DeLacourt in any way, shape or form. She really is like that.

Sunday 12th May

Time unknown

We're on the plane. We've been flying for about two hours now, and I can't pretend our journey has been entirely smooth so far. The coach journey from Woking was OK, though we really crawled along. I kept checking my watch, worried about the time. Luckily, Gex slept most of the way, he's not used to getting up before midday. He woke just as we were nearing Heathrow and needed to go to the loo.

'Hold it in,' I said. 'We're nearly there.' The last thing I needed was for him to get stuck in the toilet on the coach and make us miss the flight.

'I can't hold it in. 'I've got IDS.'

'Iain Duncan Smith?

Gex looked at me, baffled.

'The Pensions Minister?'

'Nah,' he said. 'The fing where you have to keep going to the loo.'

'You mean IBS, irritable bowel syndrome?'

'Not half,' he said, holding his tummy.

'It might help if you ate some vegetables once in a while,' I said.

'I'm not eating no veg in America,' he said. 'It's all GM.'

I started to reassure him about the safety of food in the US but he really did need to rush off. The driver seemed to speed up after that, I'm guessing he was anxious to get to the terminal and air out the coach.

* * *

The real trouble started once we arrived at the airport.

'Which desk do I go to to check in?' I asked a tired-looking BA person. He glanced at my ticket and pointed to a line full of angry-looking people which snaked around Terminal 5, out of the door and possibly all the way to Terminal 4.

'Um, are you sure? It's just that I have Executive Club tickets?'

'That's the Executive Club line,' he said, walking off.

'Wow, how long must the line be for economy?' I said to Gex. 'Mum and Dad had better hurry up.'

So we waited, and waited and waited. Gex chatted animatedly about gangs and turf and hos.

'You know you can buy guns in off-licences there, innit?' he said.

'Don't talk about guns in the airport,' I hissed.

'Why not?'

'Because people will think it's suspicious,' I whispered, nodding towards a security guard, who was watching us.

'*You're* looking suspicious,' he said.

'Well, I am *now*,' I said impatiently. 'But only because you started talking about guns.'

'Shh,' he said. 'Keep it down.'

Some more waiting. Gex started yawning loudly. After nearly an hour we were almost at the front of the queue. I checked my watch.

'Just as well we came an hour earlier than we needed to,' I said.

Gex stared at me, shocked. 'You tricked me.'

'You would have been late,' I pointed out.

'Brothers don't lie to other brothers, man.'

'Don't call people brothers when we're there. Especially black men.'

'Racist.'

'I'm not a racist. You are not black, they will think you are taking the piss.'

I was now getting seriously worried about Mum and Dad. I was starting to suspect the queue for Executive Club was the same as the economy line. Which was irritating, and it was now even longer than it had been when we'd arrived. There wouldn't be enough time for them to get to the front of the queue and get on the plane.

Just as we arrived at the front of the queue there was a huge kerfuffle behind us.

'Excuse me, excuse me. Coming through.'

A stocky lady in a tight-fitting blazer unhooked a rope and ushered my parents through. People who'd been queuing for over an hour tutted.

'Oh my goodness, thank you so much,' Mum said to the blazer lady. 'OUR CAR BROKE DOWN,' she called out so the queue could hear.

'Don't worry, we'll get you on your flight,' the lady said with a smile.

Mum turned to me and gave a panto wink. 'Car broke down?' I asked when the lady had gone. Dad was chuckling wickedly.

'Works every time,' he said.

'God, you two are such phonies,' I said. 'I'm tearing up your nomination for Pride of Britain this year.'

'Next!' someone was yelling. We all shuffled down to the check-in desk. Dad got there first and thrust out his ticket. 'I have a bad knee,' he said. 'I need a bulkhead seat so I can stretch it out.'

The man said nothing but jabbed keys furiously for a few minutes. Some of those keys sounded like they were going to fly into bits under the attack.

'No bulkhead seats available,' he said eventually. 'You need to get here earlier for those.'

'Our car broke down,' Dad said, outraged.

'Sorry about that,' the man said and continued destroying his keyboard.

Dad looked at Mum. 'I can't fly for six hours without any leg room.'

Clatter clatter clatter went the keyboard.

'Can he have an aisle seat on the left?' she asked. 'Then he can stretch his leg out into the aisle.'

The man looked up from his assault.

'You're not supposed to stretch your leg out into the aisles,' he said.

'I have a weak bladder,' Dad said quickly. 'That's the real reason I need the aisle.'

The man's eyes narrowed then.

'What is the problem exactly, sir?' he said. 'Your knee, or your bladder?'

'The knee was a decoy,' whispered Dad. 'I was a bit embarrassed. It's a prostate thing.'

The man looked unmoved, so I looked at my watch and sighed loudly. 'You can have my seat, Dad,' I said. 'In Executive Club.'

He looked at me. 'Really, son?'

'Yes, it has extra leg room.'

'Are you sure? You've been banging on about your Club Class seat for days.'

'Yes, but you have a bad knee and a prostate issue.'

Dad's face lit up and he looked at me as if he were about to slaughter a sheep in my honour. 'Thank you, Ben,' he said. 'I really appreciate it.'

I turned to Gex and shrugged. 'So I guess we're in economy after all.'

'You are,' he said. 'I'm in Executive Club.'

My mouth dropped. *Judas!* 'But don't you think Mum and Dad might want to sit together?'

'I don't mind,' Mum said.

'I'm happy to sit next to Gex,' Dad said, heaving a suitcase onto the weighing belt.

'He has IBS,' I said quickly.

'Well then, the poor lad definitely needs to go in Club,' Dad said. 'There's always a queue for the toilets in economy.'

I sighed. This is not how things were supposed to turn out.

Later; somewhere over the Atlantic

Mum is snoring softly next to me. I can hear Dad and Gex laughing a dozen rows away in EXECUTIVE CLUB CLASS, I'm sure I saw an extremely attractive flight attendant up there pouring something fizzy earlier, before she pulled the

58

curtain across. Mum and I got a cold cheese roll each from a grumpy old steward who keeps walking into my elbow. Mum felt sorry for me and gave me her roll and now I feel a bit sick. Also, the compression socks are perhaps a little too tight. I'm now worried about my circulation. No point avoiding deep vein thrombosis only to end up with gangrene.

I'm also obsessing over something else. Needles in my hand luggage. When we were checking our bags in, the keyboard killer asked me if I had anything sharp in my hand luggage.

'Like what?' I asked.

'Like a knife, or needles?'

'I have some needles,' I admitted.

'Are they for prescription medicines?'

'No, for fuschia stitch.'

'What?'

'For knitting. They're knitting needles.'

He gave me an odd look.

'OK, you'd better pack them in your hold luggage.'

'Really? I asked. 'It's just that I was going to work on my knitting on the plane. I get anxious sometimes and it calms me.'

'Sir,' he said. 'I have a long queue of people waiting.'

'Fine, fine.' I unzipped my bag and shoved the needles and half-finished Hoopie in.

'What else do you have in your hand luggage?' he asked.

I shrugged. 'Passport, tickets, my Kindle, my Stiletto.'

He jerked back. 'You have a Stiletto?'

'Yeah,' I said, grinning proudly.

'Why?'

I shrugged. 'They're cool. You can play games with them.'

He shook his head. 'It needs to go in the hold luggage, I'm afraid. 'Is it in a sheath?'

'A case, yes. Does it really need to go in the hold?'

He blinked in surprise. 'Well, you can't use it in the cabin, obviously!'

'No, I suppose not,' I said. So that went in the suitcase too and I watched it sail off down the conveyor belt.

I had this irrational fear that I'd never see it again.

I huffed and puffed in my seat. I was caught in a vicious circle. I was anxious at having been parted from my knitting; the only thing that could relax me was my knitting.

'What is it?' Mum said, dragging her eyes away from her book.

'Nothing,' I said grumpily. 'Just felt like doing some knitting to pass the time.'

Mum nodded, and a tiny smirk appeared.

'You are a weird and wonderful boy, Ben. Don't ever change.'

I sighed and fiddled with the in-flight entertainment controls.

'I'm going to lose myself in a few episodes of *Breaking Bad*,' I told her, plugging in the ear-phones. 'Let me know when they come round with the hot flannels.'

1.32pm US time

I'm writing this in a 6' x 8' cell. They've allowed me a pencil and a sheet of paper but nothing else. They even took my shoes and belt. They'll send me to Gitmo, I know it.

Here's how it happened. After the plane landed, we all shuffled out into the terminal and queued up for Immigration Control. I was a little worried about Gex. He doesn't actually have a criminal record thankfully, as the moped incident in Holland and Barrett happened when he was only fifteen. Then he got off with a caution after the Martini Rosso thing. But US immigration is notoriously thorough, and Gex, who was well ahead of me in the queue, has a tendency to lie just for the hell of it.

I stood on my tiptoes and tried to see him. I could see Dad, but not Gex. Had they already taken him off to a quiet room? A man in a dark suit and an earpiece stood to one side and watched me carefully. I realised I was probably acting suspiciously and made myself look casual and stop peering ahead.

Dermot O'Leary's voice-over started again. 'Tension is high at JFK Airport. If Gex is considered to be an Undesirable Element and refused entry to the country, Ben might face a difficult choice.'

Mum was beside me, making her passport disappear and re-appear. Then she started making my passport disappear. One minute it was in my hand, then it was gone and I was holding a red silk handkerchief.

'Stop!' I hissed. 'You'll probably get arrested.'

'Sorry,' she said. She reached behind my ear, pulled out a ten-dollar bill and gave it to me.

The man in the dark suit had now transferred his attention to my mother. He was frowning, his hand hovering over his walkie-talkie thing.

Mum gave him her winning innocent smile, though, and he nodded amiably.

I rolled my eyes.

'How are you feeling?' she asked me.

'Anxious,' I replied, looking for Gex again.

'Just relax, Ben,' she said. 'Enjoy yourself, OK?'

Then I saw him, he was at the booth showing the man his passport. The officer asked him a question. Gex replied and the officer stared at him, disbelieving.

But then the man gave Gex his passport back and waved him through.

'Now I can relax,' I said as I was called up.

I smiled as I gave the officer my passport and immigration card. He looked like a proper New Yorker, stocky and slightly grizzled. He had a great hat with shiny silver badges. Behind and to one side were cops wearing holsters with guns.

The man scanned my passport and stopped, looking at the screen.

'You have a criminal record,' he said.

Suddenly I felt nervous. I saw Mum walk through the booth next to me, the lady officer there basically just waved her through.

'I'm on probation,' I said. 'Ms Gunter sorted it all out.'

He looked at me, unsmiling. 'Ms Gunter?'

'She's my probation officer. She said she was going to sort it out with the Home Office.'

'Listen, kid,' he said. 'Criminals are not allowed in this country.'

I laughed (first mistake). 'I'm not really a criminal,' I said. 'I mean, technically I stole something, but –' (second mistake). I stopped abruptly at his stern expression.

'You think this is funny, kid?' he asked, getting to his feet.

'That came out all wrong,' I said, flustered. 'It was really just a big misunderstanding. I like knitting now.'

(Third mistake.)

What a mess. I'd been so busy worrying about Gex I'd forgotten to worry about my own situation. How am I supposed to keep up with all the things I have to worry about?

'I think we need to ask you a few questions, young man,' the officer said. He stepped out of his booth, and gestured to me to stand aside. 'If you don't mind?'

And then another officer arrived and asked me to come with him and everything went blurry and they took my shoes and my belt and gave me a Styrofoam cup of water and left me here in this cell. If I was Walter White from *Breaking Bad*, this kind of situation would be a mere nuisance.

But I am not Walter White. I'm Ben Fletcher. And I want my mum.

2.03pm
Roberto and Jack just came to see me. Roberto and Jack are immigration officers and are trying to 'get to the bottom of my situation'. Apparently my parents have been told where I am and they are waiting in the airport until 'the matter can be resolved'. An armed officer stood to one side, like in *The Shield*. I kept waiting for Roberto to ask the guard to leave so he could 'talk' to me alone . . . Roberto is young and good looking. He's full of energy and scowls a lot. Jack seems to be the Good Cop. He's grey and avuncular and keeps

disappearing to get cups of coffee for everyone. They've been in and out three times now, asking me questions about my conviction and the details on my landing card.

I'd got over my initial terror after an hour or so and was now bored out of my skull.

'Why have you come to the US?' Roberto asked, for the fifth time.

'For KnitFair USA,' I explained. 'I won a knitting competition. I wrote it all on the card.'

Honestly, why do they give you the card to fill in if they're not going to read it?

He sat back in his chair, his eyes narrow.

'You expect me to believe that?'

'Do you really think I'd make that up?' I replied.

Roberto made as if to speak but Jack interrupted. 'OK,' he said. 'I can't see as anyone would admit that unless it were true.' I could have sworn he smirked at Roberto then.

'Look, phone Ms Gunter,' I said. 'She'll tell you I'm not a terrorist.'

'This is the probation lady?'

'Yes.'

'But you don't have her number?'

'It's in my phone, in my suitcase,' I explained. 'If you get me my suitcase, I'll find you the number. Or just call 192 192.'

After a pause Jack spoke again. 'We gotta go make some calls. Come on, Robbie.'

Robbie looked annoyed to be called away, but he stood and walked to the door.

'You want anything?' Jack asked. 'Cigarettes? A burger?'

'No thanks,' I said tiredly. 'I don't smoke.'

I wish I'd said yes to the burger, though. It had been a long time since the cheese roll.

2.47pm

Roberto came back alone after a while carrying my landing card. He sat opposite me and stared at me coolly.

'Um. Did you phone Ms Gunter?' I asked after a long silence.

'Oh, we phoned her all right,' he said.

There was another pause.

Another silence. This time I waited.

'Hey, sonny,' he said, leaning forward. 'I don't give a rat's ass about your goddam shoplifting.'

'OK,' I said cautiously. That was something.

'Do you know why I don't care about it?'

I shook my head dumbly.

'It's because you wrote it on the card,' he said, stabbing his finger down on the document. He held it up and pointed to some text at the bottom. 'What does it say here?'

I leaned forward and peered at the card. 'It says it is a federal offence to provide incorrect information on this document.'

'Yeah, goddam right it says that.'

I waited.

'And you signed it,' he said.

'Yes?' I wasn't bored any more. My heart was pounding, I felt sick and hot.

'So you say that everything on this document is the God's truth?' he said, leaning back.

'Erm, I think so?' I said, now not at all sure, but wondering what I could have got wrong.

He glared at me, then looked down at the card. 'Question seven. Are you, or have you ever been a member of a group or organisation engaging in political agitation, terrorism or other unpatriotic activities?'

'Right?'

'And you ticked . . . ?'

'No.'

He smiled; a look of triumph flooded his face.

'So why is it, Mr Fletcher, that when I look at your security profile, I see, in bright green letters, that you are a member of a proscribed organisation?'

I sat, frozen in horror. What on earth?

'It must be a mistake,' I said. 'Joz tried to get me to join the young Lib Dems but it was fifteen pounds and I told him to stick it.'

'Are you saying the British security agency made a mistake?' he snorted. 'GCHQ got it *wrong*?'

'Well, yeah, I think that's very likely.'

He sniffed.

'So I guess you're going to tell me you're not a member of KAW?'

'What? A member of what?'

'K – A – W,' he repeated. He pulled another piece of paper from his pocket and slammed it on the table before me. I looked down at it.

It was a printout of an online application form, completed with my details. An application for . . .

I laughed. 'Knitters Against Weapons!' I said. 'KAW! I'd forgotten I'd even joined up. It was free. I get emails from them sometimes asking me to knit flowers for peace.'

'So you admit you are a member?'

'Well yes, but seriously . . . it's a group of knitters.'

'Campaigning for disarmament,' he finished.

'That's not illegal, is it?'

'It's unpatriotic,' he snapped. 'It's goddam unpatriotic.'

'Why?' I asked, genuinely mystified.

'Why? What happens when we disarm?' he spat. 'Do you think Omar the Terrorist is going to disarm too?'

'I hadn't really thought it through, I suppose,' I said.

Jack appeared then, carrying a Styrofoam cup of coffee. He set the coffee down on the floor, then crouched down and took the lid off.

'Do you think you can knit a flak jacket out of . . . wool?' Roberto continued.

'No, probably not,' I admitted.

'Can you crochet a tank?'

'You can't,' I admitted.

He shook his head. 'You socialists make me sick.'

'Jesus Christ, Robbie,' Jack said, tearing open a sachet of sugar. 'Let the kid go already.'

Robbie held up the landing card. 'He lied, Jack. He's a member of a proscribed . . .'

Jack reached up and took the card from Roberto, tearing it into shreds.

'What the hell? Roberto cried, looking like he might punch Jack. 'Do you know how many federal regulations you just broke, Jack? You've gone too far this time!'

I glanced over at the armed officer standing against the wall. He looked bored, like this happened all the time.

'Sorry about this,' Jack said to me. 'You're free to leave, sir.'

I didn't need to be told twice. I stood, leaving the incandescent Roberto picking up shreds of landing card as I legged it.

'Hey, kid,' Jack called as I reached the door. I turned.

'Welcome to America,' he said.

Then he winked.

5.12pm

I've been allowed to enter mainland United States after a few hours of cross-Atlantic extradition treaty discussions between the Deputy Director of the Department of Homeland Security and Livvie Hutton, Ms Gunter's junior assistant at West Meon Probation Services.

For all Claudia Gunter's efforts to clear this trip with the Home Office, you'd think she could have called the Americans and let them know I was coming. The really galling thing is that Gex just sailed right through without a problem while I was sat in Gitmo on the Hudson for four hours.

My problems didn't end there, either. I got through to find Mum sitting in the arrivals lounge, on the phone, laughing. She saw me and quickly ended her conversation.

'Oh, Diablo. Ben's here. Got to go,' she said. 'See you on Wednesday.'

'Ben, are you OK?' she asked, putting her phone away.

'I've been better,' I replied, feeling like Cool-Hand Luke. I really wished Megan could have been there to see how icy I was, rather than Mum. Still, she gave me a hug and I felt better.

'Where's Dad?' I asked.

'He and Gex have gone to the hotel.'

'Charming.'

'They're both very, very excited about being here and frankly, they were doing my head in, so I told them just to go. There didn't seem any point in us all waiting.'

'Have they taken my suitcase?' I asked, looking around for it. Mum's suitcase was there, but not mine.

'Ah,' she said. 'That's the other thing. No one can find your suitcase.'

'You're kidding.'

I knew it. I knew it, I thought. I knew that worrying wasn't for nothing.

Mum shook her head. 'Sorry. Brandi's over there now trying to sort it out.'

Brandi! I'd forgotten about Brandi.

'The airline people said they think your bag was left at Heathrow,' Mum went on. 'They'll send it to the hotel when it turns up.'

'Oh great, when will that be?'

She shrugged. 'Tomorrow maybe?'

'But my knitting's in that suitcase!'

'Look, here's Brandi.'

I looked up and did a perfect double take. Walking towards us in heels came a girl, who looked a few years older than me. She was pretty. And she had a lot of hair. Layer upon layer of it. All swoops and waves and fringes. I'd like to be able to describe her hair better but I really don't think words could do it justice. Just take it from me. There was a lot going on.

'You must be Ben!' she cried, noticing me. 'I'm so sorry you were held up for so long.'

'No problem,' I said casually. 'Just doing their job..'

'The thing is,' she said. 'We had a very big terrorist attack here a few years ago. And everyone's been *really* careful ever since.'

'You mean the attacks on the World Trade Center?'

'You heard about that? We call it 9/11.'

'Yes. It was a fairly significant global event.'

'Even in England?'

'Yes. Even in England.'

She smiled at me and I had to fight not to do another double take. Her teeth! They were amazing! So white, so straight. I found myself pursing my lips so as not to horrify her by the state of mine. Just as well Miss Swallow hadn't come as my chaperone. Her teeth aren't exactly her best feature, as I think I might have mentioned before. Personally I don't mind her crooked canines but I fear they might be a bridge too far for some Americans. I immediately felt guilty for the unfair comparison. Teeth aren't everything, I reminded myself. Jessica Swallow is the most beautiful woman in the world, even with her dental deformities. But then Brandi smiled again and I'm afraid to say I went into a bit of a daze.

'Any luck with the case?' Mum asked her.

'What? Oh no,' she said, face back to sad mode again. 'They say it will probably be here tomorrow. They'll send it to the hotel in a cab.'

I sighed.

'Did it have important things in?' Brandi asked.

'Just my clothes,' I said. 'Oh, and my phone. And my knitting!'

'Just relax,' Mum said. 'You can survive twenty-four hours without your knitting.'

'I'm not sure I can.'

'Let's just get to the hotel,' Mum said. 'You can have a shower and some food.'

'What am I going to change into?'

'You can borrow some of your father's clothes.'

'No way.'

'Or Gex's?'

'OK, I'll borrow some from Dad.'

I felt a bit better once we were in a cab and racing through the weekend traffic towards the Big Apple. I snuck a few covert glances at Brandi. In addition to having extraordinary hair and spectacular teeth, Brandi smells amazing. She talked a lot as we drove, telling me things I already knew. 'Many people think that *New* York is the capital of the United States, but it isn't. That's a city called Washington.'

'Oh yes?'

'That river there is called the East River,' Brandi said. 'On the other *side* of Manhattan is the Hudson. Manhattan has water pretty much all the way around. It's a bit like an island.'

'Manhattan is an island, isn't it?' Mum whispered to me. I nodded.

'That pointy building over there?' Brandi went on. 'That's the Chrysler building. It was built a long *time* ago. It's very famous . . . These are traffic lights here.'

'Uh huh,' I nodded. 'Traffic lights, OK.'

* * *

The hotel is on West 38th Street, close to the Hudson and just a few blocks from Penn Station and Madison Square Garden, which is where KnitFair is happening in just a few days. Brandi didn't come into the hotel. She said she was already seriously late for her date that night, but before she headed off in the cab, she gave me a folder with media engagements in it. She promised to come and collect me in the morning.

When we arrived, there was no sign of Gex. Dad came down to the lobby as I was checking in and told me Gex had dropped off his bag in the room we were sharing, and then immediately gone out.

I sighed. 'Where did he go?'

Dad shrugged. 'He turned left.'

'This is not good,' I said. 'Why didn't you stop him. You know he's got the wits of a toddler?'

'Nah. He's a big boy,' Dad said. 'He can look after himself.'

'Have you met Gex?' I asked.

Dad seemed distracted though. A bit agitated, too. He was grinning and sweating a bit.

'Are you OK?' I asked as we walked to the lift.

'Jet lag, I suppose,' he said. 'And I took some codeine for my knee. And I drank a bottle of your sister's car-sickness medication for the flight. Feel a bit funny, actually.'

'Maybe you should go and lie down.'

'Yeah, maybe just for a bit,' he said, and we headed for the lifts. Or elevators, as they're called here.

'Don't think much of this hotel,' Dad said, as we waited for the next elevator to arrive.

72

'It's three star,' I pointed out defensively.

'Out of how many?' he asked. 'Twenty?'

We got into the elevator.

'Fourteen,' I said, but Dad had already pressed 11 for some reason. Then he hit 15 by mistake, and then, in trying to correct his error, he lurched against the wall and accidentally pressed 3, 4 and 5 with his good knee.

'Sorry,' he said, blinking furiously. Mum watched him calmly as the doors closed, then reached across and pressed 14.

'Thanks, Mum.'

The room I'm sharing with Gex is quite nice. Tidy and clean. This is probably because Gex hasn't been in it much.

There's a small bathroom, two single beds and a little kitchen area with a sink and a minibar. The prices of the items in the minibar are eye-wateringly expensive. Apple juice for $8. Small cans of beer for $13. A Hershey's chocolate bar for $6.50. I'll have to watch Gex to make sure he doesn't get stuck in. I had a shower, and watched a bit of CNN, and I felt a bit better. Brandi had given me a fold-out map of Manhattan and I checked where all the important places were. KnitFair USA at Madison Square Garden. The Priapia offices on 5th Avenue. Bloomingdales on 59th and Lexington. I was so excited. I wished Megan was here.

OH MY GOD I forgot to skype Ms Gunter! This is what happens when you rely on phones to remind you to do stuff. (Note to Megan Hooper.)

I raced down to reception to ask if they had a PC I could use, and they directed me two blocks down to an internet café.

By the time I got there, I realised I didn't have any money, ran to a cashpoint and back again, it was 6.43pm NY time, or 10.43pm in West Meon. Luckily I had Ms Gunter's Skype ID on an old email.

The screen blinked into life and she glared at me.

'I'm sorry!' I said. 'I've had the worst journey.'

'It's nearly 11pm, Ben. I'm getting ready for bed.'

I peered closely at the screen and realised she was wearing a nightie.

'I was held in a little cubicle at JFK for four hours,' I pointed out.

'Spare me the excuses, Ben,' she said. 'I get excuses all day, every day.'

'Wow, you're really snippy,' I said.

'I'm sorry to hear you've had a tough time,' she said tiredly. 'But, Ben, you can't leave it this late tomorrow, OK?'

I was too tired to argue with her, despite the fact that it was her incompetence that has made this day such an unmitigated disaster.

'Fine, so I have officially checked in,' I said wearily. 'Can I go and have my dinner now?'

'Please do,' she said, yawning. 'Say hi to your parents, won't you.'

She hung up. Not before I caught the final volume of the *Fifty Shades* trilogy face down on her bedside table.

She's a dark horse, that Ms Gunter.

My parents and I finally ate at a diner opposite the hotel called Dino's. We were a bit freaked out by an old tramp who rattled a cup at us after we came out of the hotel. Mum gave him a quarter but he didn't seem happy with that. So Mum and I ran across the road to escape. Dad had a bit of trouble crossing the road, though. Talk about a rabbit in the headlights.

'Hurry up, Rain Man,' Mum called. In the end I had to go and drag him across while a yellow taxi honked at us.

'They have a friendly sound, American car horns,' Dad said, waving at the driver, who gave him the finger in response.

After we'd been seated in a booth, I ordered a Philly cheesesteak sandwich. Mum had mac and cheese and Dad had wonton soup, which was an unusual choice for his first meal in a Manhattan diner, but that's my dad for you.

Our order was taken by an exhausted-looking waitress, wearing a name tag which told us her name was Denise. She was quite pretty in a tired kind of way, and I made sure I placed the order, just in case Gex had been right about American girls liking English accents. She didn't seem to notice though, just scribbled everything down and stumped off, bashing into a pot plant as she went.

'I wonder where Gex is?' I said.

'He's probably texting you,' Mum said.' Only you don't have your phone.'

'Don't remind me,' I said. 'I think I'll buy a new one tomorrow.'

The Philly steak was fantastic, but I was put off my food slightly by Mum and Dad, who had suddenly gone completely mushy with one another. They were staring into each other's eyes, playing footsie under the table and giggling like school children. When the double entendres started it was the final straw.

'Fancy a munch of my burger?' Mum asked him.

'Maybe later,' Dad said, smirking. 'Would you like to try my wonton?'

'Not here, please,' I hissed. '

'We're just sharing food,' Mum said innocently.

'Yeah,' Dad agreed. 'Lighten up'

'Look, it's great that you're all . . . into each other at your age,' I said. 'But just tone it down, OK? It's not like you're on honeymoon or something.'

Mum gave me a tender look.

'Sorry, Ben. You must be wishing Megan was here. Can't be much fun making do with a couple of gooey old fogeys?'

'Not at all,' I said, through gritted teeth. 'I've never had so much fun.'

Monday 13th May

There was a knock on my door at 8am. I pulled on the robe I'd found in the bathroom and shuffled to the door. Peering through the spyhole I was almost blinded by the sight of white teeth filling the view. Squinting, I opened the door.

'Hi, Ben,' Brandi said. 'Did I wake you?'

'No,' I lied. I had in fact managed to get off to sleep sometime after 3am. Gex had still not returned and I woke a few times during the small hours, worried. I hoped he was with his cousin but without my phone there was no way of telling. Why on earth had I put it in hold luggage? It had of course occurred to me, soon after my bag disappeared into the bowels of Heathrow airport, that the check-in man and I had been talking at cross purposes. He'd thought I meant a stiletto *knife*. Not a Stiletto phone. The older generation doesn't keep up with phone trends, clearly.

'Would you like me to wait *downstairs* for you?' she asked. 'While you get ready?'

I stared blankly at her.

'Your media commitments? We have two newspapers and three magazines to see this morning. So, up and at 'em!' she said cheerily. There was a note of panic in her voice. She was clearly wondering what kind of media-illiterate knitting weirdo she'd been lumped with here.

'No,' I said. 'I'm nearly ready, come in. Excuse the mess.'

I led her into the room and kicked a pair of Y-fronts under the bed.

'Sit here,' I said, indicating an armchair. 'There are no tea-making facilities, I'm afraid.'

She gave me a funny look. 'You want tea?'

'Well, I usually have a cup in the mornings,' I said.

'So phone room service,' she said, looking puzzled.

'Oh, I don't want to cause a fuss,' I said. 'No time anyway. Interviews to do and all that. I'm going to have a quick shower. I'll be right with you.'

I was back out in ten minutes, still in my gown. It was only when I'd dried off that I remembered I didn't have any clothes, other than the clothes I'd worn the day before. I couldn't put those on again. I'd done a fair bit of sweating in that interview room. And I might have dropped a bit of the cheesesteak down my front.

I'd have to bite the bullet and borrow some of Gex's gear.

'I'll be back in a minute,' I told Brandi, dragging the suitcase back into the bathroom again. 'Make yourself at home.'

Brandi gave me a quizzical look, then picked up the remote and got stuck into *Judge Judy*.

Inside the bathroom I opened the suitcase.

It was worse than I'd feared. I was greeted by the strong smell of Lynx Africa body spray. On the top of the pile of clothes was a new Adidas tracksuit. White with black piping. Under that was a selection of Burberry caps, then a pair of low-slung jeans. A couple of hoodies, some long rapper-style T-shirts, another tracksuit, this time in gold with red piping, then some bling, pants and socks and at the very bottom, a belt with studs. Sighing heavily, I grabbed the jeans, the belt and one of the hoodies. After another moment's hesitation I took a pair of boxer shorts.

I didn't want to wear white socks with my brown shoes and that stumped me for a while, until I remembered the orthopaedic stockings. Of course! Thank God I'd used a charcoal wool for those.

Now. Could I be sure the boxers were clean? Gex wouldn't have packed dirty underwear, would he? But did I dare sniff them to find out? Eventually I put them on back-to-front, just in case. The idea of my boy band touching an area of fabric that had first touched Gex's boy band made me gag.

Next, the jeans. By tightening the belt I could make the jeans ride higher on my hips but that left my ankles and too much of the orthopaedic stockings exposed. So I let the jeans drop a little and covered my hips with the longest hoodie. If

I didn't lean forward I wouldn't be revealing my underpants. Sorry. *Gex's* underpants.

I made my second entrance of the morning and if Brandi thought my look was anything but suavely sophisticated, she didn't show it.

There was a knock at the door.

'That'll be room service,' she said, moving to the door and opening it. A waiter pushed a trolley in. Thankfully Brandi slipped a note into his hand, relieving me of that terrifying duty. So you did tip room-service waiters. Good to know. I didn't see how much she'd given him though. All the notes are the same colour here, frustratingly.

'I got you a cup of tea,' she said. On the trolley was a tray with a pot of tea and three metal cloches. 'And a little breakfast.'

'Wow,' I said.

'I wasn't sure what you liked so I got you pancakes, bacon and eggs and porridge. These are traditional *breakfast* foods in this country.'

'Thanks,' I said. 'Have you had your breakfast?'

'I'm on the 358:2 diet,' she said. 'You don't eat anything for three hundred and fifty-eight minutes, which is nearly six hours, then you have to eat as much as you can in two minutes, then you don't eat for three hundred and fifty-eight minutes again, then you eat for another two minutes solid, and so on.'

'Wow, sounds complicated,' I said, shovelling pancake and blueberries into my mouth.

'It's all about controlling your metabolic rhythms,' she said. 'I read this book.'

'I bet you can eat quite a lot in two minutes,' I said, thinking about it. 'I mean *one* can eat a lot in two minutes, not just *you*. I mean, definitely not you. I bet you eat like a bird.'

'Well,' said Brandi, looking quite pleased. 'I try and keep in shape.'

'You're succeeding!' I said, much too loudly, then pretended to choke on a bit of pancake to cover my embarrassment.

It had suddenly got slightly awkward.

'Oh, by the way,' she said when I'd finished my choking fit. 'There was a call while you were in the shower.'

'Oh yes?'

'I think he was from New Zealand or something. He had a strange accent. His name was Gets, or Kecks or something.'

'Gex,' I said. 'He's not from New Zealand, he's from Southampton.'

'I knew it was somewhere exotic,' she said. 'Anyway, he said to say he's fine and staying with his cousin and why aren't you answering your texts?'

'I lost my phone,' I said through a mouthful of pancake.

'I know that, I told him. He laughed.'

'That sounds like him.' I was relieved to find he was still alive at least.

I left a message for Mum and Dad and we went downstairs and out onto the street. I was excited about my first full day in New York. I felt like I was *doing business*, though perhaps not so much like Gordon Gecko. More like Ugly Betty. Still, things worked out all right for her, in the end. I was thrilled and nervous. I took in a great lungful of air and was immediately overwhelmed by a foul stench. I coughed and gagged.

'Got any change?' a man asked, rattling a plant pot at me which he seemed to be using to collect change. It was the same tramp who'd shadowed us as we'd waited to cross the road last night. He was a bit freaky looking, with staring eyes and a faded tattoo of Astro Boy on his temple. I dug in my pocket. A quarter hadn't been enough to get rid of him last night. But I didn't want to give him too much in case he became my new best friend.

'Come on, Ben,' Brandi called. She'd found a cab and was inside, the door open for me. 'We've got a lot to do.'

I gave the homeless man a dollar.

'You're not supposed to give them money,' Brandi said. 'It only encourages them.'

'I'm hoping it'll encourage him to leave me alone.'

'So did you look at the list of media commitments?' she asked. I was too busy taking in my surroundings to pay much attention. Our driver was called Tarasalak Clontarf. He glowered at me from the ID photo stuck to the window behind his head. We hadn't got very far. The traffic had suddenly snarled.

'Yes. Sort of. No,' I admitted. 'I'll look now.' I opened the folder and looked at the first page. Then the second page. Then the third, and the fourth.' Do I have to do all of these?' I asked.

'I'm afraid so,' Brandi replied. 'Is there a problem?'

'There are just so many,' I said as the cab finally turned onto 5th Avenue and crawled a few metres uptown. 'You signed the form authorising us to arrange publicity,' Brandi reminded me anxiously.

'Did I?'

'Yes,' she said firmly. Through the window behind her I

81

could see my Personal Tramp shuffling down 5th Avenue. I now saw he carried a Macy's bag as well as the plant pot. I ducked down before he saw me.

'Am I really such a big deal to warrant all these interviews?' I asked. 'Who's going to be interested in my story?'

'A *lot* of people,' Brandi replied, turning to look at me. 'People love a feel-good story like yours. Especially when it's a boy doing something . . .'

'Unstereotypical?' I suggested. 'Girly.'

'That's right,' Brandi replied seriously. 'Something that breaks conventions. You're a pioneer.'

'Well, I don't know about that,' I said, going red.

'Pioneers built this country,' Brandi said, suddenly passionate. 'People who took a chance. People who escaped their English oppressors . . . sorry . . .'

'That's OK.'

'. . . and came here to build a new life, to follow their dreams.'

'Steady on,' I muttered, embarrassed. 'I knit. That's all. Nothing world-changing.'

'Ben,' she said. 'You can realise your dreams here. It's that kind of place.'

Uplifting stuff for 9.15 on a Monday morning, you might think. And only undermined slightly by the presence of my tramp, who'd suddenly appeared at the window behind Brandi, rattling his plant pot.

'Anyway,' Brandi went on. 'Most of the interviews won't get used.'

'Oh,' I said, slightly deflated.

'This is the circuit,' she said. 'You have to go through it in the

82

hope that you get one or two hits. That's the way things work.'

I was really nervous as we turned up at the first round of interviews, in a big, slightly shabby office block on 56th Street. The building was mostly occupied by magazine companies. I saw three different junior editors, working for three different craft and knitting publications, each with a slightly different focus.

There was:

> *Let's Knit and Crochet*
> *Crochet and Knitting World*
> *Knit and Crochet, USA!*

I picked up a copy of *Crochet and Knitting World* to check the cover stories.

> *Marine-O Woollens – Practical garments to keep our military heroes warm this winter*
> *Primary Colours – Donkey or elephant? How to knit your party's emblem before the elections this fall*
> *Needlepoint Break! – 5 different patterns for that perfect surfboard cover*
> *Cast Off – We meet the dressmakers of Les Mis and find out how they create those gorgeous rags*
> *Angora Management – Robert De Niro drops by to talk about how knitting helped him to control his temper on set*

What's that? Robert de Niro knits? Amazing! How would Dad take this news? I wondered. Could go either way. Either he'll be pleased to hear his son's knitting love affair is shared by one of his favourite actors. On the other hand it might trigger some kind of mid-life crisis to have his illusions so cruelly shattered. He's still not forgiven Gavin Henson for competing in *Strictly Come Dancing*.

There was a Cellophane packet stuck to the front of the magazine with some cheap acrylic needles and some thin yarn. I saw the needles were a US 10.5 size. A good size for knitting Hoopies or scarves. Maybe these would do for me until my bag turned up. I asked the receptionist if I could take a copy and she shrugged and nodded.

I was interviewed by three young interns separately, each of whom had a huge smile pinned to her face which couldn't quite disguise the boredom underneath. *This is not what I went to journalism school to do*, their body language said. I sympathised. I didn't really want to be there any more than they did. Most of the questions were about me being a boy and how unusual it was to find a boy who knitted and were my parents very accepting? And so on.

No surprises there.

After that we got in another cab, me clutching the magazine, and went across to 58th Street, two blocks over. It would have been quicker to walk, and I could have done with stretching my legs, but when I suggested that Brandi gave me a look as though I'd suggested we travel by magic carpet. On the way, Brandi talked non-stop. 'Some people call New York the city that *never* sleeps,' she said. 'By that they mean that it's like a twenty-four-hour city, do you know what I mean?'

'I think so.'

'There's always something going on. I love it here.'

'Are you not from here originally?'

'No, I'm from Washington State. Not Washington DC. A lot of people get those confused.'

'Really?' I asked. I wondered if she thought I was dim, or just didn't want to take any chances. Rather than feeling patronised, I quite liked the way she didn't make the assumption that I knew everything about the US. Or indeed anything about the US.

The next interview was with a newspaper. The *Herald*. Again, it was a young, intense-looking intern named Miranda who asked me questions. She seemed fascinated by the fact that I actually knew how to knit and asked me to give her a demonstration.

'I'm sorry,' I said. 'The airline lost my bag, so I don't have my knitting with me at the moment.'

She seemed disappointed. 'Well, maybe you could give me your number and we could meet up tomorrow night and you can show me your stuff.'

I hesitated.

'I don't think that will be possible,' Brandi said, stepping in. 'Ben is very busy.'

'I'm not that busy,' I said.

'Yes you are,' Brandi said. 'Especially tomorrow night.'

'Well, what about . . . ' the intern began.

'If you'd like to watch Ben knit,' Brandi said coldly. 'You

can come along to KnitFair USA this weekend. Ben will be demonstrating his skills there.'

'Will I?' I asked.

'We need to talk about that,' Brandi said.

Brandi wrapped things up after that, which was a relief.

'Aren't we near Bloomingdale's?' I asked as we left the offices.

'That's right,' Brandi replied. 'You wanna pop in?'

'I want to look at the knitting gear,' I said.

So we went in, and oh my days.

Bloomingdale's knit shop is to Pullinger's what Jessica Swallow is to Susan Boyle. Sorry, Natasha, but that's the truth. There were so many varieties of wool. Types I'd never heard of. Colours that don't exist in other countries. Weaves that had dropped through a portal from another dimension. Rack upon rack of crochet hooks from around the world. Specialist, exquisite hand-carved needles in long cardboard boxes like from Ollivander's wand shop in Harry Potter.

I could have stayed in there for hours. Brandi just stood, texting absently and watching me at the same time, one eyebrow permanently raised. Eventually she coughed and looked at her watch. I bought some basic merino wool in blue and white, Hampton FC's colours. No needles. I needed to conserve my money and I had the free needles to get me by for now. I was glad I'd bought something though because it meant I got a huge paper Bloomingdale's shopping bag, which I'd really wanted. I put my magazine into it and grinned at Brandi.

'Ready?' she asked.

'Ready,' I said. 'Let's go.'

On the way out I couldn't help but notice a lovely knitted top with a cowl that was slightly reminiscent of the Hoopie. I stopped to admire it. I was pleased to see that the design wasn't close enough to the Hoopie to raise any awkward questions about copyright, but close enough to suggest that hooded tops were most definitely in.

After that we went to a radio station. Now that was fun. I was getting the hang of all the questions by then and felt confident I would know what to say. I thought there'd be all sorts of preparation and release forms to complete and someone to explain what swear words I wasn't allowed to use and so on. But not a bit of it. They just ushered me straight into the studio, and the DJ, whose name was Craig something, ignored me for a bit while he chattered inanely and then played a song. As the music faded he began talking over the top.

'And we're back on the Craig something show on WKPP morning and today we have Ben Felcher with us. Ben, tell us why you're in town.'

'Erm, it's Fletcher.'

'OK, Fletcher, tell us why you're here.'

'Er, I'm here for KnitFair USA,' I said. 'I won a knitting competition in England and one of the prizes was a trip to New York.'

'What were the other prizes?' he asked.

'A book of patterns, a voucher for wool and needles, some champagne, but I'm not old enough to drink so I got fizzy apple stuff instead.'

'So you knit?' he said. He wasn't watching me as he spoke. He was flicking his way through a stack of CDs.

'That's right.'

'Do all boys knit in England?'

'No. Not at all.' I wasn't sure I liked Craig.

'How long have you being doing this?'

'Oh, not long. Nine months maybe.'

'You must be an expert by now, huh?'

'Well, I don't know. But I've got pretty fast. That's how I won.'

'So this is speed knitting?'

'Speed is one of the criteria on which you're judged. There's technique, creativity, accuracy . . .'

'Yeah, yeah. What I don't get, about knitting,' Craig said, now shuffling through a different rack of CDs, 'Is what is the goddam point?'

'Er . . . well. I find it relaxing.'

'Because, tell if I'm wrong,' he said. 'But they have machines that can knit, right?'

I definitely didn't like Craig something.

'Yes, of course.'

'And they're more accurate, and they got better technique than a person?'

'Well, maybe, but there's creativity . . .'

'But that's just down to the guy who programmes the machines, yeah? He does the creativity.'

'Well, I suppose.' I was getting a little cross with Craig by this point. It wasn't as if I was some crooked politician. Or some businessman caught with his hand in the till. I was just an English boy in New York.

'And you're no way near as fast as a machine.'

I shrugged. Not wanting to answer.

'That's right, isn't it? The machine is much faster.'

'Depends on the machine,' I replied sullenly. 'Depends on the knitter.'

'Wait,' he said, stopping his search for a song to look at me finally. 'You think you can beat a machine?'

I shrugged again.

'You're shrugging. He's shrugging. You can knit faster than a machine? That's what you're telling me?'

I don't know what made me do it. Maybe because I didn't want him pushing me around, maybe because I felt I needed to stand up for God, for Harry and England. But for whatever reason. I leaned forward and fixed his eye.

'Damn right I can,' I said.

'That was awesome!' Brandi said, bouncing up and down as we left the building and walked out into the mild spring sunshine. Big American cars rattled by, just about every second one a yellow cab. Businessmen and women walked briskly up and down the street, carrying huge cups of coffee, talking on cellphones. People yelled at each other for no apparent reason. This was New York! I felt exhilarated. I felt as though I *could* knit faster than a machine.

Which, obviously, I can't.

Brandi took me for a celebratory bite to eat after that.

'I know this great place,' she said. 'You like *Jewish* food?'

'I don't know.'

It turned out that I really *did* like Jewish food. What's not to like? I had chicken soup with matzo balls.

'Wow,' Brandi said, watching me eat. 'You were hungry.'

'It's this town,' I said. 'Ever since I arrived I've been hungry all the time.'

'Jet lag,' Brandi said. 'I always eat like a pig when I have jet lag.'

'That's why pigs don't like to fly,' I said.

She was drinking diluted grape juice. It was still three hours before she able to eat again. I'd decided I really wanted to be around for one of the two-minute eating windows.

'How many matzo balls do you think you could eat in two minutes?' I asked. I wanted to see those amazing teeth in action.

'Thirty-two' she replied instantly. 'I really go for it. It's not a pretty sight.'

'I'm sure you're very demure, even with a mouth full of matzo balls,' I assured her, before I registered what I'd just said.

Thank God my parents weren't here.

But again, Brandi was oblivious.

'You're so sweet,' she replied. 'Thank you.'

As we came out of the restaurant I saw a giant billboard that caught my attention.

DIABLO. THE INNER SANCTUM

There was a picture of an unshaven man with lots of curly hair. He looked a lot younger, and hairier, than Dad.

'Diablo,' I said, pointing. 'My mum knows him.'

'Really?' Brandi asked. 'He's hot!'

'You mean his career is doing well at the moment?'

90

'That too,' she said, gazing up at Diablo's glowering face.

The billboard left me a little unsettled but I soon forgot about it during the next round of interviews. I felt tired after my poor night's sleep but it was kind of fun too. The irritating Craig something had got me worked up. Besides, I was determined to stay up so as to get over the jet lag as quickly as possible. We saw one more newspaper on 6th Avenue and then there was another building full of magazines somewhere on the East Side, near the river. I don't remember exactly. It was all a bit of a blur by then. What I enjoyed about it most was simply going inside the buildings to see what was inside. Waiting in reception, meeting real-life New Yorkers, being led through crowded offices with Americans talking loudly and drinking coffee. I couldn't get enough.

'Ben's loving the vibe in the city,' Dermot O'Leary intones. 'But is it really him? If he wants to make a go of this knitting business, he has some questions to answer.'

Then we arrived at the *New York Courier* offices. The windows were open, even though it was cool, and I could hear the traffic honking a few floors below. There was an older journalist there, a guy with thinning hair and braces. I've never seen someone wear braces in all seriousness before and I was too busy staring at them to really listen to his first question.

'Ben?' he said.

'Yes, sorry. What?'

'I asked how it was that you can knit faster than a machine?'

'Yes. Sorry?'

'You've said you can knit faster than a knitting machine. I find that incredible and I'd like to hear more about it.'

'Well, hold on . . .' I started, looking over at Brandi for rescue. But she was immersed in tapping something out on her phone and was no help whatsoever.

'When I said that . . .' I went on hesitantly. 'I just meant that in certain circumstances, it might be possible . . .'

'Sounds like you're back-pedalling a little,' he said, smiling. 'Can you beat a machine or not?'

'It depends on the machine,' I said. 'And the garment.' It was sort of true, I imagined. Some older knitting machines took an age to complete a row. But the new ones could complete a garment like the Hoopie in fifteen minutes. It took me an hour at my absolute best. And that had been a freakish performance, one which I wasn't sure I could repeat now.

'It's just that on the radio this morning you said you could beat a machine,' he continued, refusing to let it go. 'So when I heard that I thought maybe you were telling the truth. Because let me tell you, if you can beat the machine, you got a story. I got a story. If you can't beat a machine, then you're wasting my time, and yours.'

Honestly, this was like being at school and having Mr Grover quiz me about how much of my essay I'd cribbed from Wikipedia (answer: about 20% and it was only the one time when I'd had an anxiety attack after Lloyd Manning had cut the straps on my school bag). How exactly had it come to the point where I was being grilled by foreign journalists over my knitting prowess?

'Look, kid, I'm a busy guy,' the journalist growled. 'Can you outknit a machine or not?'

I had to set him straight. Nip this in the bud. I didn't care about the story. I hadn't expected anyone to be interested in me anyway.

I shook my head. 'I . . .'

'Yes, he can,' Brandi suddenly chimed in quickly. 'He's just being modest, aren't you, Ben?'

I gave Brandi a what-are-you-doing? look. She winked at me.

'I've seen a video of him on YouTube,' she said. 'I'll email you the link. His hands *are* the quickest thing you've ever seen. It's really quite astounding.'

'Look,' said the journalist. 'I've been fashion editor of this paper for seventeen years . . .'

'You're the fashion editor?' I asked, staring at his braces.

'I've seen knitting machines work,' the journalist went on, ignoring me. 'They are seriously quick. Especially the modern ones.'

'My boy can beat them all,' Brandi said.

I winced as the journalist nodded and scribbled something down on his notepad.

Brandi took me back to the hotel after that and we popped into Dino's for a coffee.

'That was great!' she said excitedly. 'Wasn't that great?'

'What are you talking about?' I said. 'That man thinks I can knit faster than a machine.'

'Can't you?'

'No, of course not.'

'But you told Craig that you could.'

'I just said that because he was annoying me.'

'You shouldn't let interviewers get *under* your skin,' she said. 'They do it to provoke you into saying something controversial.'

'You might have been better off telling me that *before* I did the interview,' I pointed out.

'Don't worry about it. It's not as if anyone's going to check,' she said.

'I hope not,' I said. 'I don't like lying.'

'Really? You're pretty good at it,' she said. Denise came and gave us our coffees. This time Denise smiled at me. She looked a bit perkier than she had last night.

'Did you get some sleep?' I asked her.

She laughed. 'I sure did.'

Brandi raised an eyebrow as the waitress walked off.

'What?' I said.

'Quite the ladies' man, huh?'

'No, it's just that last night . . .' I stopped. 'Oh, whatever, it's not what you think!'

'You're lying again.'

'No I'm not.'

Brandi took my hand and squeezed it. 'I'm just teasing. I think you're amazing, Ben. I really enjoyed today.'

'Yeah, me too,' I said.

Back at the hotel, I walked into my room and my first thought was that we'd been burgled by someone with reverse-OCD. Someone had taken every last item out of Gex's suitcase and distributed it carefully around the floor so that everything was exactly equidistant from everything else. Even though Gex hadn't slept in the bed last night the bedclothes were messed up and in a heap at the foot of the bed. There was also an odd smell.

Gex was sitting at the table by the window, sending a text.

'So the wanderer returns,' I said. 'I missed you. Not.'

'All right, Bellend,' said Gex, looking up from his phone. 'Whaddup?'

I shook my head and surveyed the mess again. 'Has Tracey Emin moved in?' I asked.

'Tracey who?' Gex shrugged. 'Nah. But we do have a visitor.'

I heard the toilet flush and a strange man appeared at the door to the bathroom.

'Ben, dis is Keith,' Gex said. 'Keith, Ben.'

'Yo,' Keith said.

'Hi . . . Keith,' I said, slightly nervous. Keith was a big lad with greasy hair and a huge leather jacket. So he was a gangster?

'Keith is just his gang name,' Gex said.

'Really?' I asked. 'Keith doesn't sound very . . . gangy.'

'It's a cool name here in the Apple,' Gex said knowledgeably.

'Where are Mum and Dad?' I asked.

'They went to some place called the Googlehome.'

'The Guggenheim?'

'Whatever.'

'So you the knitting guy?' Keith asked.

'Er, yeah,' I replied. I wasn't sure I was happy about Gex volunteering all this personal information about me to Jimmy Soprano here.

'My mom knits,' Keith volunteered.

'Er, OK.'

'I love my mom,' he said.

'Good,' I replied. 'Me too. I mean, I love my mom. Not your mom. Not that your mom isn't loveable also.'

Gex started whistling through his teeth, which is Gex speak for 'shut the hell up'.

'Hey, I need a coffee,' Keith said. 'Let's go to Starbucks.'

'Let me go and see if my parents are back first,' I said.

I wandered down the hall and knocked at their door, but there was no answer. They must have still been at the Guggenheim, or maybe they'd gone out to dinner. This was why it was so frustrating not having my phone. How did people cope in the 80s, before mobile phones? I shudder to think. And I worry about the human race in the event of an extraterrestrial attack. All the Martians would have to do is take out a few phone masts and we'd all forget what we were supposed to be doing and start wandering about aimlessly.

Anyway. Out the three of us went, onto the streets of New York.

For some reason Gex was nearly wetting his pants about going to Starbucks.

'We have two in Hampton,' I pointed out. 'One in the high street and one at Sainsbury's.'

'Yeah, but this is Starbucks in NEW YORK!' he said.

'It's the same!'

He shook his head. 'It's not. It's really not.'

The guy taking the orders asked for our names and wrote them on the cup. 'Dis is Keith, I'm Gex. G-E-X, and this is Bellend. BELLEND,' Gex said, pointing to me.

'Thanks, Gex,' I said. 'As ever.'

We went and sat down.

'So you live in Brooklyn?' I asked Keith cheerfully.

'Some call it living,' Keith said darkly. 'I gotta find me the exit door, you feel?'

'You don't like Brooklyn?'

'I do not.'

'You should move,' I said. 'I hear Queens is nice.'

He laughed hollowly. 'If I'm going, it has to be further than goddam Queens. They'd find me there.'

'Who would find you?' I asked. Gex was on the edge of his seat, staring at his cousin, mesmerised. There was a faint scent of man-love in the air.

Keith looked around. 'The boys.'

'What boys?' I asked. 'You mean your gang?' Gex kicked me. 'What?' I asked.

'Don't talk about gangs,' Gex said out of the corner of his mouth.

'*He's* talking about gangs!' I pointed out. 'Don't kick me again.'

Gex glared at me but said nothing.

'So, you want out of the gang?' I asked Keith in a hushed tone. Though frankly, everyone in there was talking so loudly on their phones that it didn't make any difference how loud I talked. I could have screamed that it was time to pop a cap in someone's ass and no one would have paid any attention.

Keith leaned closer to me. 'You can't talk about this stuff,' he said, eyes narrowed.

'OK, fair enough,' I agreed. 'Maybe, on balance, it would be best if you didn't tell me anything.'

'I'm in too deep,' he said, ignoring my suggestion. 'I've seen stuff.'

'Tell him about the stuff,' Gex said eagerly.

'Actually, I don't want to know about the stuff,' I said quickly.

'Have you ever watched a man,' Keith growled, 'having his kneecaps split with a –'

'BELLEND!'

'Oh, that's me,' I said, standing up.

'You Bellend?' a girl at the counter said, holding my coffee.

'I am,' I said. 'Thanks.'

'That's a cute name,' she said, smiling.

I looked at her. She seemed totally guileless. Maybe people in the States didn't know what a bellend was.

'You really think so?'

'Sure,' she said and winked. Was she. . . . was she *flirting*? 'My name's Heidi.'

'I love that name,' I said automatically.

She scribbled something on the cup and handed it to me.

'Thanks,' I said again, suddenly panicking. Should I tip a girl who was flirting with me? If so, how much? Come to think of it, was she really flirting with me or are all American girls like this? I thrust my hand into my pocket, pulled out three dollars and dropped it into a box on the counter marked 'tips'. I hate not knowing the rules.

'Thank you, Bellend,' she said, smiling

'Er, no problem, Heidi.'

98

'So there I was,' Keith was saying as I sat down. 'I had this guy dangling from the top of the building. Fifteen floors up. He was screaming and begging . . .'

'Who's Heidi?' Gex asked me.

'Eh? I don't know anyone called Heidi,' I said.

'Well, she's written her phone number on your cup.'

He reached over and turned my cup around. It was true. Heidi had written her name and number on my cup. 'Which girl was it?'

Gex and Keith immediately stood like meerkats to get a good view. I couldn't bring myself to look.

'I bet it's that great fat bird,' Gex said. 'She looks like a Heidi.'

'Or maybe the one with the zits,' Keith suggested.

'Sit down,' I hissed. 'Be cool.'

'Are you gonna call?' Gex asked, sitting down finally.

'No of course not!' I said. 'I have a girlfriend.'

Gex rolled his eyes. 'It doesn't count when you're overseas.'

'It doesn't,' Keith confirmed. 'I went to Bermuda once to pick up a package, obviously I couldn't take my girl. Oh my God, I got up to some stuff there.'

'What stuff?' Gex asked, eyes wide.

'We don't need to hear about the stuff,' I said.

'Anyways, the point is, why take sand to the beach?' Keith said.

'Damn,' I said, suddenly remembering something. 'We've got to find an internet café.'

'What for?' Keith asked.

'I have to call my probation officer.'

He sat back as if stung. 'You're on probation? What for,

man?' he asked. 'What did you do?'

'He capped a guy,' Gex said.

'No shit?' Keith said, now looking slightly alarmed.

I shook my head. 'I did not. I injured a lollipop lady, OK?'

There was a short silence, in which Gex looked at the floor and Keith picked his teeth with a cocktail stick, looking utterly bemused.

'Is that, like, code for something, huh?' he whispered.

'No. A lollipop lady is a woman who helps small children cross the road,' I said. 'It's a British tradition. A man can do it too. Whoever does it wears a white coat and is generally close to drawing their pension.'

'Whoah,' said Keith, as though I had just spoken Martian. 'That's . . . well, that's . . .'

'Pathetic?' suggested Gex.

'It didn't seem pathetic to the magistrate,' I told Keith. I finished my drink. 'Now if we're done discussing petty crime, I have some skyping that needs doing.'

'Good Lord, Ben. Are you trying to get me fired or something?'

'Sorry, Ms Gunter,' I said quietly. I didn't want Keith to hear me grovelling. They were over on the other side of the café, checking their Minecraft worlds.

'Do you know what time it is here?' she asked.

'Eveningish?' I suggested.

'It's 8.34pm,' she said.

'You're not in your nightie yet, at least,' I pointed out.

'I was having dinner,' she snapped.

'Yes. In fact, you have a little bit of spinach between your teeth,' I said, trying to be helpful.

'You promised,' she said. 'You promised me you wouldn't do this again.'

'I'm sorry. It's just that I still don't have my phone and it's been a really crazy day.'

She just glared.

'Tomorrow,' I said. 'I'll call you just after breakfast.'

'Good,' she said.

'If there's time.'

'Ben!'

'Brandi comes for me really early,' I explained. 'We have more interviews tomorrow.'

'Call me!' she said.

'That's what all the girls say,' I said, trying to make a joke out of it.

The screen went blank. She'd hung up.

I still had some time, so I called Megan. I wasn't expecting her to answer, but then the screen flickered and the connecting icon came up.

'Hey, gorgeous,' I said as the screen flicked into life.

A dishevelled-looking kid wearing a *Despicable Me* T-shirt loomed into view.

It was Marcus, Megan's little brother.

'Oh, hi, Marcus. Is Megan around?'

'No, she left a while ago,' he said. I like Marcus, he's not a sneak, and doesn't call me Bellend and try to trip me up outside Boots, like others of his age and gender are prone to doing.

'On Monday? Where's she going on a Monday?' I asked.

'Dunno, she went with Sean.'

101

My blood ran cold.

'*Sean?*'

'Yeah. Sean. I like Sean. He's cool.'

'Marcus,' I said quietly. 'Sean is NOT cool. Do you understand?'

Marcus blinked. 'Why not?'

'Because Sean wants to be Megan's boyfriend.'

'But you're Megan's boyfriend.'

'Exactly!'

'But then again, you're in another country,' Marcus pointed out.

'That doesn't mean anything!' I snapped. 'Why does everyone think it matters what country you're in?'

'OK, relax, dude.'

'Look, I need you to keep an eye on her and . . . and, *Sean,*' I said. 'Tell me if she goes out with him again, OK?'

'Maybe,' he said, toying with me.

'I'll bring you back a . . . what do you want from New York?'

'A baseball cap.'

'Mets or Yankees?'

'I don't care.'

'OK, you got it. Deal, Marcus?' I said.

'Sure,' he said.

I turned off the monitor and sat back in my chair, my stomach churning. How could she do this to me? was my first thought. But then I told myself that it could be a misunderstanding. I'd jumped to the wrong conclusion once before about Megan and Sean. But what could they be doing out together at 8.45pm on a school night?

* * *

Gex and I parted company with Keith, who said he had some 'business to take care of' in the Bronx. When we got back to the hotel I checked hopefully at reception to see if my bag had turned up.

'Sorry, Ben, it hasn't,' Jasmine told me. 'Once it comes, you'll be the first to know, OK?'

There was, however, a parcel waiting for me. I opened it in the room; there was a note from Brandi.

Hi Ben,
This is my old phone, it has some credit left. Thought
you could use this while you're waiting for your
luggage. My number is on Speed Dial 1! Call me any
time.
Brandi

'Where did you get that from? Gex asked as I pulled out last year's BlackBerry.

'Brandi sent it,' I said.

'My days, Bellend, the ladies is all over you,' Gex said. 'Can I have your sloppy seconds, innit?'

'Don't be disgusting,' I said. 'She's my PR agent. She needs to be in contact with me for business reasons.'

'She'd like to do the business wiv you,' he said.

'Stay out of there!' I yelled as he opened the minibar. 'I've counted everything in that minibar and if there's anything missing when we check out, I'm making you pay for it.'

'Good luck with that,' he said. 'I ain't got no money. Oh

man, I want to try a thirteen-dollar beer. That's got to be good.'

'It's not expensive because of the quality,' I told him. 'It's just normal beer with a huge mark-up.'

'Come on, Ben,' he said. 'We're in New York, like in the song.'

'The City that Never Sleeps?'

'Eh? No. Concrete Jungle Where Dreams are Made of.'

'Alicia Keys? Really? I was thinking more Frank Sinatra,' I said.

'Who's Frank Sinatra?' he asked and I had to hit him with a cushion. That led to a full-scale pillow fight which went on until Gex leapt up on my bed and one of the springs went twang.

'What should we do now?' I asked, when we'd got bored of that game.

'We can go to a bar,' Gex said.

'We're not old enough,' I pointed out.

'Keith can get us fake IDs, easy,' he said.

'Gex, we have to be careful,' I said. 'Immigration will be watching me. Mrs Gunter has put her career on the line so I can go on this trip. If I screw up then I might go to jail and she might lose her job.'

He sighed while I picked up the BlackBerry and checked what apps it had. Skype was there. I carefully entered Ms Gunter's phone contact details into the phone memory and set up the reminder system again.

Then there was a knock at the door. Mum and Dad had finally turned up. They asked if we wanted to join them for dinner in Little Italy. Gex looked slightly disappointed but smelled a free meal so he grudgingly accepted and changed into his best tracksuit.

104

I'm loving Little Italy. It's just like in the movies. I spent the meal staring at other people, convinced I'd seen them in something. Even though I can never remember actors' names, I can always remember what they've been in before.

'That guy was in *Breaking Bad*,' I said. 'I'm sure of it. And I'm sure that lady was a zombie in *The Walking Dead*. She has a little more colour now.'

I had veal Parmesan, because that's what people have in films set in New York. I was a little disappointed with Mum and Dad's choice. They ordered spag bol which, as I pointed out, you can get in Hampton.

'What's the point of coming to New York and eating English food?' I sniffed.

'Spag bol is Italian,' Mum argued. 'Ooh, these bread sticks are long.'

'Your mother likes a nice long –' Dad began.

'No!' I snapped. 'Not in front of Gex.'

Keen to change the subject, I asked Mum about Diablo and was he coming to the hotel?

As soon as I mentioned his name Mum looked a little sheepish and Dad frowned.

'He's invited me to go and see his show,' Mum said. 'In Times Square.'

'That's great, isn't it?' I said.

'He only sent one ticket,' Mum went on.

'Backstage pass,' Dad added, raising an eyebrow. 'I've never had a backstage pass from your mother.'

Gex suddenly choked on his fusilli and we all had to slap him on the back until he stopped.

'Are you going to go?' I asked Mum when he'd got over it.

'Of course she is,' Dad said. 'Not often you get invited backstage by a rich, handsome megastar.'

'Dave, you're being silly,' Mum said.

'Have I said you can't go?' Dad replied.

Mum rolled her eyes. 'We'll talk about this later,' she said.

Despite my parents letting themselves down with their behaviour, dinner was pretty good. I could grow to like veal Parmesan. Mum and Dad wanted to go dancing after dinner and asked if we wanted to come with them. There are a number of things I can think of that would be less enjoyable than going to an 80s club with my parents. Most of them involve having parts of my body sliced off and fricasseed before my very eyes. We politely declined and they seemed grateful, almost sprinting off down the street, hand in hand.

I was tired and to Gex's irritation decided it was time to head back to the hotel. Gex talked me into going into the bar in the lobby to try and get them to serve us alcohol but I blew it by asking if they had Horlicks. He was furious.

'I'm tired,' I said. 'I'm still jet lagged and want an early night.' Then Keith phoned and Gex said he was going off to meet him.

'Did he only invite you?' I asked, sniffing. 'What about me?'

'Probably won't mind if you come, innit,' Gex replied uneasily.

'I wouldn't want to be the gooseberry.'

'And you did say you was tired.'

'I see.' I hadn't really wanted to go out but I felt a bit as though everyone was abandoning me. Especially Gex. He was my fifth, no, sixth choice! And here he was swanning off with *Keith*. 'It's all Keith this, Keith that,' I muttered to myself in the lift.

I made the most of it though and picked up my knitting once back in the room. I put on a bit of jazz. Relax the shoulders, Ben. Forget about Megan and Sean. Lose yourself in the knitting.

Tuesday 14th May

2.11am

A noise woke me. I'd dropped off in the armchair, the needles still in my hands.

I heard the noise again. Someone whooping. A woman. Then I heard a loud bang and some furious shushing. I went to the door and opened it. My parents were on the floor in the corridor, my father on his hands and knees, shoulders rocking with silent laughter, Mum was astride his back, like he was a horse, one hand over her mouth to keep the giggles in – unsuccessfully, I might add.

'Who are you, and what have you done with my parents?' I said grumpily.

'Ben!' Dad cried. 'My boy!'

'SHHHHHH!!' said Mum at 100 decibels.

'Sorry, sorry,' Dad said.

'Knee feeling better, is it?' I asked. 'Do you know what time it is?'

Dad lifted his wrist to look at his watch. Unfortunately, this unbalanced him and the two of them collapsed to the carpet,

Mum shrieking. They lay there for a while, unable to hold the laughter in. I watched them, stony-faced. There are few things less appealing than watching other people laugh about the fact they've just woken you up. I shut the door and left them to it.

Clearly the Diablo dispute has been resolved.

Gex still hadn't returned by breakfast time this morning. I guessed he'd stayed with Keith in Brooklyn. I didn't bother knocking on Mum and Dad's door. After their embarrassing performance last night, I hoped they were hiding shamefully in their room.

While I waited in the lobby for Brandi to pick me up, I went over to speak to Jasmine.

'I'm sorry, Ben,' she said before I'd had the chance to say anything. 'Your bag still hasn't turned up.'

'I guessed that was the case,' I said. 'You will let me know if it arrives, won't you?'

She looked at me steadily for a moment, then hitched up her smile and nodded.

'Yes, Ben,' she said. 'You'll be the first to hear.'

Brandi arrived then and I said goodbye to Jasmine, who flashed me a smile. I got in the cab and we drove downtown. We were a few minutes early for the meeting, so we went for a quick walk down Wall Street, towards the river and Battery Park.

'Why is this area called the Battery?' I asked.

She hesitated before speaking, seemingly unsure of the answer. 'I guess this is where they keep the electricity?' she said.

'Hmmmm.' That didn't sound likely to me, but I didn't pursue it.

Brandi and I did a few more interviews. There were a couple of small newspapers and one more magazine. I was getting quite good at them by then. I started making jokes and telling anecdotes. Brandi would smile and give me the thumbs up. We finished early and grabbed a sandwich for lunch. Brandi was going back to her office after that so I'd have some time to myself. I was looking forward to it. I'd intended to go and see the Empire State Building, then maybe a museum or two if there was time.

'Now,' Brandi said as we came out of the café. 'I have another interview lined up for you tomorrow morning. Another radio station.'

'I can't do tomorrow morning,' I said. 'I have an appointment to see someone at Priapia.'

She looked at me, eyes wide. 'Priapia? They're huge.'

'I know,' I said. 'They own Virilia, who own my whole school.'

'No Ben,' she said. 'I mean really huge. Like Alec Baldwin huge. To give you an idea, they make more in a year than all the countries in Africa put together.'

'How do you know that?'

'They're one of our clients. So who are you seeing then?' she asked.

'A guy called Robert something.'

'Robert D'Angelo?!'

'Yeah, that's the guy. It's just an informal chat.'

'Robert D'Angelo is head of their clothing arm,' she said. 'He's an *important* guy.'

I swallowed. 'Is he? Mr Hollis said it would be quite casual.'

She raised her eyebrows. 'Ben, this could be really huge.'

'Why does everything have to be huge?' I asked, really starting to worry now. 'I don't like huge things. I like things that are small to medium, or slightly larger than normal at a push.'

I think she could see I was starting to get anxious. 'Don't worry,' she said. 'You'll knock 'em dead. Just be yourself.'

I bit my lip and looked up at the grey sky, or the little of it visible through the trees of the park. It was just starting to rain. I told myself Brandi was right. Being myself had got me this far, after all. I was concerned though that I didn't have anything much to show them at the meeting tomorrow. I had started on another Hampton FC scarf but that wasn't going to interest the CEO of the clothing division of an Africa-sized multinational.

In fact, I could only really think of one thing that I might be able to show them that would be of any interest at all. And I'd need to show them a completed garment.

I was going to have to knit an entire Hoopie.

Tonight.

Later

I went back to the hotel. No time now to visit the Empire State Building if I wanted to give myself enough time to knit the Hoopie. Thankfully, I had enough wool now, thanks to my trip to Bloomingdale's. There was a message on the answering machine. It was Mum and Dad, they were in the lounge bar downstairs and did I want to join them? I took my travelling clothes and Gex's boxer shorts down to the laundry room and left them there washing while I went up to say hello to my parents.

I found them playing Scrabble on the iPad. Dad had just put down HOLE on a triple-word score.

'Four letters?' I tutted, sitting down. 'You always waste triple-word scores.'

He glanced at Mum, who grinned.

'Feeling OK?' I asked. 'Sore heads at all?'

'We had a lie-in,' Dad said, winking at Mum.

'Breakfast in bed,' she said.

'Stop right there,' I said, sighing. 'You two are so tiresome.'

'We're just enjoying ourselves,' Dad said. 'It's like a second honeymoon for us.'

'The first one wasn't all it could have been,' Mum said.

'What was wrong with it?'

'Let's just say there was another person who spoiled the fun,' Dad said.

'Dave,' Mum said, shaking her head.

'What? Who?' I asked.

'Never mind,' Mum said. What had he meant by that? But then the waiter came over and Dad asked me what I wanted.

'Coke, please,' I said.

Mum and Dad looked at each other.

'What?' I said.

'Make that a Diet Coke,' Dad said to the waiter, inexplicably.

I watched them play their game for a while and had a good moan about having to knit the Hoopie at such short notice.

'I'll be up half the night finishing it,' I said.

'Most of the time you complain you don't have enough time to knit,' Dad said. 'Now you've got all night to do it and you're still not happy.'

'FLAPS,' said Mum, putting her tiles down.

'Good one,' Dad said.

'Waste of an S, though,' I said absently.

The waiter brought my Coke and I took a contemplative sip.

'Maybe I should cancel this meeting?' I said, not that anyone was listening.

'LIP,' Dad said. 'I'm putting my LIP on your mother's –'

'Stop that, stop it,' I barked, suddenly realising what they were up to. 'I told you you weren't allowed to pay Rude Scrabble any more!'

'That was in England,' Dad said, while Mum's shoulders shook with mirth. 'It doesn't count when you're in another country.'

'Don't you start,' I said.

'Anyway, it's not Rude Scrabble,' Mum said. 'It's Semi-Rude Scrabble. All the words have to be suggestive, without crossing the line into outright filth.'

I looked at the board. 'ROD,' I said. 'SLICK, JOB . . . hold on. ELBOW? What's rude about ELBOW?'

Mum and Dad looked at each other and burst into giggles again.

'I don't understand,' I said. 'But I'm sure it's disgusting all the same.'

'Molly's not here,' Mum said. 'Lighten up. Maybe you can help me?'

She showed me her letters. XDEBUTT

'Is there anything you can see there that I can put on your father's HOLE?' she asked.

'This is such fun,' I said coldly, as she and Dad rolled about in tears. 'But if you'll excuse me, I have to get to work.'

I stalked out and went up to my room. I helped myself to a full-fat Coke from the minibar and grabbed the freebie needles.

I had work to do.

11.43pm

Gex interrupted my knitting half an hour ago. He's being vague about what he's been up to but he smells of KFC.

I was a bit cheesed off with him actually and I think he picked up on it.

'What time do you call this, then?' I asked.

All right, Mum,' he said.

'I thought you'd be staying at Keith's?'

'He had some stuff to do, innit,' Gex said vaguely.

'I hope you're not getting up to no good.'

He shook his head. 'Nah, nothing like that.'

'I'm just not sure I trust Keith.'

'He's a good guy,' Gex said. 'We're going to a bar tomorrow night. You're coming too.'

'No, I'm not.'

'Bruv,' he said shortly. 'You can't say no when I ask if you want to come out then get annoyed with me because I'm not around.'

'I'm not annoyed,' I sniffed.

'Yes you are,' he said. He was telling the truth. 'Come out

113

with us tomorrow, yeah? You want to see the real New York? Keith will show you.'

'I'll think about it,' I said.

I realised that Gex was examining the clothes of his I'd been wearing. I'd folded them and left them on an armchair so I could wash them tomorrow.

'You been wearing my clothes, innit?' Gex asked.

'Yes, Sherlock.'

'Thought you was looking fly.'

'Thanks, mate. Hope you don't mind?'

'Naw. Don't mind. As long as you aren't wearing my boxers, man,' he laughed.

Uh-oh.

'Don't be a prat,' I said. 'As if.'

'Cos that would be like wrong,' he continued.

I laughed a little too loudly at this, but I think I got away with it.

'No way would I ever wear your boxers, Gex!' I lied. I'll have to sneak them, washed, back into his suitcase when he isn't looking.

Where is my LUGGAGE?!

I'm now writing this in the bathroom because Gex claimed he needed his beauty sleep. Honestly, who does he think he is, Lady Gaga? Might have to finish the Hoopie on the toilet. Not ideal, but needs must.

Wednesday 15th May

9.03am

It took me hours to finish the Hoopie last night in that bathroom. Tell the truth, I'd been a little distracted by what Dad had said in the bar. Who was this person who had spoiled their first honeymoon? Mum hadn't wanted him to talk about it. Had she had an affair with Diablo? It must have happened around the time they got married.

And that got me thinking. Which is rarely good.

Diablo has curly hair. Mine's kind of curly, or wavy at least. Dad's hair is straight, what's left of it. Could it be true? Could I be Diablo Junior? What with that distraction, and the jet lag, I went slowly and made a few mistakes. When I'm in tune and on song and pumped with mojo, etc. I can knit like a Time Lord. But the slightest distraction and I knit like a Dalek. It also didn't help that I'd had to work in the bathroom.

There was a man waiting for me in reception who had chauffeur written all over him. He was stocky and wore a blue uniform with fetching brass buttons. He was quite young, maybe in his early twenties, and he held his peaked cap and a piece of paper with *Mr Fletcher* written on it.

'I'm Mr Fletcher,' I said, approaching him. I was already worrying if I'd need to tip him. And how much? Why can't they just add the service charge to the bill like they do at Pizza Express? Or have a rule where you can just add a quid and round it up?

'Good morning, Mr Fletcher.'

'Just call me Ben,' I said, holding out my hand.

'Good morning, Ben,' the man said, shaking it.

'Good morning . . . ?'

'Trey,' he said, grinning a huge grin. 'My name's Trey.'

Now Trey had great teeth. Not as magnificent as Brandi's, mind you. No one had teeth like Brandi's. But really quite special nonetheless. Why was a man with teeth like that driving a boy with teeth like mine? It would never happen in England.

America is a superpower not just in terms of weaponry and economics. It is also a Superpower of Teeth. If the state of a nation's teeth were used as a measure of its standing in the world, then the US is miles ahead of anyone else. British teeth, by comparison, are like the various territories of the British Empire; neglected, crumbling, dropping out one by one. They say China is the new kid on the block in superpower terms, but if they really want to compete with the US on all fronts they're going to have to put some serious investment into their dental infrastructure.

'Can I take your bag?' Trey asked. I was holding the Bloomingdale's shopping bag. The only bag I had big enough for carrying the bulky Hoopie.

'That's OK, I'll hang on to it,' I said, clutching the bag tightly. We were only going a few blocks but I wasn't taking any chances.

Trey led me outside and opened the rear door to a huge black Cadillac with tinted windows. I felt like a crime boss. We pulled out into traffic, a taxi giving us a welcoming blast of his horn.

'Screw you!' Trey screamed at it.

I knew the Priapia Offices were on 5th Avenue, what I hadn't realised was that they were in the Flatiron Building, that iconic piece of 1920s architecture shaped like the incredibly thin wedge of cheesecake Mum always asks for before helping herself to seconds.

'Oh my God,' I said. 'I can't believe I'm actually going to be inside the Flatiron Building.'

'It looks better from the outside', Trey said. 'Everything's all screwy inside. None of the furniture fits, and the plumbing is a nightmare.'

Trey pulled up out front and hopped out to open the door for me. You've got to tip a man who opens a car door for you, even I can see that. I fumbled in my pocket as I got out but Trey cleared his throat and shook his head. OK, so no tip for a chauffeur, but a tip for a taxi driver? Maybe because I'm a guest of the company? How does that work? The minute I think I'm getting the tipping thing someone changes the rules. It's not doing my nerves any good. He walked me into reception. I was starting to feel nervous. Mr Hollis had said this was going to be an informal chat. But the building was opulent, the receptionist was beautiful, they'd sent a chauffeur to pick me up. How informal could this be? I got a text from Brandi.

Good luck with your big meeting. Knock 'em dead!

Brandi was clearly another one who seemed to think this was my big chance. I was glad I'd washed my clothes. Imagine turning up here wearing my father's chinos with the frayed cuff.

'I'm gonna go park the car,' Trey said. 'I'll wait and pick you up after your meeting.'

'Thanks, Trey,' I said.

'Hey, good luck in there,' he said, looking genuinely anxious for me.

Was everyone trying to make me as nervous as possible? They were acting like I was going to play a game of chess with Death.

'It's just an informal chat,' I said, dry-mouthed.

Trey shook his head. 'You're seeing Robert D'Angelo, right?'

'That's right.'

'That guy doesn't do informal chats. You've got fifteen minutes of his time, which is the most valuable piece of real estate in this goddam city.'

I swallowed. I didn't want to have this meeting. I wasn't ready. There were three dropped stitches in the Hoopie sample.

Without Trey it suddenly seemed very quiet. The receptionist tapped at her keyboard. Suddenly feeling I needed to break the silence, I spoke up.

'I hear you have trouble with your plumbing,' I said. She looked up at me in alarm.

'I mean, in the building,' I explained quickly.

'Oh,' she replied. 'Yeah, we do.'

Her phone buzzed and she answered it quickly, no doubt relieved to not have to talk to this weird English kid any more. Why can't I just learn to keep my mouth shut?

'Mr D'Angelo and his colleagues will see you now,' she said, hanging up. 'Take the elevator to the eighth floor.'

Colleagues?!

'Knock 'em dead, kid,' Trey said as he came back, chucking me on the shoulder. He watched as I made my way to the lift then he called out.

'One shot!'

The lift doors opened on the eighth floor and I was met by another beautiful lady. 'Ben Fletcher? I'm Gloria Tevez,' she said, extending her hand.

'Like the footballer,' I replied, shaking her hand.

'Excuse me?' she asked.

'Oh, I mean soccer player,' I said.

'There's a soccer player called Gloria Tevez?' she asked, interested.

'No, his name is Carlos. And he's a man. Doesn't matter.'

Shut up Ben, shut up.

Please come through,' she said, as though I hadn't just acted like a prat. 'We're all excited to meet with you today.'

'Me too,' I said. Though for excitement read scared witless.

Gloria led me into a room shaped a bit like a cartoon wedge of cheese, with a table squashed into the thin end of the wedge. Two men and a woman sat facing me. It was like the *Dragon's Den* studio had been rammed into the bow of an America's Cup yacht. The window behind them looked out towards the Empire State Building, framing it perfectly. If a team of top scientists had designed a scenario with the sole purpose of causing me maximum anxiety, they would have come up with something very much like this. Though they would have painted it cerise, of course, a colour which also brings me out in hives.

Gloria asked me to take a seat on this side of the table, then she moved around to the other side, the weird geometry of the building meaning she had to squeeze her way past the end of the table.

'Please take a seat, Ben,' one of the men said. 'I'm Robert D'Angelo.'

'Hello,' I said. I sat on the chair and clutched my Bloomingdale's bag on my knees.

'This is Miles O'Flynn, and this is Liz Hanson.'

'Hello, hello,' I said.

'You've already met Gloria Tevez,' he said.

'The soccer player,' Gloria said, with a taut smile.

'Ha ha. Yes.'

'So, Ben,' Robert said. 'What have you come to show us today?'

Suddenly, I didn't want to open the bag. I had no idea what they were expecting, or what they were hoping for, but I was convinced the Hoopie wasn't it. These people were in charge of buying for the textiles and clothing arm of a multinational corporation. I was a beginner knitter from Hampton who apparently couldn't even spell Hampton. What could I offer these people?

Nonetheless, here I was. Here they were. I had to show them something. Mr Hollis, Mrs Tyler, Brandi, my parents. Trey. They all wanted me to give it my best shot.

So I pulled out the Hoopie.

'This is my design,' I said. 'I call it the Hoopie. It's like a hooded cardigan with a loose knit.'

'Could you bring it here, please?' Liz asked. I laid it on

120

the table and the four of them began poking it, peering at it, subjecting it to a forensic analysis. You know those dreams you have, when you're naked at school and all your friends are looking at you and laughing, and then Miss Swallow walks in and then you realise it's not Miss Swallow, it's actually your MUM?

Anyway. That's how I felt. The Hoopie was such a personal thing. And this was far from the finest example.

I watched as Robert fingered a hole where I'd dropped a stitch.

'You knitted this by hand?' he asked.

'Yes, I'm sorry about the dropped stitches. My room-mate was trying to get to sleep and kept throwing cushions at me because of the clicking. I went and finished it in the bathroom, hence the toothpaste on the sleeve.'

'You finished this last night?' Gloria asked, looking up at me. She wore those trendy big glasses, making her nice eyes look huge, like a woman from a manga comic.

'I knitted the whole thing last night,' I said.

'You knitted the whole thing in *one night*?' she asked, eyes even wider. She began scribbling on a pad sitting next to her. But the weird thing was, she didn't look at the pad as she wrote. She just carried on looking at me with her massive eyes, her hand writing away as if it had a mind of its own. It was disconcerting, to say the least.

'Yes. I can do one in less than an hour if I'm really in the zone,' I said. 'That's how I won the Knitting Championship.'

Robert sat back in his chair and regarded me thoughtfully. 'Yeah, I heard about that,' he said.

Liz was whispering to Miles, who was tapping away on a tablet.

'You know what else I heard?' Robert asked.

'Um, no?'

'I heard you can knit faster than a machine.'

Oh no.

'Well, I . . .'

'I didn't believe it at first. But I don't know . . .' he looked down at the Hoopie. 'Maybe you can.'

I shook my head. 'I need to explain, I –'

'So you run a business?' Gloria cut in, her independent hand still scribbling on the pad.

'Yes. I mean I sell these on Etsy. I also do tank tops and football scarves.'

'How many employees?'

'Erm. Just . . . just the one, really. Just me.'

Miles and Liz stopped talking. Robert dropped his pen. They all stared at me. Even Liz's independent hand stopped writing.

'No employees?' Miles asked.

'Er, no?' I said, wishing I could be giving a different answer.

'How many machines?' Robert asked slowly.

'Machines? Er . . . I don't have any machines, as such,' I admitted.

'Let me get this straight,' Robert said. 'It's just you?'

'Yes.'

'And everything knitted by hand?' As he asked this he pointed to the dropped stitch in the Hoopie.

'That's right.'

Robert shook his head and sat back in his chair, looking

away. If this was *Dragon's Den* he would be out.

'Have you considered buying some machines?' Gloria asked slowly.

'I've got nowhere to put them,' I said. 'Though I suppose I could get rid of the ziggurat.'

'You could rent premises,' she pointed out.

'I need cash for that.'

'How much do you need?' Miles asked, a finger poised over his tablet.

'I don't know.'

'You don't know!? Where are your revenue projections? Where's your five-year plan?'

'I haven't really done one.'

Miles looked disappointed. He sat back.

'You've got a good design here,' Liz said. 'But how many of these can you knit by hand in a week?'

'Not so many at the moment,' I admitted. 'I have exams in July. I'm doing AS levels. I had to turn down a couple of orders in fact. Tank tops and scarves are quicker.'

'What's your margin on a tank top?' she asked.

Thank God. I knew this one. Thirty per cent.'

'And on a scarf?'

'About fifty per cent.'

And what was your profit last year?'

'I haven't been going for a year. My profit last month was £67.'

Liz stared at me for a while. Then she sat back in her chair. No more questions, m'lud.

'Thanks so much for coming in, Ben,' Gloria said silkily,

standing up. It looked like she was out as well.

'Sorry,' I said, meaning sorry for wasting their time. I stood and she helped me get the Hoopie back in the Bloomingdale's bag while the other three sat quietly, the only sound the cheerful honking in the streets below.

I shook hands with the others and Gloria walked me to the lift.

'Goodbye, Ben,' she said.

'Goodbye.'

'Good luck with the Hoopie,' she said. 'It really is a great design.'

'Thank you,' I said. 'Good luck with Juventus.'

'How did it go?' Trey asked excitedly as I walked back out into reception. He was leaning over the desk.

I shook my head. 'I think I missed my one shot.'

'Oh damn, seriously?'

'Yeah. I wasn't prepared,' I said. 'I thought . . . oh, it doesn't matter.'

'Hey, don't worry about it, dude,' Trey said. 'There'll be another opportunity.'

'That's not what you said before.'

'That's true,' he said. 'That probably *was* your opportunity.'

I sighed.

'Come on,' he said. 'I'll take you to a bar, we can get drunk.'

Once I'd explained to Trey that I was underage and didn't much like alcohol anyway, he took me back to 38th Street and parked outside Dino's.

'Hi, Ben,' said Denise, pointing us to our usual table in the window.

'Hi, Denise,' I replied.

'Bad day?'

'It's that obvious? Could I get a flat white?' I wasn't in the mood for flirtatious banter, even though Denise was wearing a nice low-cut top.

'Make that two, honey,' Trey said.

'So,' Trey said, once Denise had gone. 'You wanna talk about it?'

I shrugged. 'Not much to say. I wasn't ready. I mean, I'm not ready. I'm small potatoes, you know? I shouldn't be having meetings with big multinationals. I'm just a boy with one design and not enough time.'

'So, hire more people,' Trey said.

'I can't afford to pay people with the revenue I'd be getting. It takes too long to knit each Hoopie.'

'Can you mechanise? Like Henry Ford?'

I shrugged. 'I suppose. But are people going to want to buy a Hoopie if it's not hand-knitted? People want home-made. They can get cheap machine-bought stuff in the supermarket. I can't compete with that.'

'Hold up. I need to ask: what the hell is a Hoopie?'

So I showed him.

'This is beautiful,' he said, feeling the wool. 'You knitted this by hand?'

'Yeah, there are a couple of mistakes.'

'My girlfriend would love this.'

'Pity she wasn't one of the Dragons,' I said gloomily.

'What's that?'

'Never mind. You know what? Take it,' I said suddenly. 'It's yours. Give it to your girlfriend.'

'Are you serious?'

'Sure. I want you to have it.'

He looked at me long and hard. 'You're a good kid.'

'Thanks.'

'Seriously,' Trey said. He reached into his pocket and handed me his card. 'You call me any time. You need driving somewhere. I'm at your service.'

Denise brought our coffees. 'Here you go, boys,' she said.

'So you got a girl?' Trey asked. Or a guy?'

'A girl,' I said quickly. 'Definitely a girl.'

'What's her name?'

'Megan.'

'She pretty?'

'Yes she is.'

'So how come she didn't come with you?'

'Her grandmother is unwell,' I said. 'Her family needs her.'

Trey raised an eyebrow. I took a sip of my coffee.

'Yeah. I know how that sounds,' I said. 'And I'm worried she's going off me.'

I told Trey all about my concerns with Megan and Sean. As I poured my heart out, I noticed Gex outside peering in through the window. Keith stood behind him looking up and down the street as if he was waiting for someone. I waved at them and they both came in and sat down and I introduced them to Trey. To his credit, Trey wasn't too appalled by Gex's appearance, even though Gex's jeans were so low slung that

126

the tops of his Primark underpants were fully visible.

'You gotta fix it, man,' Trey continued after the introductions were complete. He licked coffee foam off his spoon.

'Fix what?' Gex asked.

'Megan's been seen with Sean,' I said.

'Sean?' Gex spat. 'Not *that* guy again.'

'You can't let this Sean guy just walk in there and steal her away,' Trey said. 'What a dick!'

'I'm not sure there's much I can do.'

'You want me to fix this guy?' Keith asked, cracking his knuckles.

'What did you have in mind?' I asked.

'I could arrange for him to have a little visit from some friends.'

'You got friends in East Hampshire?' Gex asked eagerly. 'Sean lives in Liphook.'

This meant nothing to Keith, of course.

'I saw someone use a lip hook once,' he said, a faraway look in his eye. 'The guy paid up.'

'I think sending the Mob around might be a little heavy-handed in any case,' I said. 'We don't know what's been going on, exactly.'

'Call her,' Trey said. 'You got a phone?'

'I have a BlackBerry,' I said.

'Call her now.'

So I did. I skyped her. To my surprise, she answered straight away.

'Hi, Ben,' she said cheerfully. 'How's the Big Apple?'

'It's amazing,' I said. It was so good to hear her voice. She

127

was blurry on the little screen but she looked great. 'I've done some interviews and . . . stuff.'

'Is Gex there?' she asked.

'Yes, unfortunately.'

'*Ask about Sean!*' Gex hissed. I shook my head. It wasn't the right time.

'Where are you?' she asked, peering at the camera.

'I'm in a diner.'

'Are you eating Philly cheesesteak again?'

'No, just coffee. But I might have Philly cheesesteak for lunch.'

'Have you had any fruit and veg since you arrived?'

'A little. But mostly just Philly cheesesteak.'

'Are you going to come back looking like Eric Pickles?' she asked.

I laughed. 'No, I have a fast metabolism, I never put on weight.'

Gex made a strange sound then. A bit like a strangled laugh. I gave him an odd look.

'I have a fast metabolism too, said Megan, laughing. 'My body converts food very quickly into fat and stores it on my thighs.'

I glanced up at Trey; he was listening to all this with narrowed eyes.

Denise walked by and swiped an empty water glass off the table. Then she leaned across me to grab another one on the far side.

'Who was that?' Megan asked.

'That was Denise, the waitress.'

'She's pretty.'

'Is she? I hadn't really noticed.'

'You didn't notice that she just flopped her breasts out in your face?'

'She was reaching for a glass.'

'I told you, Ben,' Megan said, with a little sideways smile. 'Watch out for American girls.'

'The nerve,' Gex muttered. He made a grab for the phone, but I slapped his hand away.

'What about *Sean?*' Trey asked loudly.

'What?' Megan asked. 'Who was that?'

'Just some guy at the next table,' I said.

'Yeah, what about Sean?' Keith asked.

'*Two* guys at the next table,' I said. 'Anyway, better go now, Megan.'

'OK, Ben,' Megan said cheerily. 'Thanks for calling.'

'Speak soon, miss you,' I said quickly, fighting Gex off at the same time. I hung up.

'What are you doing?' Trey asked. 'Call her back. Why didn't you ask about Sean?'

I shrugged. 'It just seemed like everything was OK. I didn't want to start a fight.'

'I don't get you English,' Trey said. 'You never want to start a fight.'

'That's not true,' I said defensively. 'We've started loads of fights.'

'Yeah, but I'm saying YOU need to start a fight.'

'That's not me,' I said. 'I'm more of a drawn-out cold war kind of guy. I have a spy.'

'You know what I think?' Gex said slowly.

129

'Go on,' I said guardedly.

'I think Megan sounded a little too happy.'

'Yeah? Well, maybe she was happy that I called?'

'Maybe,' Gex said, eyeing me coolly. 'Or maybe she's hiding something.'

'Nah,' I said confidently.

But now I can't stop thinking about what he said. For a girl who's supposed to be worried about her family, she did seem very smiley.

The sooner I touch base with Marcus the better.

On the way back over the road to the hotel, Gex and Keith in tow, I spotted my homeless guy again. He saw us and ran in our direction.

'Homeless guy,' Gex yelled. 'Run!' We sprinted into the hotel lobby just in time. As I stopped to get my breath back, the BlackBerry buzzed.

Call me. I'm sorry. G.

Maybe it was Brandi's boyfriend or something. I frowned. I had to too much to think about to analyse who the mysterious G was right now.

Up in the room I skyped Ms Gunter. She was eating a Wagon Wheel and looking much more cheerful.

'Hello, Ben, how are things?'

'Fine thanks.'

'No more trouble from immigration?'

'Funny,' I said. 'But I'm not ready to laugh about that just yet.'

'Fair enough.' She took a large bite of her Wagon Wheel. 'How are your parents?'

'They're fine. Dad still seems to be struggling with jet lag. Mum told me that yesterday he walked into a glass door at Macy's. Then he got into an altercation with a busker but refuses to tell me exactly what happened there.'

'And your friend?'

'Gex? He is spending a lot of time with his cousin. Who I think is a bad influence.'

'Be careful, Ben,' Ms Gunter said. 'If this cousin is trouble, then you need to keep well clear.'

'It's fine,' I said calmly, though I was already worrying about spending the evening with Gex and Keith later. I should probably hole up in my hotel room with a film or something. Stay out of trouble. But someone needs to keep an eye on Gex and make sure he doesn't do anything stupid. From an entirely selfish point of view, it wouldn't look good on my probation report to be a known associate of the infamous Gex the Strangler.

2.09pm

I met Brandi for lunch in Dino's. She'd called to say she had something exciting to show me. When she walked into the diner, carrying a towering pile of newspapers and magazines, she was smiling so much her face was like a lighthouse, her teeth like shining searchlights.

'Take a look, Ben. Take a look,' she said, dropping the pile onto the table. I started looking through the newspapers. Brandi had circled the relevant articles. They were all about me.

Boy vs Machine

Ben Fletcher is an unusual young Englishman. Not content with being the first ever male winner of the British Knitting Championships, he has now embraced a new challenge: taking on the knitting machine industry itself.

'I'm faster than any machine,' Ben told me when I spoke to him on Monday. 'Machines are destroying the industry. I want to see a revolution. I want people to take knitting back from the big corporations, the industrial megaliths. I want to see it return to a cottage industry, where women and men can produce unique, quality, bespoke garments and sell them directly to one another.'

I phoned Morgan Fairfax, CEO of KnitTech Industries in Calumet City, and put this idea to him.

'We've heard this socialist pipe-dream before,' says Fairfax. 'The idea that we can, or should revert to a pre-industrial age is ridiculous and potentially damaging. The knitting machine is here to stay. Our company saw a 23% growth last year. And the idea that a boy could knit faster than a machine?'

Fairfax laughs. 'I'd sure like to see that,' he says.

'This is terrible,' I said. 'I never said all this. I've been misquoted.'
There were more like that. I was even the cover story in one

magazine, *Garment Worker*. Brandi held it up proudly.

'Front cover!'

'How many people read *Garment Worker*?' I asked, hoping it would be a few dozen.

'I don't have the figures for *Garment Worker*,' Brandi said. 'But you'd be surprised. These trade publications have a loyal readership. *Meat Packer*, for example, has a circulation of thirty thousand.'

'Great.' I said.

'This is fantastic *publicity* for the KnitFair, Ben!' Brandi said, eyes shining as she read an article in the *Times*.

'But the stories aren't accurate,' I protested. 'For a start, it was the All UK Knitting Championships, not the British Knitting Championships.'

'Yeah, like there's a difference,' Brandi said.

'There's a big difference,' I said, coldly.

'Anyway, you won a knitting contest,' Brandi said, pointing to the article. 'They got that right.'

'Junior division.'

'It doesn't matter.'

'It matters to me!'

She held up the paper. 'Ben, you're in the *Times*!'

'But under false pretences!' I cried. Why couldn't she see this wasn't good?

'Ben, Ben, Ben,' Brandi said, reaching over the table and taking hold of my shoulders. I found myself mesmerised by all the teeth and hair being in such close proximity. 'It's better if they get the story wrong. That way, you can go to other newspapers and put the story straight.'

'OK,' I said. 'Let's do that. For a start I'm going to tell them I can't knit faster than a machine.'

'Ah,' she said. 'I'm thinking maybe it would be better if you didn't tell them that?'

'Why?'

Denise came, Brandi ordered a mineral water.

'Let me guess,' Denise said, looking at me. 'Philly cheesesteak.'

'Er, oh, go on,' I said. As she left I saw the homeless guy wander past outside the glass front. He peered in towards me and I hid behind the menu. Was he stalking me?

'It's just that I had a call from the Craig something show,' Brandi went on, ignoring my odd behaviour. 'Do you remember Craig something?'

My eyes narrowed. 'Oh yes. I remember Craig something. He started all this.'

'So they're really keen on doing an *event* at KnitFair, they'll sponsor it, in association with Priapia.'

'What sort of event?' I asked suspiciously, having flashbacks to the terrifying KnitBowl at the London Knitting Fair.

'Boy. Versus. Machine,' she said, theatrically holding up the cover of the *Times* again to illustrate.

I stared at her, shaking my head, hoping this was a dream.

'Do you get it?' she said. '*You*. Knitting against . . .'

'. . . a *machine*, yes, I get it,' I said. 'I'm not doing it though.'

'Really?' she said. 'I *thought* you'd love the idea.' She put on her sad face, which I'm slightly ashamed to admit, really does work on me.

'Strangely, I don't love the idea,' I said.

'There'll be prize money if you win,' she said. 'I think a

thousand dollars.'

'I won't win, though,' I said. 'So that's not going to help. Did you *really* think I'd love the idea?'

'Why not,?' she said. 'Ben, you're amazing.'

'I'm not amazing,' I said. 'I'm just an English boy . . .'

'. . . in New York,' she finished for me. 'You're an English Boy in New York! And what did Sinatra say about the Big Apple? If you can *boom* make it here, you'll make it *boom* anywhere.'

'I'm not sure he had knitting in mind,' I said.

'Listen, kid,' she said. 'You're from *Great* Britain. There's got to be a reason there's a *Great* in there.'

Bless her, she was trying so hard. 'That's true,' I said, rubbing my chin.

'And,' she said. 'Imagine if you beat the *machine?*'

'Brandi, I'm not going to beat the machine,' I said. 'I'm not Gary Kasparov.'

'Who?'

'Er, a chess player. Like Bobby Fisher?'

'Bobby Fisher? Did he sing "Don't Worry be Happy"?'

'Yeah, that's the guy,' I sighed. 'Anyway, I'm not him.'

'Look, you've got to do something,' she said. 'The sponsorship from Priapia didn't come . . . hasn't come through yet. We need the publicity and you need to do something at the fair.'

I said nothing. She crossed her arms. We glared at each other for a while.

'So, if you don't do this, then what exactly *are* you gonna do at the fair?' she asked.

'Have you seen me zumba?' I suggested.

* * *

135

'So here in the US we are a democracy,' Brandi said after my food had arrived. She was drinking her bottle of mineral water and eyeing my fries hungrily. We'd decided to change the subject.

'Oh yes?'

'We have two political parties, the Democrats and the Republicans.'

'I've heard of them,' I said.

'Have you?' she asked, surprised.

'Oh yes. Obama is a Democrat. He's the President, but the Republicans have a narrow majority in the Senate.'

'Wow!' she said, her eyes bright. 'You know about US politics!'

'A bit,' I said modestly.

Brandi looked impressed. 'So what do you want to do this afternoon?' she said.

'Don't we have interviews to do?' I asked.

'Not at the moment,' she said. 'I'm waiting on a couple of calls. I have to go into the office this evening but we have a few hours.'

'Oh great,' I said. 'What do you suggest?'

'Have you ever heard of a game called baseball?' she asked.

I had Brandi check the street before we left Dino's, to make sure the homeless guy wasn't going to accost me.

'How will I recognise him?' she asked.

'He wears a grey trench coat and a red polyester jumper,' I said. 'And he smells worse than the toilets at an asparagus factory.'

'OK,' she said. 'Got it.'

'Also, he has a bird skeleton in his beard if you think you need a further visual clue.'

She popped out and back in again quickly.

'He's not there,' she said.

'Great,' I replied, walking out into the watery sunshine. Brandi started waving for a cab.

I sighed with happiness as I took in the street scene. Crawling traffic honking merrily. A plump cop giving directions to a lady with a pushchair. A gaggle of tourists waiting at a bus stop. And up the street, rapidly approaching . . .

Oh crap. My homeless guy. Thanks a lot, Brandi. I ducked behind a planter but it was too late, he'd spotted me. Brandi was still waving fruitlessly for a cab.

'I got some advice for you,' he cried. I could smell him already. I grabbed Brandi and pulled her away down the street.

'Let's take the subway,' I said.

'The subway?' she protested. 'But we can put the cab on expenses.'

'I just want to experience all that New York has to offer,' I said, glancing back over my shoulder as I hurried her down the sidewalk. The homeless guy was still coming, but he seemed burdened by the plant pot and Macy's bag and couldn't keep up.

We made it safely down onto the platform and hopped on a 7 Train heading to Queens. Brandi found us two seats and I sat, looking around excitedly as we headed off. It was a long way and the train stopped at a lot of stations. As we rattled along, I noticed the man opposite me was falling asleep.

He'd slump slowly to the side, then suddenly jerk awake and straighten up. Then a few seconds later he'd lean to the left, his head drooping dangerously close to the shoulder of the man next to him, who I could see was aware of the situation but was pretending to be reading a book. I nudged Brandi and we giggled together at the sight.

There was a bit of a walk from the station which I was pleased about. I felt I hadn't done enough walking so far on this trip. In fact, I was puffing a little from the steps up to the street. Maybe I should cut down on the Philly cheesesteaks.

The BlackBerry buzzed as we walked in the weak sunshine. A text.

Hi Ben, I hope you don't mind me contacting you directly. My name is Melanee Chang and I work for the American Knitting Guild in publicity. We're huge fans of yours and would love to meet with you to discuss some possible events? It could be great for the profile of your business and we would be able to connect you with some very important people in the North American Knitting and Crochet world. Please reply by email or you can call me on 555 678 9451. I hope to hear from you soon! Melanee

'Look at this,' I said, showing Brandi the screen.

She quickly scanned the text.

'That bitch!' she hissed. She looked up at me. 'Seriously, Ben,' she said. 'You do not *want* anything to do with the American Knitting Guild.'

'I thought you worked for the American Knitting Guild?'

Brandi glared at me. 'I work for the Knitting Guild Association of America,' she said.

'They're different?'

'Yes they're different,' Brandi said grimly. 'They used to be the same organisation. But there was a . . . a big fight, kind of. Like when the Catholics and the Protestants had that disagreement.'

'You mean a schism?' I said. 'It was slightly more than a disagreement.'

'Well, so is this,' she said. 'They wanted to change the *fundamental style* of knitting in this country.'

'To what?'

'To the European style. Like they use in Canada.'

'And Europe,' I pointed out.

'Do they?'

'Yes,' I said. 'I knit in the European style.'

She hesitated, perhaps wondering if she'd offended me. 'I'm not saying it's not a *legitimate* style, in other countries. But it's not the American way.'

'Is it banned here?' I asked, slightly worried I now had to keep an eye out for the agents from the Department for Homeland Knitting.

'No, of course not,' she said. 'It's available as an alternative method, of course. But it shouldn't be the primary method, that's what we're saying. They, the so-called American Knitting Guild, wanted to change what was taught to young American knitters. The Standards, do you see?'

I had no idea knitting could be so political. But America's that kind of place. People feel strongly about things. And knitting is important.

3.15pm
I love New York. I love hot dogs. I love baseball. I love the fat guy behind us who yelled at Brandi in a good-natured way because her big hair was obstructing his view. Brandi didn't seem particularly interested in the game. Very few people were as far as I could make out, apart from the fat guy behind us who kept groaning every time the announcer gave any team news.

'For the NEW YORK METS, pitcher Jimmy Consuela!'

'Oh my God,' the fat guy cried. 'Not Consuela. My mother could knock him outta the park.'

'That man is the pitcher,' Brandi explained unnecessarily. 'He throws the ball at the other man, who tries to hit it with the stick.'

I looked around at the crowd. Brandi had explained this was a family-fun day, hence the early start. There were a lot of children here and a lot of people dressed up in animal costumes for some reason. Despite the fat guy's concerns, Consuela seemed to do the job for the Mets as three Oakland batters duly struck out and there was a change of innings.

'At bat for the Mets,' the announcer crackled. 'Bobby Johnson.'

The man behind howled in frustration. 'Johnson? You gottta be kidding me.'

Johnson hit a foul.

'I want my money back!' he cried. People really cared here. In the stands at Hampton FC everyone moaned constantly, but with no real belief that the team might actually improve. The guy behind me clearly thought his team could, and should, do better.

The next ball Johnson duly cracked clear into the stands, which quietened his critic for a while.

'That's called a home run,' Brandi told me.

Mets 3, Pittsburgh 1.

I'm never, ever going back to Hampton FC.

After the game I remembered to buy a Mets cap for Marcus. I'm running a little low on money. I'd had to buy the wool to replace the wool in the lost suitcase. And I've bought a toothbrush and a couple of pairs of boxers because I can't keep wearing Gex's. He'll find out if I'm not careful and that's really not going to look good. There was nothing for it but to go and see my parents tonight and ask them for some money. If I could find them, that was.

As we left the stadium amid streams of happy New Yorkers, the BlackBerry buzzed again. I'm a lot more popular here in the States than back home.

Please call me. Whatever I've done. I'm sorry. I don't deserve this. G

'Brandi,' I said. 'I forgot to mention this before, but I've had a couple of messages along these lines.' I showed her the phone.

Brandi looked furious, and snatched the phone off me.

'That bastard,' she said.

'You know who it is?'

'Oh yeah. I thought I'd blocked all his numbers.'

I put my hand on her shoulder lightly. And suddenly, before I knew what was happening, she'd turned and squashed her face into my chest, sobbing uncontrollably. I had no choice but to put my arms around her and pat her back comfortingly. This all happened in the middle of the flow of fancy-dress wearing pedestrians trying to get to the subway. I'm afraid we caused a bit of a blockage.

'There, there,' I said. I hadn't felt this uncomfortable since that time I found Freddie off his face in the garden at Isobel Knowles's end-of-term party and I had to help him get his clothes back on. Got to say though that I preferred this situation. Even if Brandi's enormous hair was all in my face and making me want to sneeze.

'I'm sorry, Ben,' she said. 'He's an ASSHOLE!'

'There, there,' I repeated, smiling apologetically at a giant turkey who was trying to get by.

'Why are all men assholes?' she asked, pulling back and wiping her eyes. I fumbled for a tissue in my Bloomingdale's bag.

'I guess it's just how God made us,' I said, somehow thinking this was comforting.

'You're not an asshole, Ben,' she said. 'And thank you for the tissue.'

'Do you want to talk about it?' I asked.

She shook her head. 'No, not here, not now. I gotta be professional.'

All things considered it would be better if I didn't tell Brandi the next time G leaves a message on my phone.

* * *

Brandi and I parted at 38th Street and she told me she'd be in contact once she had more news about the other media engagement she was trying to arrange.

When I got back to the hotel I found Keith and Gex in our room lounging around in the armchairs. I could tell something was up as soon as I entered because they first went very quiet and then started giggling.

'Hello,' I said cautiously. 'What have you two been up to?'

'Nothing,' Gex said.

'Playing cards,' Keith said.

I walked over to the coffee table, which was strewn with Coke cans.

'This place is a tip,' I said. 'Why is it always me who has to do the tidying around here?' Then, as I picked up one of the cans I sniffed it.

'Vodka!' I said. 'I knew it! I can't leave you two alone for five minutes. Where did you get the boo . . .' I trailed off, looking towards the minibar. 'Oh, please tell me you haven't?'

'Haven't what?' Gex asked innocently.

I rushed to the minibar and opened the door. The miniatures were all there. But hold on. I grabbed a bottle of vodka and examined it.

'The seal's broken!' I cried. 'This has been opened.'

'Probably the cleaner,' Gex said sheepishly.

'I can't believe you guys have done this,' I said, checking all the bottles. 'I have to pay for these.'

'Brandi's paying, innit?' Gex said.

'WE DON'T KNOW THAT!'

'Chill, Ben,' Gex said, belching. 'We filled up the vodka

143

bottles. And the Scotch.'

'You had Scotch too?' I cried, pulling out a tiny bottle of Bell's and examining it in the fridge light. 'What have you filled it up with?'

'Er, tea?' Gex said. Keith was stifling laughter.

'Don't lie to me, Gex,' I said, standing up and pointing a finger. 'You know full well there are no tea-making facilities in this room.'

'Honestly, Ben,' he said. 'It's tea.'

'Then why is it so yellow?' I demanded.

'It's Canadian,' Keith said. 'Canadian tea.'

Unscrewing the cap, I took a careful whiff which confirmed my suspicions.

'Firstly, Gex,' I said, furious. 'You are a liar and a thief. Secondly, you are disgusting, and thirdly, you need to drink more water, you are clearly dehydrated.'

'Lighten up,' Gex said. 'It's just a few bottles.'

'Look, homeboy,' Keith said, trying to placate me. 'Stealing a couple of miniatures is nothing. Did I tell you about the time me and the boys held up a Savings and Loan?'

I decided to go down to the lobby at that point to cool off. I needed to skype Ms Gunter and didn't want to do it with them in the room.

I saw Dad, sitting alone at the bar. He had a drink in front of him and was looking at his phone forlornly. I walked over.

'Hi, Dad,' I said cautiously. 'Where's Mum?'

'Times Square,' he said evenly.

'Diablo?'

'Diablo.'

'Are you two . . . OK?' I asked.

'We're fine, Ben,' Dad said. 'Just fine.'

But he didn't look fine. What if something happens between Mum and Diablo? Magic can be very romantic. He might pull flowers from his sleeve. She might pull a glass of champagne from behind his ear. Anything might happen.

Poor old Dad.

Dermot O'Leary popped up inside my head again. 'It's not just Ben who's having concerns about his relationship,' he said in a concerned tone. 'Ben's parents seemed happy, but is there something he's not being told?'

I felt a bit sick as I walked down the street to the internet café. Though whether this was from the thought of Mum and Diablo together in a false-bottomed wardrobe, or the fourth hot dog I had at the Mets game, I don't know.

Speaking of hot dogs, I had a bit of trouble doing my buttons up today. I'm certainly getting more USA around the waist. I'm puzzled by this. I've only been here a few days. I've only had four Philly cheesesteaks, maybe five. Four plates of waffles. How can I be putting on weight so quickly?

It must be all the vegetables. They're so bloating.

I drank a Diet Coke while I skyped Ms Gunter. Neither of us had much to report and the call was over pretty quickly. Once I'd hung up I skyped Marcus, hoping to catch him before his bedtime. He answered.

'Hi, Ben,' he said. 'Did you get the cap?'

'Before I answer that, Marcus,' I said. 'Has she been seeing Sean?'

'Yes,' he said immediately. My heart skipped a beat.

'When?'

'Did you get me the cap, or not?'

'Yes, yes, I got the cap,' I said impatiently. 'When did Megan see Sean, Marcus?'

'Last night. He came around while I was having my dinner and him and Megan went off together.'

'They might have gone to the hospital together?' I asked hopefully.

'Hospital?'

'To see your gran?' I said.

'Is Gran in hospital?' he asked, bottom lip wobbling. 'What's wrong with her?'

Uh-oh.

'Um. Just a routine . . . thing,' I said hurriedly. 'I'm sure she's fine.'

'Mum's coming,' Marcus said. 'Gotta go.'

'OK. Thanks. Oh, and, Marcus, keep a lid on things, will you?'

'I will,' he said.

As he switched off the monitor I wondered if his eyes looked a little moist. I hope I haven't worried him about his gran.

Thursday 16th May

12.31am

It's late but I can't sleep. I'm worried about Gex. I've come back on my own from the Big Night Out. Keith went off to pick up his car from a car park nearby. He came back and collected us just after 8pm in a maroon-coloured Cadillac so big and shiny it resembled a float in a small town parade. He parked so badly that not only did it take up the No Stopping bay opposite the hotel but one of its tail fins blocked half of the next lane as well. He picked up quite a few friendly honks and beeps during the time it took us to come downstairs.

'Could you walk any slower?' he asked as we got in.

'Blame Gex,' I said. 'He wouldn't come out of the bathroom.'

'I got IVF,' he mumbled.

'IBS,' I sighed. The seat I was on was so deep my feet didn't touch the floor.

We pulled out into the cheery traffic, turned right and the float rumbled up the street.

'Tell Ben what you were telling me yesterday,' Gex said to Keith. 'About how you watched that guy get whacked off.'

'He didn't get whacked off,' Keith replied quickly. 'He got whacked.'

Gex was silent for a moment. 'What's the difference?' he asked.

'Let's change the subject,' I said. 'I'm uncomfortable with either definition.'

'OK,' Keith said. 'You're gonna love this place we're going, Ben.'

'It's not further than 110th Street, is it? I'm not crossing 110th Street.'

'No, not that far,' Keith said. I sat forward a bit. I could hardly hear him all the way up the front of the float. The radio was playing Motown and I have to admit I was feeling pretty excited about the evening.

'So, here's my theory about why girls like British guys,' Keith said as we drove.

'Go on,' I said.

'It's like in movies,' he said. 'The British actor is always the bad guy. Like Alan Rickman, or Anthony Hopkins, or Hugh Jackman.'

'Hugh Jackman is from Australia.'

'Like there's a difference.' Keith said impatiently. 'Anyway, so all these British guys in movies, playing bad guys?'

'Yeah?' I said.

'Girls *like* a bad guy.'

I waited for more. 'Is that it?'

'Yep.'

'That's your theory?'

'Yeah, what do you think?'

'It's brief, which is good. But I don't think it holds water,' I said. 'For a start, not all British actors play bad guys. What about McNulty in *The Wire*?'

'He's not British!'

'Yes he is. So is the guy who plays Stringer Bell.'

'You are so full of crap.'

'There are loads of British actors playing Americans. What about Hugh Laurie in *House*?'

'He's American!'

'He most certainly is not.'

'Listen to his voice, man.'

'He's putting on an American accent!' I cried.

'Anyway, Greg House isn't such a good guy,' Gex said.

'He's sort of good and bad,' Keith agreed.

'Half British, half American,' Gex said. 'Half good, half evil.'

'The other way around, I think,' Keith said after a brief consideration.

'Anyway,' I said. 'There are loads of American bad guys.'

'Like who?'

'Ted Bundy?' suggested Gex.

'No, in films,' I said.

'Hannibal Lecter?'

'Welsh. Anyway, the point is, I don't agree with the theory that girls always like bad boys.'

'Course they do,' Keith said. 'They like guys who are tough and strong and who can protect them.'

'This is why I need a gun,' Gex said.

'You don't need a gun,' I said.

'OK, let's have a little bet tonight,' Keith said, changing lanes without indicating. 'Ben, you be all nice and lah-di-dah with the ladies. Take 'em for a waltz and a two-step and a three-step. Dance the Pride of Erin if there's room. Gex here, on the other hand, will treat them like dirt. Ignore them, yawn in their faces. That sort of thing. We'll see who has the most success.'

'Oh man,' Gex said. 'This is going to be great.'

'Neither of us is going to have any success,' I pointed out. 'We're just a couple of losers from Hampton. Gex is wearing a gold tracksuit. I am wearing my father's chinos.'

'Yeah,' Keith said. 'But you got those British accents going on.'

* * *

We left the huge car in an alley around the corner and made our way to the club. There was a man outside in a filthy string vest. He stared at us blearily as we walked past, into the doorway and down the tatty staircase. The club didn't actually look too bad once we were down there. It was dark, very dark, with coloured floor lights and pretty good music.

'The thing about this club,' Keith yelled as we stood at the bar, waiting for service, 'is it attracts a certain type of lady.'

'What type?' I asked.

'Well, let's just say that the typical customer here is what you might call . . . vintage?'

'In a fashion sense?'

'No, more in an age sense.'

I looked around. Keith was right. The girls I could see weren't girls. They were women. Most of them looked like they might be in their thirties, or forties. I saw a small group looking at us. One of them said something and they all laughed.

'That's why it's so dark in here,' I said.

'Three beers,' Keith said to the young barman. 'And three whiskey chasers.'

'No whiskey for me,' I said. 'And do you have any non-alcoholic lager?'

'No,' the barman said.

'Ooh, what about a highball. Can you make a highball?'

'No,' the barman repeated. He plonked three bottles of beer and three shot glasses on the counter. Keith slapped a note down on the table and drank his whiskey.

'I'm never going to get my highball,' I said, sniffing the whiskey dubiously.

'This is the sort of bar,' Keith said, 'where ladies come who are looking for a summer–spring romance. Or maybe even autumn–spring.'

'That one over there is well past autumn,' Gex said, looking at a blonde slumped at the bar. 'Her hair has a bit of snow in it.'

'Why have you brought us here?' I said as Keith led us over to a booth at the back of the club.

'Two reasons,' he said. 'One, because of the sort of place this is, they don't check IDs too closely. Not guys' IDs anyhow, you feel?'

'And the other reason?' I asked.

'I think I've already explained,' he said, indicating the autumnal ladies at the next table.

'We're here to pick up older women?' I asked, horrified.

'Oh man,' Gex said, barely able to hide his glee. He drank his whiskey too quickly, did an enormous hiccup and knocked his beer off the table.

We'd been there around fifteen minutes when three women from the group who'd been laughing at us earlier came over to chat. Gex ignored them; he'd found a toothpick from somewhere and was turning it over and over using just his lips and teeth.

So it was down to Keith and I to chat up Cherry, Monique and Yasmin. I decided if we were going to play this game I was going to do it properly. Especially as this was a game I really didn't want to win. If I acted in a completely non-threatening manner then no woman could possibly want to get off with me. Not that they would anyway. But at least this time I'd have an excuse as to why I hadn't got off with anyone.

'Do you like knitting?' I asked Monique, who reminded me a bit of Mrs Frensham. I can't really imagine Mrs Frensham in a place like this, I have to say. She hates young men. She's not that keen on old men either to judge by the things she says about the octogenarian who lives next door.

Monique gave me a look.

'Knitting? How old do you think I am?' she asked.

'You don't have to be old to knit,' I said. 'I'm a keen knitter, myself.'

'I don't knit,' she said.

'Oh, shame.'

'I do a little crochet sometimes,' she admitted.

'Ah, now I've just begun to get into crochet,' I said. 'I'm not sure it's for me though.'

I didn't get to hear Monique's response though, as Cherry broke in.

'You're British!' she said. 'I love the British accent.'

'That's so cool because I love the American accent!' I replied enthusiastically.

I caught Gex's eye, I think he might have been wishing he was in my shoes, playing the cheeky English lad card. It already seemed to be the more successful approach. Obviously I didn't want anything to happen! Especially not with Monique, but you know how it is. No one wants to strike out completely. In any case, I don't think I could ever play the bad boy. I like a chat too much. And I get churned up inside if I think I've been rude to someone.

Keith bought me a litre glass of ginger beer as it was clear I wasn't going to drink the actual beer he'd bought me. I gulped it down gratefully. It was surprisingly thoughtful of him but after a while all the liquid sent me to the little boys' room. Gex had to make a trip as well, due to his IBS which didn't make the experience any more pleasant, I can tell you for nothing. Thankfully there was a man in the loo handing out towels and he had a large selection of aftershave bottles which he sprayed frantically in the direction of Gex's cubicle.

As I washed my hands, the towel man spoke.

'You having a good night, my friend?'

'You know what?' I said, taking a towel. 'I am. I didn't think I would, but I like it here.'

He wore a neat waistcoat and a small moustache. I find myself drawn to neat people. 'You got your eye on a lady?' he said. 'I got some scent here with musk.'

'No musk for me, thanks,' I said. 'I have a girlfriend back in England. I'm just here for a drink and a chat.'

He shrugged. 'In that case, put this one on.' He held out a tiny bottle from the back of the tray.

'What's this?'

But we were interrupted by Gex, who came out of his cubicle pulling up his gold trackie bottoms and walking gingerly. The toilet attendant grabbed a bottle and pumped a few sprays into the air.

'It has a secret ingredient, from the Amazon,' he told me.

'What's so special about it?'

'It makes people trust you,' he said, winking. 'They feel like you're their friend. No sexy stuff.'

'OK, why not?' I said and squirted a few blasts onto my wrists and neck.

'Does it, like, make chicks jam their hand down your pants?' Gex asked.

'No. This is what you're looking for,' the attendant said, picking up a different bottle. 'It has pheromones from the Costa Rican love toad.'

'Love toad?' Gex asked, wide-eyed.

'That's pretty spooky, Gex,' I said. 'It's as though it was created just for you, eh?'

'Sick!' Gex said, as usual not getting the irony. 'How much?'

'For you, sir, ten dollars a squirt,' said the attendant.

'Ten dollars?' Gex cried.

'Take it or leave it,' the man said.

Gex gave it five seconds before prodding me in the arm. 'Pay the man, Ben.'

'Seriously?' I gaped at him. But it was too late, the man had squirted some onto Gex's wrist. It didn't smell great to me, but I'm not a female love toad. And to be honest, it was a lot less offensive than the odour coming from the cubicle Gex had just vacated. Gex left in search of lady toads, leaving me to rummage through my pockets for notes. I paid the man, and feeling confident for once, gave him a nice tip.

'Thank you, sir,' he said, smiling.

I came out and ran straight into into a large lady stood outside the toilets. At least I think she was a lady. She looked a bit like Groo from *Despicable Me*.

She was obviously waiting for me, as she gave me a huge smile and linked her arm through mine.

'I want to show you something,' she said.

'Erm . . .' I began nervously. 'Have we met?'

Where was Gex when I needed him? Where was Keith?

The lady looked behind her to check the coast was clear and ushered me to the end of the corridor, by the cigarette machine. She was a lot bigger than me and wore a suit that was very tight across the bust. I was in trouble.

'I need you,' she said urgently.

'Look, I only came along to keep an eye on Gex,' I said. 'I'm not looking for any kind of seasonal romance.'

'I'm in such a mess,' she said, shaking her head. 'I don't know where it all went wrong.'

'I'm not sure I'm the right person to . . .' I said, backing away and bumping into a pot plant.

'I think you are,' she said, fixing me with a hungry look. She jammed a hand into a large suede bag and pulled out a tangle of wool and needles.

'It's supposed to be moss stitch,' she said. 'But I keep losing track of what I'm doing.'

Oh thank God.

My heart resumed beating and I took the tangle from her.

'Yes,' I said, peering at it in the dim light. 'You've missed a few rows.'

'Should I just start again?' she asked, crestfallen. 'I spent ages.'

'I think you might be able to salvage some sections,' I said. 'Let me have a look at it in the light of the glitter ball.'

She told me her name was Ursula, and I took her back to our table to join the other ladies. Ignoring Gex's glares, I repaired Ursula's sweater as best I could. Then Monique pulled out her crochet from somewhere and began showing me the basics. After a time Gex was dragged onto the dance floor by Yasmin.

And Keith danced with Cherry.

As for me, I spent a happy hour or so stitching and bitching with the rest of the ladies. They were all very interested in the KnitFair. I even told them about the challenge of me knitting against the machine and they all thought I should go for it. It's obviously a very go-for-it kind of place, New York.

Keith sensibly walked away from Gex, who was cavorting on the dance floor, twisting and hopping in the middle of a dozen or so mature women like an ambulant handbag, to bring back some more drinks for our table.

'What is that?' Keith asked, pointing at the work.

'It's crochet,' I said. 'I'm just learning how to do it.'

As I spoke, I saw a middle-aged man enter the bar and look around angrily. He spotted something, or someone on the dance floor and stalked in that direction. I suddenly had a flash of anxiety. I watched the man as he headed straight for Gex, who was slow-dancing with a lady in leopard print. Not Cherry, some other random lady. The man grabbed the leopard-print lady's wrist and pulled her away from Gex. The lady shrieked and Gex fronted up to the newcomer, who was at least two inches taller and looked well-built. Say what you like about Gex, but he's got bottle. 'What the hell are you doing with my goddam WIFE?' the man spat at Gex.

'The lambada,' Gex replied coolly.

'My baby don't lambada with nobody,' the man said.

'Yeah, well . . . nobody puts Baby in the corner,' the slightly drunk Gex replied.

'Oh, for heaven's sake,' I muttered. And then Baby's husband took a swing at Gex, who ducked just in time. Keith leapt on the man's back and tried unsuccessfully to pin his arms.

The man roared and swung wildly in my direction. Instinctively I raised my arms to protect myself, only then realising I still held Monique's doily and hook, which were knocked out of my hands as I fell to the floor.

Baby shrieked again, her husband howled and I looked up to see him clutching his fist. Four inches of crochet hook were sticking out of the space between his first and second knuckles. The music suddenly stopped, and there was a deathly silence. A droplet of blood fell from the man's knuckles, splashing onto the dance floor. 'Oh God, I'm *really* sorry,' I said, picking up the crochet and holding it out towards him in case he felt he needed a holey bandage.

The man moaned and fell to his knees, staring at his knuckles, unable to believe what had happened to him. How was he going to explain this to his insurance company? Did they pay out for knitting-related injuries?

Outside on the street we heard a siren.

'Five-Oh coming!' Gex screeched and suddenly we all panicked and rushed for the exit.

'My crochet!' Monique yelled as I ran past, but I was too stunned to react and it was only later that I realised I still held it in my hand. The man in the singlet watched us clatter back up the stairs and out of the door, then we sprinted around the corner to the car.

Which wasn't there.

'Dude, where's your car?' Gex said.

'Oh crap,' I hissed, as another siren sounded, closer this time. Keith said we'd better head for the subway.

'What about your car?' I asked as we scurried along 84th Street.

'It's probably been towed,' Keith said. 'I gotta call the pound.'

'You can crash at our hotel if you want?' I offered.

'I ain't crashing anywhere, yet,' Keith said, stopping and turning. 'The night is young.'

My heart sank. 'Where are we going, now?' I asked.

'Jersey,' Keith said.

'Just to be clear, I am not going to Jersey,' I told Gex. 'The A train takes us back to the hotel.'

'And the B train takes us to Jersey, innit,' Gex replied. He clearly didn't want to call it a day yet, either.

The three of us were standing on the platform of the subway at 86th Street. Gex and Keith were planning to go to some dive to drink and play cards, as Keith put it. Gex was clearly thinking this was his chance to be initiated into Keith's gang.

'You wanted to see the sights, Bellend,' Gex said. 'Now's your chance, bruv.'

'Jersey wasn't exactly top of my list,' I said. 'In fact, it was more like not on my list at all. I've heard it's a bit rough.'

'Nah,' Gex said. 'Keith says his crew have the whole district locked down tight. No one's gonna touch us cos we're in the gang.'

'You and I are not in a gang,' I pointed out. 'And to be honest, I don't think Keith is either.'

'*What?!*'

'He's all mouth. Gangstas don't talk about capping people while ordering a Starbucks Mocha Frappuccino.'

A fast train rattled by, electrical flashes lighting up Gex's thin face.

'He's not scared of nothing. He's protected.'

'Protected from *reality*. He ran like a girl when we heard that siren.'

'Look, I'm going. You in or not?'

'No, Gex,' I said. 'I'm drawing a line. Here's the line.' I pointed to a cracked line of tiles on the grimy floor.

'I'm crossing the line,' he said, stepping over it.

'Fine,' I said. 'I'm also crossing it.' I stepped over the line as well.

'I'm taking the B train tonight,' he said.

'I'm taking the A train tonight,' I replied.

It was then that I realised we'd both need to cross the line again to get to the right platforms.

'We should of done this the other way round,' Gex said.

'Yeah. Look, stay out of trouble, OK?'

'Don't worry about me,' he said, and perhaps still a little drunk, gave me a hug.

I felt bad all the way home on the rattly train. Should I have gone with him, to keep him out of trouble? I think I should have gone with him.

2.45am

I just had a call on the BlackBerry.

'It's Keith. You gotta get here, man.'

'What? Who? What?' I said. 'I have jet lag.'

'It's Gex. He's in real trouble.'

159

Immediately I was wide awake. 'What happened?'

'Just get down here.'

'Put Gex on the phone.'

'He can't talk right now.'

'Is he alive?'

'For now. But he's in too deep, man.'

'Oh God. Should I call the police?'

'Nuh huh! No cops.'

Keith gave me the address. I thought for a minute how would I get there. Emergency or not. I don't think I had enough money for a cab ride all the way to Jersey. Also, I wasn't that keen about going on my own. I thought of getting Mum and Dad up, but they'd call the police.

Brandi is a girl and shouldn't be exposed to danger. Megan is also a girl and two thousand miles away. In the end I called the one person who seemed like he'd be there for me in a crisis.

'I'll meet you in your lobby in twenty minutes,' Trey said after I'd woken him up and told him everything. 'Don't worry, Ben. We'll find your friend.'

I was sick with worry and self-recrimination as I dressed. Why had I left Gex? Why hadn't I dragged him back home with me? The night staff were watching me curiously as I waited downstairs. Especially when Gex's belt buckle felt a little tight and I had to loosen it.

I saw Trey's car pull up and rushed out.

'Thanks for coming,' I said and gave Trey the address.

'Sheesh,' he said. 'That's one rough neighbourhood.'

I checked my phone, there was a message. Private number.

160

I want my Michael Bublé albums back. Can we meet up? G

Another message from Brandi's ex. I deleted it and scrolled back through the log until I found Keith's number. I hit call but it just went straight to voicemail.

It seemed to take forever to reach the address. Jersey looks close on the map, but even at this hour there was plenty of traffic around and a lot of the streets were single lane. People were walking on the road, some making threatening-looking gestures at the car as it went by.

Eventually Trey pulled over. 'We're here,' he said, peering out of the window at the shop front and sagging canopy. It looked like a restaurant. The windows were heavily draped and a tarnished single pole stood outside, a frayed velvet rope trailing from it forlornly. The place looked deserted. A faulty street light flickered on and off overhead, adding to the *Day of the Dead* atmosphere.

He's in too deep! Keith had said. I checked my phone again but there was no message. Even Brandi's ex had given up for the time being.

'Whatever we find in there, we stick together, right?' Trey said, sounding like Russell Crowe in *Gladiator*.

'OK.' I nodded. I've never felt the need to breathe into a paper bag to control my anxiety until that moment. I was absolutely petrified.

Trey waited until the street was clear then he got out and, after taking a deep breath, I followed. Trey walked to the door and found a buzzer, which he pressed.

There was a long pause and he was just about to press it again when a voice crackled out.

'Who are you?'

'Taxi. Here to collect a couple of guys.'

'Who?'

'Keith and Gex,' Trey said coolly.

There was another pause, then a buzzer sounded and the door clicked unlocked. As we entered, a drunk walked past behind us cackling softly to himself. I shivered. Inside was a restaurant with the chairs up on the tables. It looked like it might have been cosy during the day, when everyone was slurping down spaghetti vongole, chins greasy, wine sloshing in old-fashioned glasses. But right now, in the small hours, dimly lit, it looked like the sort of place where good guys got whacked.

A short fat man poked his head out of a door at the back.

'Through here, Tony wants to see you.'

Trey and I looked at each other nervously and followed the man.

It was a large room with a round table in the centre. Around it sat six men, including Gex and Keith, who were looking up at us, with terror on their faces, mixed with relief. I was immensely relieved to see that Gex was apparently unharmed. A pack of cards lay on the table along with poker chips. Everyone had a stack of chips except for Gex. Another man stood at the back of the room with his hand inside his jacket. Everyone was watching us except for one man who was shuffling the pack.

'Tony,' the fat man said to the shuffling man. 'These are the guys.'

'Taxi,' Trey said.

'Why are there two of you?' said Tony without looking up.

'Security,' Trey said.

The man looked up at me.

'He's your security?'

The card players laughed.

'He's tougher than he looks,' Trey said.

'I doubt that,' the man said, and he stood and walked over to me, looking me up and down.

I swallowed. A trickle of sweat rolled down my spine. Gex stared at me, wide eyed.

Tony leaned closer and closer to me and took a large sniff. I remembered the neat guy in the club. The trustworthy aftershave! The pheromones! Tony leaned back, nodding slightly, and I felt I'd passed the first test. If I get out of this, I told myself. I'm going back to the MILF Club and doubling the towel guy's tip.

'What you got in the bag, tough guy?' Tony asked.

It was only then that I realised I was still clutching the Bloomingdale's bag. I must have grabbed it instinctively when getting out of the car.

'Oh, nothing. Just personal items.'

The man fixed me with a hard stare. The man at the back of the room straightened and pushed his hand further into his jacket. I couldn't help but notice there was a bulge in the jacket over the left breast.

I swallowed and reached into the bag. Everyone stiffened. Three of the card players reached into their jackets.

I pulled out my knitting. There was a long silence.

'What is that?' Tony said, eventually.

'It's called a Hoopie,' I replied. 'It's my design, a hooded cardigan.'

'No. I mean is it yarn-back? Backward loop?

'Oh. It's just straight knit and purl, just with chunky needles. . . . You knit?'

'I sure do. Those are some big needles.'

'10.5s. The cardigan is designed to have big holes.'

'I never heard of a knitting bodyguard before,' Tony said.

I've never heard of a knitting Mob boss before, I thought, but didn't say.

'I find it relaxes me,' I said, acutely conscious that everyone in the room was watching me intently. I wasn't feeling at all relaxed.

'Yeah me too,' Tony said, and came over.

'Do you mind?' He held out a hand. I passed him the Hoopie and he inspected it closely.

'Well,' said Keith. 'I think it's time we were going.'

'Sure, no problem,' said the standing man with the lump in his jacket. 'Once you've paid up.'

'Right,' Keith said. 'So how much do we owe?'

'You owe thirty dollars. Your friend in the tracksuit owes one hundred and sixty-five dollars.'

'How much?' I spluttered.

Gex shrugged. 'I had a full house. Sal went all in, I had to borrow to match his bet. I couldn't lose.'

'Sal had four kings,' Keith said. 'So you did lose.'

'How much you got?' Trey said, pulling out his wallet.

'Thirty-five,' I replied, throwing it down on the table.

'I got a fifty,' Trey said.

'Me too,' Keith said, adding that to the pile.

164

'Fifty-five short,' the man with the bulge said.

'We could go to an ATM,' Trey said. 'Get the rest.'

'Your friend stays here until you get back,' bulge man said, nodding at Gex, who looked terrified.

'Wait,' Tony said, looking up at me from the Hoopie. 'You knit a lot of these, kid?'

'A few,' I said nervously.

'OK. How about you knit one for me and we forget all about the money your friend owes.'

'Sure, of course,' I said, relief flooding through me. 'Is it a gift for your wife?'

'Nah. My mistress.'

'Right,' I said, trying to look totally down with this information. I'll just need her measurements?'

'No problem, Tony said. 'She's 44, 28, 45.' As he spoke, he outlined an hourglass figure with his hands. The other card players nodded appreciatively behind him. 'She's a whole lotta woman, *capiche*?'

'*Capiche*.'

'I'm seeing her Saturday night,' he said. 'So I need it by then.'

'No problem,' I said, already panicking about when I'd have the time to do it. My only hope was adjusting the one Tony had in his hands. It would save on wool too.

But Tony was scrutinising the Hoopie with a worrying frown.

'Everything OK?' I said. 'You like that one?'

'Sure I do, except for the colour,' he said. 'I'll need it in her favourite colour.'

Damn.

'And what is that?' I asked.

'Cerise.'
'Cerise?'
'Cerise.'

Trey laughed all the way back to Manhattan. He found the whole episode hilarious. Unlike the rest of us.

'So, Keith. Do you remember earlier, on the phone,' I said. 'I asked you if Gex was alive?'

'Yes?'

'And you said *for now*. I thought you meant he was in danger of losing his life.'

'What? No way. I meant he was nearly out of chips.'

'Right. But you can see how I might have got the wrong end of the stick?'

'I guess.'

'You guess?'

'Yeah.'

'But you're saying now that Gex was actually in no danger at all?'

Trey exploded with another fit of giggling.

'The worst they would have done was threaten to pull out a couple of fingernails unless he paid,' Keith said.

'Just threaten?'

'Yeah. Unless he didn't pay.'

'Now I've got no money left,' I said. 'My immediate problem, to add to all my other problems, is how the hell am I going to buy six rolls of cerise wool, which I'm allergic to in any case, so I can spend a day indoors knitting a Hoopie for a crime boss to pay off your gambling debt.'

Trey swerved across the turnpike as he doubled over, laughing.

'Watch the road, Barry Chuckle,' I said.

'I'll just shoplift your wool from Bloomingdale's, innit,' said Gex.

'You are *not* shoplifting from Bloomingdale's!' I roared. 'You've caused enough trouble as it is.'

'Can't you borrow it off your parents, then?' Gex shrugged.

'I'm not asking my parents. They don't have much money either.'

'You could ask your girlfriend?' Keith suggested.

'Megan doesn't have any money,' I said.

'Not Megan, the girl with the hair.'

'Brandi is not my girlfriend.'

'She wants to be,' Keith said.

Gex snorted.

'Also,' I said, changing the subject. 'We have to pay Trey back.'

'Ah, don't worry about it,' Trey said. 'I had a blast.'

'I'm paying you back,' I said.

He looked over at me and grinned. 'Tell you what, you get that big deal with Priapia, and then you can pay me back.'

'I'm not getting any deal,' I said. 'I told you, I made a mess of the interview.'

'That's not what I heard,' Trey said. 'I was driving Robert home last night and he made a call. Your name was mentioned.'

'Really? What did he say?'

'I can't tell you. I've already said more than I should have. But you should prepare yourself for a call.'

'When?'

'Tomorrow, I guess, he said he needs to talk to you before the fair. He's got a plan.'

Dawn was breaking by the time we got back to the hotel. Gex was still sheepish and went to bed quietly. I made up a bed for Keith on the floor using cushions from the armchair. While Keith was in the bathroom, Gex sidled up to me and mumbled something unintelligible.

'What? What did you say?' I asked.

'Just wanted to say thanks,' he said quietly, looking at the carpet. 'For coming to get me and that.'

This was unexpected and a bit embarrassing. Gex never apologises. I was touched.

'Never mind,' I said. 'You're a mate, after all.'

Then we both looked down at the carpet awkwardly, until the door to the bathroom opened and Keith came out. 'Room service for anyone?' he said.

'Absolutely not,' I said, back to outraged disapproval. 'I think it's time you both went to sleep.'

Later, I lay in my own bed, my mind awhirl, listening to Gex and Keith snoring and the chirping traffic thirteen storeys down. I was thinking about the crazy night I'd just had, about what Trey had said, but most of all about the fact that I'd somehow agreed to knit a hooded cardigan for a Mafia don in New Jersey.

In cerise.

9.17am

We wanted to sleep in the next day, but Mum and Dad had other ideas.

'We've hardly seen you since we arrived,' Dad said as I squinted at him over the threshold. At least Mum was here, and the two of them were still talking. She hadn't run off with Diablo.

'Well whose fault is that?' I asked. 'You've been out and about dawn till dusk having fun, while I've been going to interviews and tidying up after Gex.'

'Get dressed,' he said, unsympathetic. 'We'll meet you in Dino's in ten minutes.' As I closed the door, Gex was sitting up in bed, looking at me oddly.

'What?' I said.

'You is getting the chunk on, bruv,' he said.

'I am not.'

'It must be all them Philly cheesesteaks.'

'I've only been here a few days,' I pointed out.

'You have eaten a lot of Philly cheesesteaks.'

'Only three. Maybe four,' I said. 'Anyway, I don't get fat, I have a fast metabolism.'

'It's slowed down,' he said, rolling over and plumping his pillows.

I looked at my belly. The T-shirt I was wearing did seem a little tight.

'It's probably jet lag,' I said. 'I'm not worried.'

Keith made his excuses and slipped off before breakfast to track down his car. While Gex snoozed, I texted Brandi to ask if there were any interviews to do today or whether I had the day for sight-seeing. I still hadn't even been to the Empire State Building! The phone rang straight away.

'Hey, babe,' I said, feeling a bit Hollywood.

'Hello? Mr Fletcher?'

'Oh, sorry, yes, this is Ben Fletcher.'

'This is Robert D'Angelo of Priapia Textiles.'

'Hello, Mr D'Angelo. How are you?' Suddenly the nerves were back.

'I'm well thanks, Ben. I told you I'd give you a feedback call following your meeting with us earlier this week.'

Had he said that? I couldn't remember.

'Ben, can I be honest with you?'

'Please do,' I said. That didn't sound good. People only ever ask if they can be honest with you when they're about to tell you something you don't want to hear. Like you have pongy breath, or you're just not cut out to be a test pilot. Or both.

'We think you need to do some more work on your business proposal.'

'OK, what sort of work?'

'Well, you need to actually have a business proposal for a start.'

'Point taken,' I replied. I wondered if I should tell him he needed to work on his 'informal chat' skills.

'We didn't feel you were adequately prepared for the meeting. It wasn't clear how you intended to monetise your enterprise, what your short-, medium-term and long-range goals were, or even what level of funding you were looking for.'

I wondered if I was allowed to hang up now? I should have

170

been at Dino's eating waffles. Maybe I should shout down the phone: 'Yeah, well, screw you, buddy. I'm gonna make it big in this town, then I'm gonna buy you out and fire your ass.'

'Having said that, we LOVE your design,' he went on.

'You do?' I said, taken aback. 'Well, that's nice.'

'And . . . and we've been watching the news reports about you, Ben. About how you're going to outknit a machine.'

'About that –'

'We like your approach to publicity, Ben,' he said before I could explain. 'Your business plan sucks, but you're damn good at publicity.'

'That's all down to my people,' I said quickly, glancing over at Gex, who I suppose is one of my people. He was still in bed, scratching his bottom.

'I wanna make you an offer, Ben. I want to make you a very nice offer.'

'Really?'

'Really. I want the rights to that design. I want world rights. And I'm prepared to pay a lot.'

'Wow!'

'Yeah, wow!' he said. 'And I want your name, and I want you to sign a contract to provide me with more designs.'

I jumped up and down in silent glee.

'But it comes with a condition.'

Of course it does.

'Ben,' he said.

'Yes?'

'You got to make me some sales at the fair. You can take a table in our stand on Saturday. I'll fix up some appointments for you.'

'Wow, that sounds amazing.'

'And one more thing, Ben.'

'Yes?'

'You got to win against that machine.'

There was a very long pause.

'This is all about the story. Your story. If the machine beats you, then there's no story. No story, no more publicity. No publicity, no Hoopie.'

'I see,' I said.

'I'm sorry to be blunt, Ben, your design is amazing. But I'm afraid that's not enough. You think it over. You have my number.'

'OK,' I said. 'I will.'

'But don't leave it too long,' he said and hung up.

In the diner, Mum had found another article about me in the newspaper and showed me over breakfast.

BRIT KNITS

Ben Fletcher, 17, claims to be able to knit faster than a machine, but is this possible? Ben famously knitted an entire sweater in an hour to win the final of the UK Knitting Championships. Now he's here in New York and is bullish about his chances of outknitting the latest machines, proving that hand-knitting is best and ushering in a new era of cottage industry crafting. We spoke to Dr Singh, a bio-mechanical expert from the University of New York. We first asked, what makes a fast knitter?

'What we see in studies of experienced knitters is a huge variety in speed,' Dr Singh says. 'Some people knit fast. Some people knit slow. Interestingly, there doesn't seem to be much difference between slow knitters and fast knitters in bio-mechanical terms. Technique yes, but this isn't like sprinting, or weight-lifting where people are limited by genetics or gender. Most people's fingers work pretty much the same. And given equivalent, good technique, in theory there's no reason one person should be faster at knitting than someone else.'

So how does he account for the difference in speeds witnessed. Why is Ben Fletcher so much faster than the average knitter?

Dr Singh taps his head. 'It's all up here,' he says.

'. . . It's a mental thing,' Mum read out.

'So mental,' Gex said.

'This is why I was so fast at the AUKKC final,' I said. 'Everything just clicked into place. In my head, I mean.'

'You were Zen,' Mum said.

'My yin and yang were balanced,' I said.

'Your arse and your elbow were in alignment,' Dad added.

'So that's the key,' Mum said. 'You need to have your head together. Then you can do it.'

I wanted to ask Mum about Diablo but I thought it might be awkward with Gex sitting there. And Gex looked to be in for the long haul. Once he realised Dad was paying, Gex ordered bacon, eggs and hash browns with extra toast. I didn't eat much for breakfast. This was for a number of reasons I will list in no particular order.

1) I was worried about Megan and Sean.
2) I was worried everyone would laugh when the KnitMaster 3000 opened a can of whoop-ass on me.
3) I was worried about Diablo and Mum's backstage pass.
4) I was worried about knitting the cerise hoopie for Fat Tony considering I didn't have any money to buy wool.
5) Dad is a revolting person to sit opposite while eating.

Since he got punched in the face by the busker, Dad has developed a habit of leaving a bit of food on his fork after withdrawing it from his mouth. I think it hurts him to really bite down on the fork with his top lip, so he's only lightly closing his lips as he pulls it out. That's disgusting enough, but then he insists on picking up more food with the same encrusted fork and offering it to me for a taste. 'I *would* like a taste,' I said after a pause. 'But do you mind if I use my own fork?'

'Yes I do,' he said. 'That's been in your mouth.'

'Well, *that* one's been in *your* mouth,' I pointed out. 'And if I have a taste, then it'll have been in my mouth too.'

Mum sighed.

'Well, let me scrape it off onto your plate, then,' Dad said, before dumping a noxious-looking lump of waffle onto my plate, glistening with his saliva.

Anyway, I didn't eat much.

After breakfast we took a walk. Mum hadn't been to Bloomingdale's yet and was very excited at the prospect.

'I used to keep up with fashions by glancing at the window displays on the high street as I walked past every day,' she said. 'But since Peacock's shut I feel I've lost touch with the latest styles.'

I wanted to go and have another look at the knitting department and was hopeful I could get Mum to buy some wool for me. We weren't in any particular hurry and took a wander through the park. The leaves were fresh and green. Full of promise for the summer to come.

'Heard any more from the Magic Circle?' I asked Mum.

'Yes, I'm to appear before a tribunal to explain myself,' she said worriedly. 'Until then, I'm not allowed to perform any magic.'

'What happens if you do?'

'I'll be cast out of the Circle,' she said.

'But what does that mean?

'Some venues won't hire anyone outside the Circle. It's a little like a union. I'd probably have to go back to doing kid's parties like in the old days.'

'Would that be so bad?'

'The money's not great,' she said. 'Your father would have to work more hours.'

Dad looked up at this, panicked. 'We are going to get this sorted out, Susan.'

We were passing some teenagers throwing a frisbee and a mis-throw sent the pink disc wheeling in our direction. Dad leapt like a stung horse and sprinted a dozen steps to catch it, inches from the ground. He then returned it to the clapping teenagers before jogging back to us.

'Ta-dah,' he said.

'What happened to the knee injury?' I asked.

'Ow,' he said, clutching it quickly.

I glared at him but wasn't able to quiz him further on the mysterious disappearance of his injury because Mum had spotted a group of men playing a game.

'Ooh,' she said. 'Three-card Monte.'

We watched for a while as tourists tried the game. It was quite simple, you had to pick which of three cards was the Queen of Hearts. The man running the game would show you the three cards then turn them face-down and switch them around quickly a few times to confuse you.

The first couple of times he did it the man playing won. Then the man bet more money and lost.

'I've seen this before,' I said. 'It's a scam. They let you win at first, then the guy hides the queen and switches it for another card.'

'Keep watching,' Mum said.

The first player walked off grumpily, and another took his place. This guy lost the first game. But put more money down.

'Sucker,' I said.

He lost the second game and I expected him to walk away, but instead I heard him say, 'One more try,' and he threw down another $10.

176

The guy dealing began switching the cards. I watched his hands carefully. He was quick. But I thought I could follow the queen. If he'd switched the queen with another card, then this would prove it. The man pointed to the card I was watching and the dealer flipped the card to reveal . . .

The Queen of Hearts. The man had won. The dealer shrugged and handed him a few notes. The man walked off quickly, clearly delighted to have got the better of the shyster. Still, something seemed wrong to me.

Mum strode forward to take his place.

'Mum,' I said. 'I don't think this is a good idea.'

'I'd like to play, please,' she said, brightly holding out a ten-dollar bill.

'OK, Kate Middleton,' the man said, taking the note and dropping it in a cigar box full of notes which rested on the edge of the table.

'Hardly,' Mum said, giggling.

I sighed.

The man showed the three cards and began his switcheroo. Over, under, over again, switch and slide. He moved his hands with the speed and grace of an experienced knitter. I thought I could see the pattern. The queen was on the right.

Mum pointed to the card on the right. The man flipped it. The queen.

'Double or nothing?' the dealer said. 'You can afford it, Duchess.' The guy must have been seventy-five years old. He wore a little waistcoat and a cloth cap and looked like he might have been an extra in *Ocean's Eleven*.

Mum pulled out a twenty-dollar bill and dropped it on the

table. The dealer snatched it and dropped it into the cigar box. Again the man showed the queen before beginning his elaborate routine. A small crowd had gathered around us.

Again, I watched his hands closely. Again it seemed to me I knew where the queen was. This time on the left.

Mum pointed to the left-hand card. The man grimaced and flipped the card. The queen.

'You're good at this game,' he said.

Mum held out her hand for her winnings.

'Give me one more chance to make my money back, huh?' the man said. 'Double or nothing again?'

Mum hesitated.

'Come on, Mum,' I said. 'Let's go.'

But Mum reached into her pocket and pulled out forty dollars. She reached across and placed it in the cigar box. More people had stopped to watch. There were now a couple of dozen. The man licked his lips nervously and began switching cards again. This time, his hands were quicker. He flicked here and there and the routine was different. But I thought I could follow it. The queen was in the middle.

Mum tapped the middle card firmly.

I was watching the guy's face. He grinned briefly and in that instant I knew Mum had been suckered.

'Sorry, Your Highness,' he said and flipped the card.

It was the Queen of Hearts.

The man stared at it like it was a death certificate with his name on.

Mum grinned. 'You're right,' she said, holding out her hand. 'I *am* good at this game.'

The man stood, staring at the card, then up at Mum. It was clear what he was thinking. How the hell had the queen ended up there?

'One hundred and twenty dollars, please,' Mum said, still holding out her hand.

The dealer man glanced over at someone in the crowd. I thought I recognised him as the man who'd 'won' earlier. The man shrugged.

'Come on, buddy,' someone else called. 'Pay the lady.'

The dealer frowned and opened up the cigar box. He counted out the notes and reluctantly passed them to Mum.

'Thanks,' she said before walking away. Dad and I trotted after her, I looked back to see the old dealer scratching his head in puzzlement. His accomplice was watching us go.

'That was amazing,' I said when we were safely away. 'How did you do that?'

She looked up at me as we walked. 'I could see where he was putting the queen when he wanted to switch,' she said. 'He was slipping it under the cigar box. When I gave him the forty dollars I took it out again. Then when I tapped the middle card I switched it with the queen. Simples.'

I gasped, shocked. 'You cheated!'

'No, he cheated,' she pointed out. 'I just evened things up.'

Dad's one of those people who's never quite got the hang of walking. At least not when there are other people walking nearby. You can't get past him easily in a corridor, it's all 'Scuse me, sorry. Haha. Shall we dance?' And when you're out on the street, walking next to him, he'll keep veering into you for no reason. He trips up every thirty feet, he walks too close to people in front of him and stops suddenly and turns around so people behind bump into him. He's not great at standing, either. In London, he always stands on the wrong side of the escalators. I mean, how can he not see that EVERYONE else stands on the right? There are signs all over the place saying stand on the right. Then when he gets to the top of the escalator he just stops there and looks around while people pile up behind him falling over. There's a sign at Waterloo underground that says *135 days since the last accident at this station.*

Needless to say, Dad last went to London 136 days ago. He's a menace.

New York is not designed for people like my father. While it's true the pavements are mostly pretty wide, there are a lot of people on them. I think New Yorkers are taught to walk properly from an early age; everyone's very good at nipping in and out of the stream of pedestrian traffic. There are bumps occasionally, of course, and people abuse each other in a good-natured manner but on the whole, the system works. At least it did until Dad arrived.

'Where are you going?' Mum says, grabbing him by the collar as he wandered into the path of a group of schoolchildren. Then he floated off in the other direction and collided with a businessman, spilling his coffee. 'Watch it, buddy!' the man spat.

'What's wrong with you?' Mum asked, shaking her head. 'Is it your knee?'

* * *

Eventually we arrived at Bloomingdale's and split up, agreeing to meet back near the 59th Street entrance in an hour. Dad went off to look at Lycra and Mum went off towards the lingerie section.

'Where are you going to go?' I asked Gex.

'I'll come with you,' he said.

'Really? I'm only looking at wool and needles and stuff.'

He shrugged. 'Ain't got any money anyway.'

So along he came. He sat on a low display while I fingered the wools, cooing appreciatively, and was remarkably patient when I spent a good twenty minutes picking up needles of various sizes and makes, trying to find the perfect Hoopie needle.

I looked up at him at one point to find him shaking his head sadly at me.

'Can we go now?' he said eventually.

'I've found them,' I said.

'Found what?'

'The needles I'll buy if I win the prize money at the DeathMatch.'

I showed him. Two 10.5-size faux-ivory Spry in their Ollivander's box. But these could create genuine magic. 'The weight, the balance, the feel of them. If I had these . . . well, I'd be smoother, I'd be quicker, I'd make fewer mistakes.'

'They make that much of a difference?' Gex asked.

'Oh yeah,' I replied, gazing down at the needles.

'How much are they?'

I showed him the price tag and he nearly exploded.

'You is paying fifty dollars for knitting needles?' Gex was looking utterly baffled as my phone rang.

It was Brandi, giddy with excitement.

'We've got Donovan, we've got Donovan!'

'Who's Donovan?'

'Who's Donovan? He's only the presenter of the third highest-rated afternoon TV talk show in New York state.'

'Wow,' I said, though it didn't exactly sound like *The X-Factor*. 'I'll send a car,' she said. 'Do you have any . . . suitable clothes?'

'None,' I answered confidently.

'OK, I'll come now,' she said.

'I'm not at the hotel,' I said. 'I'm in Bloomingdale's.'

'Perfect,' she said. 'Stay right there. I'm on my way.'

12.47pm

I've got to say, shopping for clothes is extremely tedious. I understand now why Dad locks himself in the toilet every time Mum suggests going in to town. As soon as Brandi arrived at Bloomingdale's, Gex made his excuses, and a few suggestive gestures behind Brandi's back as he left. I texted Mum and told her I'd see them back at the hotel later.

'Wow!' Brandi said as I came out of the changing room. 'Lose the tie.'

'But I'm going to be on telly,' I said.

'That's why you've got to look good,' Brandi said. 'Shame we don't have time for a haircut.'

She stepped over as I loosened the tie and began messing with my hair. She was standing very close and smelled amazing. She undid the top two buttons on my shirt.

'They'll fix your hair in make-up, anyway,' she said. 'Try these shoes.'

I put the shoes on and she stood back to appraise.

'How do I look?' I said.

'You look hot,' she said.

'Well, it is very warm in here.' I said.

'No, I mean . . . you look . . . great,' she said. But she wasn't even looking at the suit, she was looking into my eyes when she said it. She was behaving a bit oddly.

'OK.' Brandi held up the credit card. 'Anything else you need?'

'Well,' I said, eyeing the card, then glancing over towards the knitting section. 'There is one more thing . . .'

1.21pm

'It's a very bright colour,' Brandi said, inspecting the wool I'd just bought. We sat in the back of a yellow cab heading uptown.

'Tell me about it,' I said. 'It's cerise, and it gives me a headache.'

'So why did you buy it?'

'It's for a . . . client,' I said. 'Someone very important. That's the colour he wants.'

'See, Ben,' she said. 'New York's rubbing off on you. You're hustling.'

And just then, in the back of a cab, in a new suit, a beautiful blonde by my side, eight balls of the finest wool on my lap, I wondered if maybe she was right.

Unfortunately the headache got worse as we crawled downtown. The traffic was slow and Brandi looked nervous, which made me nervous. I rubbed my temples. I shouldn't have looked at the wool.

'You got a headache?' Brandi asked.

'It's the wool,' I said. 'I don't suppose we have time for lunch?'

''Fraid not,' she said. 'Hang on.'

She dived into her handbag and pulled out a pill bottle. 'Try these,' she said, handing them to me. 'I get them from Canada.' She passed me a bottle of water and I swallowed two of the pills.

'Just take one,' she said.

'One? I had two.'

'Really? They're kind of strong. Especially on an empty stomach.'

'You said take these. Not take *one* of these.'

'Oh, sorry. Well, I'm sure you'll be fine.'

'What are they?' I asked, even more nervous.

'Just paracetamol,' she said.

Brandi swept me through reception at the studios, telling everyone who tried to stop us that we were late. The headache had gone but I felt a little woozy. Canadian paracetamol is strong! We were directed to the green room, where we'd wait for my name to be called. The floor manager came up to me. She was pretty, with long black hair and wore a headphone/mic that I found quite fetching. I wobbled a bit and Brandi grabbed my elbow to steady me.

'Hi,' I said. I may have been grinning a lot. 'I'm English.'

'I know who you are,' she said shortly. She explained I would be on third. First up was a man with a hole in his stomach who apparently was able to feed bits of food in tied to a string then extract them hours later, half digested.

'Does he do that for a living?' I asked, nauseous.

'Kind of. He's an inspirational speaker,' the floor manager said. 'After him there's a guy who is going to marry a woman on death row.'

'Wow,' I said.

'Then it's you, and then finally we have the contortionist,' she finished.

I turned around to see a slim girl in an animal-print leotard sitting on the sofa reading a book. Both her legs were behind her head. I blinked a few times but the hallucination didn't disappear. What the hell kind of programme was this?

'That's if we don't overrun,' the stage manager said half to herself and checking her watch. 'We may have to bump the contortionist to tomorrow.'

'She won't mind,' I said. 'I understand she's quite flexible.'

The floor manager ignored my brilliant joke.

'Talk about a sense of humour bypass,' I said as she walked off.

'Well, I think you're funny, Ben,' Brandi said, laying a hand on my arm and giving me a flash of those amazing teeth. 'Honestly.'

'Thanks, Brandi.'

'Can I get you anything?' she asked.

'I am a bit thirsty,' I said, smacking my lips, which felt rubbery.

Brandi went off to get me a Coke. While she was gone, my alarm went off. Time to phone Ms Gunter. I needed to keep it straight. I was dimly aware I was being a bit more . . . talkative than I usually would be.

'Hi, Ben,' she said. 'Nice suit.'

'Thanks,' I said.

'How did it go last night? Gex keep you out of trouble?'

'You bet.' I grinned. For someone who hates lying I certainly do a lot of it. Maybe Megan's right about me. I'm pathological. But sometimes you just have to lie, don't you? For the greater good.

'Where are you?' she asked, peering into the camera.

'I'm in a TV studio,' I said. 'I'm going to be on the Donovan show.'

'Never heard of it,' she said.

'I think it's the equivalent of *The One Show*,' I said. 'But they told me twelve million people watch it. That can't be right, can it?'

'Everything's bigger in the States,' Ms Gunter said.

'It sure is,' I said.

'Are you OK?'

'What's wrong. Do I look ill?'

'No, in fact, you're looking very well,' Ms Gunter said.

Well? What did she mean by that? Was she calling me fat?

'It might be this BlackBerry camera,' I said. 'It's quite distorting.'

'Yes, that's probably it,' she said.

'Ben, Ben!' the floor manager called. 'You're on in five!'

'I gotta go,' I said.

'Look, Ben,' Ms Gunter said. 'Keep an eye on Gex, OK? And if he's getting into trouble, then stay right away from him. You can't afford to let him drag you down, got it?'

'Yeah, I got it,' I said impatiently, looking towards the floor manager, who was waving me on. If I didn't hurry they'd send the damn contortionist on ahead of me and I wasn't having that.

I could sense her watching me, her head twisted round like an owl's. Call me paranoid, but I did not trust that contortionist one bit.

'Ben!' Ms Gunter snapped. I looked back at her, trying to concentrate. 'I've taken a professional risk getting you into the US,' she said. 'Don't screw up.'

'I won't,' I assured her.

'Break a leg,' she said.

I turned the screen off and ran towards the stage, just as the contortionist had begun unfolding herself.

It was just as well I was so rushed because I hadn't had time to get nervous. Brandi gave me a squeeze on the arm as I went past and I was through a curtain and up onto a bright, hot stage. Jingly-jangly music played and a smallish studio audience clapped enthusiastically as I walked across the carpet, trying not to trip on the coiled cables.

Piper Donovan stood to greet me and crushed my hand with one of his meaty paws, bringing tears to my eyes.

'Ben Fletcher, welcome to America,' Donovan began.

'Thank you very much,' I said, bowing slightly.

'What do you think of New York?' Donovan asked.

I knew the answer to this one. 'New York is the greatest city on earth,' I said. The audience whooped and cheered. I had them on side immediately.

'So, you're a knitter, Ben?'

'That's right, Piper,' I replied. I knew what the next question would be. Something about it being unusual for a boy to knit, etc. etc. I had my answer all prepared.

187

'And you can knit faster than a machine?' he asked.

'That's right,' I said. 'Knitting used to be a male . . . sorry, what was your question?'

'It says on my card here that you can knit faster than a machine.'

I glanced across to see Brandi standing in the wings, next to the yawning floor manager. Brandi nodded and mouthed 'yes' at me. What should I say? The studio swam, the audience was silent and expectant, and I felt hot and cold at the same time.

'This is it,' Dermot O'Leary intoned. 'This is Ben's chance to put things right. The Piper Donovan show has twelve million viewers. He has to tell the truth.'

No, I thought. No, I can't knit faster than a machine.

'Yes,' I said. 'Yes, I can knit faster than a machine.'

'Really?' Donovan asked, grinning.

'You bet!' I said.

A lone woman whooped at the back, perhaps assuming that everyone else would be joining in.

'I thought I told you to wait in the car,' I shouted at the lone whooper. Everyone screamed with laughter. Suddenly I had the crowd right where I wanted them. I felt triumphant already!

'For Christ's sake, Ben,' Dermot muttered.

'And this is going to happen this Sunday at KnitFair USA? Is that right?' Donovan asked.

'You bet,' I said again, 'I'm going to be there. And the

188

machine's going to be there. And we're going to go head to head.'

'And you're going to win?'

'Oh yeah!' I said.

'But this is the KnitMaster 3000 you're up against,' Donovan said, reading from his card. 'This is the newest, fastest knitting machine on the planet.'

'You haven't seen me knit,' I said.

'Well, we do have some video footage,' Donovan said. 'Do you want to see Ben knit?' he called to the audience. They knew their role and screamed their approval. A large monitor flicked into life and I saw the YouTube video of me from the final of the AUKKC. There I was, my fingers a blur, the Hoopie taking shape, a goat wandering in the background.

'Wow,' Donovan said as the video ended and the crowd clapped obediently. 'You ARE fast.'

I winked. 'I'm the fastest,' I said. More cheers.

Donovan put his fingers to his ear and held up a hand for quiet. 'Now, we've got Dr Kovac from KnitCorp on the line. Dr Kovac.'

I looked up to see the man who'd been pictured in the *New York Times* article. He smiled and nodded quickly. 'Good evening, Mr Donovan,' he said.

'Now, Dr Kovac, your company, KnitCorp, manufactures the KnitMaster 3000, is that right?'

'That's correct, Mr Donovan,' Dr Kovac said with a small nod.

'Ben here tells us he can knit faster than your machine. Do you think that's possible?'

'Absolutely not,' Dr Kovac said. 'The KnitMaster 3000 can

knit a thousand rows per hour, without making any mistakes. A human, even a human as fast as young Ben here, could not hope to do more than forty or fifty.'

'Ben?'

'Well, we'll see about that,' I said insanely.

'Also, garments knitted by humans will have mistakes,' Dr Kovac went on. 'A sweater knitted by machine will be perfect, every time.'

I couldn't help myself. 'Well, Mr . . . Dr . . . Kevorkian, maybe people don't *want* perfection,' I said.. 'Maybe people like to find the occasional flaw in their sweater. Maybe people like having a hole in their sock.'

'If so, then this can be programmed into the pattern,' Dr Kovac droned. 'And my name is Kovac, not Kevorkian.'

'People don't want programming,' I said. 'People don't want mass-produced. People want character, originality, uniquen . . . *inity*!'

The crowd was on its collective feet by now whooping and cheering.

'Well said,' muttered the man with the hole in his stomach.

Dr Kovac was shaking his head, a smug smile on his face. 'I'm afraid retail sales figures don't agree with you there, Ben. People want to know what they're buying. They want their clothes well made, cheap and available quickly. Only machine-knitting can offer that reliability. Hand-knitting is a dying art.'

'Actually,' interjected the man who was marrying the death-row prisoner. 'Home crafting is on the rise. My fiancée makes and sells toilet roll covers on Etsy.'

The crowd clapped slightly less enthusiastically, perhaps

190

not sure if they should be applauding a criminal.

'She gives the money to an animal rescue charity,' he added. There was a roar.

'I look forward to meeting you on Sunday, Ben,' Dr Kovac said when the noise had died down. 'I admire your courage, but you cannot possibly win.'

'We'll see about that Dr Kev . . . Kovac,' I replied coolly. 'We'll see about that.'

The crowd went bananas and it took the floor manager ages to calm them down. I lapped it up, the glow of the Canadian paracetamol surging through my blood, the hackles on my neck raised. I was Katniss Everdeen being interviewed by that blue-haired bloke. Piper Donovan was on his feet applauding me. The man with the hole in his stomach stood, clutched his side with one hand and clapped me on the back with the other. Brandi was bouncing up and down in the wings, delirious with joy. All the while, a tiny voice of reason deep down within me was enquiring as to just what on earth I thought I was doing.

But the voice was easily ignored, and one thing was for sure.

There was no way that damned contortionist was getting on today.

'Turn it off,' I groaned. 'I can't bear it.'

We were sat in the hotel room watching a streamed recording of the Donovan show on Brandi's iPad. I was waving my hands around like a mentalist on screen, haranguing the poor Dr Kovac, playing to the audience. Gex howled with laughter.

'You had them eating out of your hand,' Brandi said

admiringly.

'I was talking absolute rubbish!' I said. 'And why didn't you tell me my trousers were tucked into my socks?'

'I thought that was British style.'

'Are those orthopaedic socks you're wearing?' Mum asked.

'It's a long story,' I sighed. 'No wonder the contortionist kept looking at me in the green room. I thought she was out to get me.'

I watched myself stand, basking in the audience's applause, face shiny, grinning like a maniac. I shook hands with everyone, acting like I'd just been nominated to run for president at the Democratic National Convention.

'Well done, Ben,' Mum said, giving me a hug.

'This calls for a celebration,' Brandi said, opening the fridge. She pulled a mini champagne out. 'Anyone?'

I eyed Gex suspiciously and he shook his head.

'I'm not sure I want champagne,' Mum said. 'I could murder a cup of tea though. I wish we had a kettle.'

'I wish we had Hobnobs,' I said.

'What are Hobnobs?' Brandi asked. ''Cause I know a British supermarket in Brooklyn. You can get all kinds of British food there.'

'Ooh, we could get proper tea,' Mum said.

'Cadbury's Creme Eggs,' Dad suggested.

'Chilli Pringles,' Gex added.

'No,' I said. 'We're here to experience life in New York. We eat Philly cheese, we go out for coffee, we have waffles and matzo balls an . . .

'Wonton soup,' Dad said.

'Er . . . exactly,' I replied.

'Maybe I could go and check it out for all of us,' Gex began.

'No,' I repeated. 'No one is going to the British supermarket.'

'All right, Ben, you've made your point,' said Mum.

'Well, we have to celebrate,' Brandi said. 'Let me take you all out for dinner.'

Mum and Dad looked at each other. 'We have tickets to *Stomp*,' Mum said apologetically.

'Well, thanks for inviting me,' I said. 'I love *Stomp*.'

'And Keith and I are going to a basketball game, innit,' Gex said.

'Does no one ever think to invite me to anything?' I protested.

'Well, I'm inviting you,' said Brandi with a sweet smile. 'Just you and me for dinner. What do you say?'

I had just enough time before dinner with Brandi to catch up with the *Knitwits!* girls. Brandi gave me the address of where to meet her later and then I took the subway uptown to Alanna and Marie's hotel, which is a lot nicer than ours. There is a homeless guy out the front but he hardly smells at all and offered me no advice when I gave him a quarter.

'So great to see you!' Alanna said.

'We heard you on the radio,' Marie said.

'You heard that?'

'Yeah, and we saw you on TV,' Alanna said.

'Oh.'

'Yeah,' Alanna said. 'Did you . . . really mean all that stuff.'

'Hmm, not all of it,' I said, I think I must have been blushing.

The girls were trying to hide their disapproval but it was clear they thought I'd been a bit of a numpty.

'Well, I was sort of hoping I could use the podcast interview to clear the air,' I said.

'I think that would be a great idea,' Marie said.

We ordered coffees in the lobby bar and found a quiet spot in the corner to record the interview.

'So, Ben Fletcher,' Alanna said. 'Here you are in the US of A. The Big Apple. How are you finding it?'

'I love it here, Alanna,' I said. 'It really is everything I'd expected and more.'

'And you've caused quite a stir since you arrived,' Marie said. 'You've been interviewed on the Piper Donovan Show, tell us about that.'

'Ah yes,' I said, pausing briefly. 'I . . . er . . .' I was suddenly tongue-tied.

'You made some comments we can all agree with,' Alanna said, coaxing me.

'Yes. I think I was right to suggest that hand-knitting had a bright future and that machine-knitting is not the only game in town,' I said. 'But I also said some things that should probably not, when all's said and done, be taken too seriously.

'Like what?' Alanna asked.

Here goes, I thought. Time to put an end to this.

'I'd like to clarify what I meant when I said I can knit faster than a machine,' I said. 'It was a reckless thing to say and any serious knitter knows it's practically impossible.'

'Hmm,' Alanna said, nodding at me in agreement. 'According to a press release from the Knitting Guild Association of

America you are going to go head-to-head in a speed-knitting contest with the KnitMaster 3000.'

'Yes, that's right,' I said. 'It's sponsored by Priapia.'

'Yes. I found that interesting, considering your views on home-crafting. Did you know Priapia are one of the major shareholders in KnitCorp?'

'Erm, no, I didn't know that,' I said.

'It just seems like you're saying one thing, and doing something else. Even if you beat the machine, the only thing you'll accomplish is to help promote the company that's doing more than any other to drive the mechanisation of the knitting industry.'

I was totally wrong-footed. She was completely right of course. But I couldn't pull out now.

'Well,' I said. 'It's just a bit of fun.'

Thankfully she let it go at that point and we moved onto other things, like animal cushion covers and the new book from ace male knitter Fabrice Gentile. I was hoping to see his lecture at KnitFair.

'Thanks, Ben,' Alanna said when we'd finished. 'It was so great to hear your views on the rise in hand-crafting. Sorry if I put you on the spot.'

'No, you're right,' I said. 'But is there a simple answer? The big clothing companies aren't evil. They give people jobs, they produce great clothes at prices everyone can afford. I just hope hand-knitting doesn't get completely squeezed out by these new super-machines.'

'Well, you didn't hear it from me,' Alanna said, 'but I heard the KnitMaster 3000 isn't all that. I heard it can't cope very well with untreated 4-ply . . .' She glanced around to make sure we weren't being overheard. 'The loose strands clog up the workings, apparently. It breaks down a LOT.'

'How do you know this?'

She tapped her nose. 'That's for me to know, Ben Fletcher. I never reveal my sources.'

'Well,' I said. 'I feel so relieved I've managed to correct the misunderstanding about me being able to beat a machine. How many people listen to this podcast?'

'Oh loads,' Marie chirped.

'I'll bet,' I said.

'Sometimes we have more than one hundred downloads,' she went on.

'Oh,' I said.

Twelve million people had watched me telling Piper Donovan I could knit faster than a machine.

I was in trouble.

When I got back to the hotel I found Keith and Gex awake and the TV blaring. Keith held Monique's bloodstained crochet, inspecting it carefully. He put it down hastily when he saw me.

'Crochet,' I said.

'I know,' he said.

'I haven't dabbled much,' I said. 'But I'm curious.'

'Uh-huh,' he said, not looking me in the eye.

'Are you . . . curious too?' I asked.

He snorted, but didn't say anything. I handed him the crochet and he took it slowly, still not looking at me.'

'It's OK,' I said. 'No judgement.'

'Girl!' Gex yelled from across the room.

'From me, at least,' I said.

'So what's so great about knitting, and crochet and stuff?' Keith asked. 'You're a fan, Tony's a fan. What's up with that?'

'It's relaxing,' I said, my stock answer. 'But it's more than that. It . . .' I stopped for a moment to collect my thoughts. What was I trying to say? 'When the pattern starts to take shape,' I went on, 'I can see I'm creating something. Something solid, something useful. Something that's real. That comes from inside me. Does that sound dumb?'

'Yes,' said Gex.

'No, I kinda get it,' Keith said, frowning at Gex. 'Maybe you could show me some time?'

'Any time,' I said.

After that I went to see my parents to ask for some money. Mum let me in. Oddly, she was wearing a dressing gown even though it was far too early for bedtime. As I walked in I noticed a Bloomingdale's bag on a chair and some frilly item of female underwear draped across the nightstand.

'Where's Dad?' I asked suspiciously.

'He's in the shower,' she said. 'We were just . . . having a nap.'

Dad came out of the shower. Spotting me he said. 'Good timing, eh, Susan?'

'I've been meaning to ask you about something, Dad?'

'It's not about bloody *Dr Who* again, is it?' he said, exasperated. 'I told you, I set it to record before we left.'

'Well, now you mention it,' I said. 'Your answers last time

we discussed this weren't entirely consistent.'

'Look, I found *Dr Who* on the TV guide screen,' he said. 'Then I hit the red record button. Done!'

'But *series* record. You have to press it twice for *series* record. Did you press it twice?'

'At least twice,' Dad said. 'Perhaps more.'

'You're only supposed to press it twice,' I said, groaning. 'If you press it again, it cancels all the recordings.'

'I'm sure it's fine,' he said.

'I'm sure it's not,' I grumped.

He's such an idiot.

'So this date with Brandi,' Mum said.

'It's not a date,' I said. 'It's a business dinner.'

'Is that a thing?' Mum asked. 'I've heard of a business lunch, but not a business dinner.'

'It's very common in New York,' I said airily.

'And she's paying?'

'Yes.'

'Good.'

'But I might need some money, just in case.'

'What, for condoms?' she asked.

'MUM!'

'OK, OK, sorry,' she said. She reached into her purse, took out thirty dollars and handed it over, eyeing me strangely. 'Have a good time. Be careful.'

'Thanks. Yeah, you too,' I said, trying not to look at the nightstand.

* * *

As I left their room the BlackBerry buzzed again. Damn you,

198

G! I thought. I opened the message. But it wasn't G. It was Melanee, the PR girl from the American Knitting Guild.

I saw you on the Donovan show. You were amazing! I'd love to meet with you soon to discuss some projects. We have some great ideas. Can we talk? Mx

I hesitated before calling. I hadn't discussed this with Brandi. She'd gone out of her way to warn me about Melanee and the American Knitting Guild. She'd been so nice to me and the KGAA had paid for my tickets and everything. Also, I was counting on Brandi to pick up the tabs for room service and the minibar. I needed her on side. She mustn't know about Melanee. But maybe she didn't need to find out.

Not without reservation, I called Melanee.

'Hi, Ben,' she said. 'Thank you so much for calling!'

'Er, no problem. You said something about projects?'

'Yes of course. I realise your time in New York is very precious but I wonder if you could spare a little time to talk with me? Face to face.'

'I suppose so,' I said. 'Now?'

'Not now,' she said. 'I have a date tonight. Tomorrow?'

'I'll be at KnitFair tomorrow,' I said. 'Could we meet up there?'

'Sure,' she said. 'Swing by our stand.

'Yes, OK,' I said. 'That sounds great.'

6.22pm

Before I got stuck into Fat Tony's Hoopie, I called Marcus for an update on the Megan situation. It could have gone better. As soon as Marcus realised who was skyping him, he looked around guiltily and leaned towards the camera.

'I'm not allowed to talk to you,' he whispered.

'Why not?' I asked. But then I heard another voice.

'Who's that?' Marcus moved aside and I saw Mrs Hooper peering at me. 'Marcus, go and wait in the sitting room,' she said curtly. Marcus scurried off.

Mrs Hooper sat and glared at me. She was magnificent when angry, but I didn't feel I should say.

'Hello, Mrs Hooper,' I tried.

'Why did you tell Marcus his gran was dying?'

'I didn't,' I protested.

'He says you did.'

'I may have let slip that she was in the hospital. I didn't know it was a secret. Sorry.'

'Why were you even talking to him?'

'He answered when I skyped on Tuesday. Megan wasn't there.'

'But you called him again?'

'Yes. Well. You see it's about Megan. I was worried about her.' There was no getting around it, so I told her my concerns about Sean.

'You were jealous of Sean, so you ask her little brother to spy on her and while you're at it tell him his gran is at death's door?'

'I don't think I used those words exactly . . .'

Mrs Hooper shook her head. 'I'm disappointed in you, Ben,' she said.

I hung my head, feeling lower than a depressive worm.

'Sorry,' I repeated. 'Is Megan cross with me?'

'I'm afraid she is,' Mrs Hooper said. 'We all are.'

'Is she there?'

'No, she's not.'

I waited for Mrs Hooper to go on to tell me where Megan was but she said nothing. My heart sank. She was out with Sean. I knew it!

'I've got to go, Ben,' Mrs Hooper said. 'I'll tell Megan you called. I'm not sure she'll want to speak to you just now, though.'

'Thanks, Mrs Hooper,' I said. 'Sorry.'

But she'd gone.

I've really screwed up this time. And it'll take more than a bit of super-fast knitting to put this right.

7.01pm

As I got ready for my dinner with Brandi (which involved stealing a fresh set of boxer shorts from Gex and liberally applying Gex's Lynx Africa to my armpits), I couldn't stop wondering and worrying whether Megan was at this very moment out with Sean. But without Marcus, how could I spy on her now? I needed another operative. Freddie was no good because he has the IQ of a goldfish, so I skyped Joz.

'Why is it dark in your house?' I asked as he answered. 'Is the electricity off again?'

'It's the middle of the night.'

'Oh, sorry,'

'Don't worry about it,' he said. 'As it happens, the electricity *is* off again. It's cold here. Mum and Dad don't know what to do, we can't afford to pay for an electrician and Southerly say there's nothing wrong.'

'Gosh that's terrible,' I said impatiently. I hadn't phoned to listen to Joz's sob story. I needed him to do my bidding by spying on my girlfriend.

'Look,' I said. 'I need a favour. I need you to keep an eye on Megan.'

'Why?'

'She's been seen with Sean.'

'Sean? I *hate* that guy.'

'Yeah, so could you please go around and see if he's at her house?'

'Sure, I'll go tomorrow.'

'No. Go now.'

'It's nearly midnight!'

'She only lives a couple of streets away from you!'

'I'll go in the morning.'

'But I think she's out with him tonight!' I protested. 'You need to catch her in the act.'

He shook his head. 'I'm not doing it.'

I thought quickly, what could I offer him?

'I know,' I said. 'What if I could solve your electrical problems?'

'You're going to fix the electricity from New York?'

'No, but I know someone who can help you.'

'Who?'

'You don't need to know the details,' I said. 'Just trust me. Will you go and check up on Megan?'

He sighed. 'Yes, I suppose so.'

'Thanks, Joz. Leave the electricity to me.'

'You'd better not be bullshitting me,' he said.

'Call me when you get back,' I said.

'He sighed. 'OK,' he said and hung up.

7.43pm

I was to meet Brandi outside the subway entrance at 29th Street and Lexington. I arrived ten minutes early and she was ten minutes late. I was wearing the suit. I'd hummed and hawed about possibly plumping for Gex's gold tracksuit with the red piping but in the end figured the suit was probably the better choice.

'Ben?'

I turned. Brandi looked amazing. She'd gone to town on the make-up and wore a tight-fitting spangly top and I would say that she was slightly overdressed if you can apply that term to someone who's wearing a skirt only four inches long.

'Hi, Brandi,' I said.

'Hi,' she said, going for the double-cheek kiss which I managed to get right for once. 'Nice suit.'

'Thanks,' I said. 'Nice . . . skirt.'

Why had I said skirt? I meant top. I was suddenly very sure that this wasn't a date but also that Brandi thought that I thought it was.

'Come on,' she said. 'The restaurant isn't far.'

'So,' I said as we walked down Lexington. 'That guy G is

still texting.'

'I'm so sorry about that,' Brandi said.

'It's OK, I'm just curious. I hope you don't mind me bringing it up?'

'No, it's fine,' she said, nodding.

'What does he do?' I asked.

'He's like, really rich. He runs his own company. He wrote some neat software for e-readers to display magazines better.'

'Oh, so to make them look glossy and bright on screen.'

'Yeah, because people like to flick through magazines, y'know, *casual* like? And he tried to make the e-reader experience feel the same.'

'Cool.'

'Yeah, and you know how in magazines you have to flick through most of the advertisements before you get to the articles?'

'I sure do,' I said. 'It's annoying! So his software makes it easier to find the articles?'

'Oh no,' she said. 'The software makes it so you have to flick through *all* of the ads before you can read the articles.'

'Isn't that quite irritating for the reader?'

'Not really, have you ever read the articles in a fashion magazine?'

'Fashion, no. Just knitting magazines, mostly.'

'Well, let's just say that the ads are usually a lot more interesting.'

'I'm confused now,' I said.

'Welcome to my world,' she said, laughing. 'I'm confused all the time.'

I looked sideways at her. I was getting used to her hair by now, and the spangly white top really suited her.

'But seriously,' she said. 'Would you mind not telling me if he texts again?'

'Of course, I'm sorry.'

'Just delete the messages please. It's just too painful to think about.'

'I will.'

'Thanks.'

'What sort of restaurant is it we're going to?' I asked, thinking it was time to change the subject.

'I chose it specially for you,' she said. 'It's British cuisine.'

'It's what?'

'British cuisine?'

'What's British cuisine?' I asked.

She looked at me, confused. 'Aren't you from Britain? I thought England was in Britain. Where is it? It's in France, isn't it? I'm such a dummy.'

'No, you're right. England is part of Britain,' I confirmed. 'I'm just not quite sure what British cuisine is. Roast beef, I suppose. Lancashire hotpot. Stilton? Terry's Chocolate Orange. Vimto?'

'They all sound delicious,' she said.

I suppose, on reflection, we do have a cuisine. I decided not to tell Brandi I was trying to avoid British food on principle while I was here. A bit of Stilton wouldn't hurt and maybe they would have Hobnobs. And Vimto.

The restaurant was a cool affair. Floor lighting, everything in shades of red, white and blue, with stylised Union Jack flags all over the place. Even though Brandi had booked, the thin maître d' kept us waiting for ten minutes or so while other people were seated before us.

'That's a bit rude,' I huffed. 'We can go somewhere else if you like. There's a diner next door. I think I saw a guy eating Philly cheesesteak in the window.'

'This is quite normal,' she said. 'You always *have* to wait.'

'Not at Dino's,' I said.

'At good restaurants you have to wait.'

'Even if you've booked?'

'Yeah, that's how you know it's a good restaurant.'

'So if they'd seated us straight away you'd have been unhappy?'

'Oh yeah,' she said, looking at her watch. 'Though having said that, if we don't order soon I'll miss my window.'

'Your window?'

'My two-minute eating window.'

'I really do not want to miss that,' I said.

I didn't think they would have Vimto, after all. It was too classy. Ribena, maybe.

While we waited, the BlackBerry buzzed. A Skype call from Joz.

'Do you mind?' I asked Brandi. She shook her head.

Joz had a strange look on his face.

'What?' I asked, my heart pumping furiously. 'Did you go to Megan's house?'

He nodded, swallowing.

'Did you see something?'

He nodded again and took a deep breath.

'What, what did you see?'

'I don't want to tell you. You'll be upset.'

A sick dread crept across me.

'Tell me,' I said. 'You have to tell me. Was it Sean?' Of course it was Sean.

But no. Joz shook his head.

'So what? Another boy?'

He shook his head again.

'What is it, Joz, for God's sake!'

'You said I had to check out her house, see what she was up to,' he said.

'Yes, so what was she up to?' I asked.

He shrugged. 'She was getting changed.'

I was silent for a moment, taking this in.

'You peered through her window?'

'I snuck into the garden,' he said. 'You know, they live in a bungalow. There was a chink in the curtains and there she was.'

I groaned.

'You said to check her out,' he protested. 'I mean, check up on her.'

'I didn't tell you to perve on her,' I cried.

'There was a chink!'

'What else did you do, hide in her cupboard? Set up a hidden camera?'

He rolled his eyes. 'It was *your* idea, Ben.'

'What did you see?' I snapped.

And there it was, the give-away smirk.

'You saw her naked, didn't you!' I gasped.

'Not entirely,' Joz said.

I could hardly breathe. It was unthinkable that Joz should have seen more of her than I had.

'How much?' I asked, not really wanting to know the answer, but knowing I couldn't bear it if he didn't tell me.

He shrugged.

'Knickers?'

He nodded. Good, at least she'd had her knickers on.

'Bra?'

He nodded again. Phew.

'The bra was on the bed,' he said.

I closed my eyes, feeling faint.

'I looked away instantly,' he said quickly. 'Almost instantly.'

'Joz,' I said. 'I'm in great pain.'

'I had to make sure she wasn't with anyone,' he pointed out.

'And was she?'

'No,' he said. 'There was definitely no one else in that room.' That was something at least.

'I've got to go,' I said.

'What about the electricity?' he asked.

'I'll think about it,' I said and ended the call before he had a chance to protest.

We finally got a table, near the kitchen. The tables were all made of glass. Frosted slightly, but not so you couldn't see through. I tried not to let my gaze slide downwards, because I sensed if I did I'd be able to see right up Brandi's skirt. Why do they make tables out of glass? Everything's on show. And they're so loud. I always find myself putting my fork down really carefully so as not to make a clanking noise. Perhaps because of all the clunks and clanks echoing around the restaurant, the waitress had an amazingly loud voice even though she was physically very small. I bet that was the first thing they asked about in the job interview. 'Can you talk LOUD? Because we've got these glass tables all over the place and it's like REALLY NOISY.'

'HERE ARE YOUR MENUS,' she said. 'I'LL GET YOU SOME WATER.'

America is a land of contrasts. People tend to be either incredibly tiny, or absolutely massive. Like French dogs. There's no middle ground. But, when it comes to speaking volume they all seem to be at the upper end of the scale.

I stared at my menu for a while.

'It's all in French,' I said, surprised.

That's why I picked this place,' she said. 'To make you feel at home.'

Baffled, I peered over the top of my menu at her for a while, but she seemed deadly serious.

'You know, Europe?' she said brightly.

'I see. Thing is, my French is a bit rusty of late,' I said, still baffled.

'Oh, would you like me to translate? *Agneau* is lamb.'

'OK,' I said, grinning. 'What's petits pois?'

'I think a type of jello.'

'Lamb with jello is a traditional English dish,' I said.

'Wow,' she replied. 'I'm not sure I'd like that. I want fish.'

'Me too,' I said. 'Let's just get *morue et frites à deux*.'

'*Morue?*'

'It's cod.'

'Sounds good,' she said, putting away her menu. 'So. I have a question.'

'Shoot.'

'So you got England, yeah, and that's in Britain, right?'

'Right.'

'So what's *Great* Britain?

'Britain is the island with England, Ireland and Scotland on it,' I said. 'Great Britain includes Northern Ireland.'

'And what's the UK?'

'That's Great Britain with all the other bits added in.'

'What other bits?'

'Er, the Falkland Islands. Gibraltar. Maybe some mouldy rocks in the Atlantic.'

'And what about New England?'

'Well . . . that belongs to you guys. That's part of the US.'

'Oh yeah, of course,' she said, grimacing. 'I'm such a ditz.'

'Not at all,' I lied. 'It's confusing. In fact, we used to own New England. Back when we had an empire.'

'You had an empire?'

'Biggest empire there ever was,' I said proudly. 'Lost it all now, of course.'

'I never knew.'

Brandi ordered some wine with our meal. I don't normally drink wine but I thought I'd better keep her company, so I had a few sips. Suddenly I felt a shove in the back as the man sitting behind me pushed his chair back. I spilt wine on the table.

I turned and cleared my throat but he ignored me, so I went all English on his ass and pulled my chair in a bit further to give him more room.

'Tell him to move his goddam chair forward,' Brandi said, noticing my discomfort.

'Oh no,' I whispered, shaking my head. 'I'm English, we don't like confrontation.'

'Hey, buddy!' Brandi yelled. The man turned.

'Do you mind? My friend can't breathe!'

'Sorry,' the man grunted and shifted his chair forward a few inches.

'No wonder you lost your empire,' she said.

She had a valid point.

'So,' she said after drinking half her glass. 'Are you excited about doing the event?'

I leaned back and put my glass down. 'I don't know, Brandi. I'm wondering if I made the right decision. You do know I can't possibly win?'

'You won't win with that attitude,' she said.

'I won't win anyway,' I said. I had to make her understand. 'It's impossible.'

'So why did you say you could?'

'Because that guy wound me up. I've been trying to explain ever since.'

She leaned across the table and took my hands, her fingers warm and soft. 'Ben. You have a special talent. I've seen you on YouTube. I've seen you in real life. You're amazing. And remember, Ben. You're in New York now. Anything is possible here.'

We stayed like that for an elongated moment, our hands entwined. I started to feel slightly uncomfortable but was saved by the ringing of the BlackBerry. I made an apologetic face, pulled the phone out and hit the receive button.

Megan's face blinked into view on the screen.

'Hello, Ben,' she said coldly.

'Hi, Megan,' I said, totally discombobulated. 'I er . . . er . . . I wasn't expecting you to call.'

'Why not?' she asked. 'When I want to find out what's going on in someone's life I tend to phone them directly. Or would you rather I'd phoned your sister instead?'

'Oh, you heard about that,' I held the phone up, facing it well way from Brandi. I did not want Megan to see who I was having dinner with. She might not understand.

'Yes, I heard about that,' she snapped. 'What the hell were you thinking?'

I was about to apologise, again, when I felt a sudden wave of irritation. Maybe it was the wine. Maybe the jet lag. Maybe I was going a bit New York.

'Well, what were you thinking of going out with Sean?' I snapped back. 'Twice?'

'What?! I wasn't going out with Sean!'

'Marcus said Sean came and picked you up on Monday, and again on Wednesday,' I pointed out. There, I thought, explain that, Megan Hooper.

She shook her head sadly. 'And did Marcus tell you what we were wearing?'

'I'm not sure I want to know,' I replied primly.

'Waitrose uniforms,' she said. 'Sean works at Waitrose too. He offered to walk me to work and back.'

'Oh,' I said.

'He thinks about others, you see?'

'And I don't?'

She sighed. 'I know you've had your mind on other things, Ben. Your knitting, this trip to New York. But I don't really feel you've been very . . . sympathetic lately. I've been really worried about Gran.'

'I'm sorry,' I said. Her entirely reasonable explanation had taken the wind out of my sails a bit. But I wasn't prepared to completely wave the white flag just yet. 'I was disappointed you weren't coming to New York with me.'

'Don't you think I wanted to?' she asked.

I shrugged.

'Of course I wanted to go to New York with you.'

'I didn't get that impression,' I said.

'Well, then *I'm* sorry.'

I smiled. 'I'll be home soon.'

'Good,' she said. 'I've missed you.'

'And I promise I'll think about your feelings more.'

'Thanks, Ben,' she said.

A huge wave of relief washed over me. It was going to be OK. We were OK.

'MORUE ET FRITES À DEUX,' the loud waitress said, clattering the plates down on the table.

'Ooh, cod and chips,' Megan said. 'Who are you there with?'

Panic!

'Oh, no one,' I said quickly. Brandi raised an eyebrow across from me.

'You're eating two cod and chips by yourself?'

'Oh, no. I mean. Mum's here. I'm eating with Mum.'

'Oh good. I was starting to get a little worried about your eating habits.'

213

'What do you mean?'

'Nothing It's just that you're starting to look a little. . . cuddly.'

'I am not cuddly.'

'Sorry, I shouldn't have mentioned it,' Megan was back to her usual, chirpy self. 'Put your mum on. I want to say hi.'

Double panic!

'She's gone to the loo,' I said. I was dimly aware of Brandi watching me intently. Maybe I wasn't so bad at lying after all.

'Oh, OK. Well, tell her I said hi.'

'Will do.'

'Actually. Since you're alone . . .' she said.

'Yes?' I said, looking up at Brandi, who was holding her knife and fork and peering anxiously at her watch. I had to end this call fast or else Brandi would miss her eating window.

'I wanted to talk to you about . . . how things have been.'

'Maybe we should talk when I get back?' I suggested.

'I just . . . well, I realise that I might have seemed a little non-commital,' she said, carrying on regardless. 'Not just about saying no to New York.'

I wanted to tell Brandi to go ahead and eat, but I couldn't do so without revealing her existence to Megan. I had to end the call.

'Look, Megan, I'll come and see you when I get back. We'll talk about this then, OK?'

'Oh, OK,' she said, blinking in surprise.

'Gotta go, speak soon,' I said.

'Bye, Ben,' she said, blowing me a kiss. 'Nice suit, by the way.'

'Thanks, bye,' I said, blowing one back.

I was on the home straight. Columbo was walking out of the door, all his questions answered satisfactorily. I was the escaped British officer about to get on the train in *The Great Escape*. The finishing line was in sight.

Then the bloke behind me shoved his chair back hard again, this time knocking me forward. The phone fell from my fingers and clattered across the table, coming to rest, face down, on the glass right in front of Brandi's plate.

I grabbed it quickly, hoping the drop had broken the connection. But no. Megan was still there, a curious look on her face.

'Whose knickers were those?' she asked.

'Mum's?' I said. I looked up at Brandi in a panic. She was trying not to laugh.

'I thought you said she was in the loo.'

'She's back.'

'Can I see her?'

'You want to see her?'

'Yes, Ben,' Megan said coldly. 'I want to see her.'

I flipped the phone around quickly, keeping it angled down. Maybe in the dim light, she wouldn't be able to tell the difference between a nineteen-year-old blonde PR assistant and a forty-six-year-old frizzy-haired magician.

'My, my, Ben,' Megan said. 'How your mother's breasts have grown.'

'I know,' I whispered. 'I think it's the menopause.'

'Who is she?'

The gig was up. The German officer had rumbled me. I'd tumbled in sight of the finish post and they were putting up a little tent around me.

'She's my PR agent,' I said, turning the phone. 'Megan, meet Brandi, Brandi, this is Megan.'

Brandi peered at the screen, sizing Megan up. 'Hi, Megan, I've heard lots about you.'

'Hi, Brandi,' Megan replied coldly. 'I've heard nothing about you.'

'I like your cardigan,' Brandi said.

'I like your knickers,' Megan replied.

'It's not what it looks like,' I said, turning the BlackBerry to face me again. 'This is a business dinner.'

'So why did you pretend you were with your mum?'

'Because I thought you might not understand,' I said. 'You were already cross.'

Megan said nothing, she just shook her head.

'I can't deal with this now, Ben,' she said. 'I can't listen to any more of your lies.'

'Don't be like that . . .' I began, but she cut me off.

'Enjoy your *business* dinner,' she said and the screen went black.

'She's nice,' Brandi said

'Yeah,' I agreed, sighing.

'What's *knickers*?' Brandi asked.

11.15pm
So. It's late. I'm back at the hotel. Brandi could see I wasn't in the best mood after the phone call to Megan so we grabbed a cab and she dropped me back.

Gex and Keith are still out. I have no idea where they

are but they've clearly been ordering food off room service because there was a tray outside the room with the remains of two meals. None of the vegetables had been eaten off one plate. Inside the room there are empty beer cans and crisp packets everywhere. I'd have to talk to Keith and make sure he paid for all of this. I'm certainly not, Gex doesn't have any money and I can't ask the Knitting Guild to cover the tab. I should have just come to New York on my own. I wouldn't be any lonelier and there'd be a lot less clutter. Though I wouldn't have the contents of Gex's suitcase to plunder either. I took another pair of clean boxers from Gex's case by way of revenge.

Friday 17ᵗʰ May

9.12am
I woke early and took advantage of the continuing absence of Gex and Keith to get on with Fat Tony's cerise Hoopie. I did about twenty minutes before the headache got too bad. After a brief internal struggle I got up and found the Bloomingdale's bag. Rummaging in the bottom I found what I was looking for. The blister pack of Canadian paracetamol. I took one and went and had a shower. By the time I'd finished the headache was pretty much gone and I felt mildly floaty. I sighed happily and got back to the knitting, only to be interrupted again by a phone call from Gex, who said he and Keith were having breakfast in Dino's and would I like to join them?

'I'm busy, Gex,' I said. 'I have to do this Hoopie. Then I'm off to KnitFair.'

'You have to come down and have breakfast wiv us,' Gex said.

'Why?'

'Cos both of us is skint, innit,' he informed me.

The BlackBerry went off just as Denise brought my waffles

Please call. I've left her for good. Like you asked. I don't know what to do now. I need to talk to you. G

Uh oh. Surely I should say something to Brandi about this? But she'd made it clear she didn't want to know about G's texts any more. What had she said? *It's just too painful to think about.* Even allowing for the tendency of New Yorkers to overstate things, it seemed clear she didn't want anything to do with the guy. Against my better judgement, I showed Gex and Keith the most recent text.

'The guy's in bits,' I said. 'I'm worried about him.'

'He shouldn't of messed her around then, innit? Gex said.

'What do you think I should do?' I asked. 'Should I tell Brandi?'

'Nah, man,' Gex said. 'I think you should hit reply, tell him where to go.'

I raised my eyebrows doubtfully but Keith nodded his head. 'Yeah, good plan.'

'Is it really a good plan?' I asked. They nodded enthusiastically, in synch.

I pressed reply and stared at the screen, thinking.

'What are you gonna say?' Keith asked.

'I don't know. I'll let him down gently, I suppose.'

'Ben's good with words,' Gex said. I glanced up at him, surprised by the unexpected compliment. 'He's a spod,' he went on, righting the universe.

I texted.

Please stop. We were great together, but it's over now. B.

Taking a deep breath, I pressed send.

'There,' I said. 'It's done.'

'Do you Brits not get the idea of a balanced diet?' Keith asked, nodding at my waffles. 'Waffles for breakfast, Philly cheesesteak for lunch and dinner.'

I shrugged. 'I like it.'

'I can see that,' Keith said, looking at my belly. I just happened to be slouching a little so maybe my shirt was pulled a bit tight.

'You saying I'm fat?' I asked.

Keith pulled a face. 'Listen. You eat nothing but waffles and Philly cheesesteak, you're gonna pile on the pounds. Law of nature.'

'Look here, Jamie Oliver,' I said. 'I'm not taking dietary advice from a citizen of the country that invented bacon milkshakes.'

The BlackBerry buzzed on the table. We all watched it for a moment. I glanced nervously at Gex before picking it up.

'It's him,' I said. 'G.'

'What's it say?'

'It says, "I can't believe you got in contact. I'm so happy. We WERE great together. When can I CU?"'

'What?' Gex asked. 'Did he not read the part about it being over?'

'I told you not to do it,' Keith said through a mouthful of egg.

'No you didn't,' I said. 'You both said I should do it.'

'Well, looks like you made the wrong call,' Keith replied.

I agreed. I was beginning to think I'd made a terrible mistake.

'What should I text back?' I asked.

'Nothing,' Keith said. 'You'll only make it worse.'

'Since when are you the Textmaster?' I asked him.

'You shouldn't screw with other people's relationships,' he said.

'They're not having a relationship,' I said, fuming at the fact that Keith had completely reversed his position. 'She's not even getting his texts. I am.'

'Ignore them,' Keith said.

'He won't be able to,' Gex said. 'This is Bellend Ben you're talking about. He always sticks his nose in.'

I stared at Judas, my mouth open. 'Firstly, no I don't,' I said. 'Secondly, you said texting back was a good idea. Both of you did.'

Gex took a mouthful of sausage to avoid having to respond. I texted back as Keith shook his head.

Don't text me any more. U will never C me again.

'There,' I said. 'That should do it.'

But the BlackBerry buzzed again, almost immediately.

I could come to your office? We could go to our bar?

'What the hell is wrong with this guy?' Gex said, leaning over to see. 'He's a nutjob.'

'Oh God. What have I done?' I said. 'What if he turns up at Brandi's office?'

'Do you know his name?' Keith asked. 'Maybe I could pay him a little visit, along with a couple of pals.'

'Thanks, Scarface, but that won't be necessary.'

'What are you going to do?'

'I think I'm going to take your advice and stop responding.'

'You wanna come downtown with us today?' Gex asked. 'We're going on a *Gangs of New York* walking tour.'

'You're paying to go on a walking tour?' I asked.

'Nah. We're just going to follow them around,' Keith said.

'I'm going to KnitFair today,' I said. 'But thanks.' I was touched to be asked.

'Do you have any tickets left for KnitFair?' Gex asked.

'You want to go to KnitFair?' I asked, surprised.

'Maybe,' he said, chewing on a piece of toast. 'It's free at least.'

'Not today, though?' I said. As nice as it would be to have some company, I wasn't sure I wanted Gex following me around making stupid jokes.

'Maybe tomorrow?' Gex said.

I shrugged and pulled out my wallet. I'd given my parents tickets for the Sunday but had a few comp tickets left. I handed one to him.

It's great that Gex is showing an interest. So why do I have such a bad feeling about this?

I stood for a moment, gazing out across the cavernous hall. Katniss couldn't have felt more excited the first time she saw the arena. I'd thought the Knit Fair at Olympia had been something special. I was wrong. At Olympia there had been rows of stands. Here there were streets. Olympia had a narrow mezzanine level for sales meetings and a café. Here there were three wide suspended boulevards with conference suites, lounge areas, bars and restaurants.

I was glad I'd come alone to this bit. No one else would have understood. I didn't have any meetings arranged for today. They were all tomorrow and Sunday morning, on the Priapia stand. Today was just a chance for me to look around and soak up the atmosphere.

I wandered the crowded streets for a while, listening to the conversations. Time flew and before I knew it I had to rush to get to lecture theatre 3 to listen to a Fabrice Gentile Master Class in which he revealed his new pattern for a Ruffled Dropped Stitch Neck Warmer. He is such an inspiration.

Later on I attended a workshop on Demystifying Set-in Sleeves. As I was leaving the lecture room, who should I bump into but Gex! Following close behind him was Keith.

'I thought you weren't coming until tomorrow,' I said.

'The *Gangs of New York* tour people chased us away,' Gex explained.

'We think they may have been genuine wiseguys,' Keith said quickly.

This didn't sound likely to me.

'Where did he get his ticket from?' I asked, pointing at Keith.

'He doesn't have one,' Gex said. 'He tailgated through the turnstiles.'

I gasped. 'You gatecrashed KnitFair?'

'Sure did,' Keith said proudly.

'Why?'

'I was interested in the crochet stuff.'

'Sure you were,' I said sarcastically.

'Ben,' Gex said. 'Why is it only you who can like craft? You're stereotyping us.'

'Whatever,' I said. 'So do you want to come to the buttons and ribbons lecture with me?'

'You're joking, innit,' Gex said, looking aghast.

'Fine, please yourself,' I said. 'Just stay out of trouble, OK?'

1.01pm

OH MY GOD, it is amazing here. Madison Square Garden is massive. This makes the London Knit Fair look like a Wednesday afternoon knitting circle at Liss community centre. There's an entire pavilion devoted to socks. I've also seen the crocheting monkey. I had to join a long queue and we all shuffled past as this tiny monkey put the finishing touches to an antimacassar. I'm no expert, but some of the flanges looked a little sloppy.

2.15pm – coffee break

Interesting.

I've just spent quite a while observing the KnitMaster stand. They were demonstrating the KnitMaster 2000 which is the model they have on sale at present. There were half a dozen white-coated boffins scurrying about adjusting machines and answering people's questions. They're not unveiling the KnitMaster 3000 until Sunday, when it goes head-to-head against yours truly. After ten minutes of watching the 2000 I was convinced there was no way I would have a chance. It was knitting a pair of trousers with an exquisitely tight weave. Quite impressive really, but all I could think of was the forthcoming humiliation of losing to this machine in a head-to-head DeathMatch. What had I been thinking, even considering the idea? Publicity was all well and good, but if you end up looking like a trash-talking lunatic then it's going to backfire, surely?

I suppose from Priapia's point of view they don't care. If the machine buries me then they get into the papers and the money they've invested in KnitMaster will bring them a good return. If a miracle happens and I win, then they'll have an option on my Hoopie design and will cash in on that.

I guess that's how you do business. Maybe I'm not cut out for that world.

I was just about to turn away when something odd happened. The 2000 suddenly stopped and let out an urgent buzzing noise. One of the technicians hopped over and started prodding and poking in the innards. Finally he bashed it on the top and it started working again, to a round of applause.

I swung by the Knitting Guild Association of America's stand after that to catch up with Brandi, who'd been quiet lately. She was in the middle of a meeting, so I hung around waiting until she'd finished, looking through brochures and catalogues.

'Hi, Ben,' she said. 'It's like Stressville, Idaho, here.'

'I was hoping you'd have time for a cup of tea,' I said.

224

'She shook her head. 'Sorry, today is my busiest day. I'll have more free time tomorrow, and Sunday of course.'

'Oh, OK.'

'Can I take a raincheck on that tea?'

'Sure thing.'

2.55pm

Have just sat down for a well-earned cup of tea on my own. There's an email I need to send. I had toyed with the idea of leaving Joz in the dark but my inherent good nature won out in the end.

Hi Mr McGavin,

I'm emailing because I need a favour and I thought maybe we could make a deal. I'll knit you a Hampton scarf if you could drop by my friend Joz's house and have a look at his electrics. The lights keep going out and Southerly Electricity say they can't find the problem.

What do you think?

Best wishes,
Ben Fletcher

That done, I sighed happily, able to relax for the first time in ages. I was looking through some of the catalogues I've picked up when I heard the most almighty crash somewhere in the hall, followed by screams. I hope Gex isn't involved. I'm on the mezzanine, so should be able to get a good view.

3.15pm

Gex *is* involved. A brightly coloured marquee has been brought down over on the far side. I can see Gex remonstrating with a group of security guards. What is he like? I'll have to go over and sort things out.

3.30pm

I made my way over to the collapsed marquee, which turned out to be the Andean Weavers' Collective stand. Mostly alpaca wools in reds and browns, now squashed. From somewhere in the wreckage, slightly muffled pan flutes could be heard, still playing. I could also hear a faint squeaking noise.

When Gex saw me he waved me over.

'I had nothing to do with it, innit,' he said. Keith stood to one side, trying to look innocent.

A security guard looked at me sternly, then he saw my VIP badge. 'You two know each other?'

I sighed. 'Yes I do.'

'Can you vouch for him?'

Hmm, let's see. I can vouch for the fact that trouble follows him wherever he goes. That it's always me who seems to land in hot water afterwards. I can vouch for the fact that he's self-obsessed, rude, unsupportive, misogynistic and likes to shoplift.

'Yep, I can *vouch* for him,' I said, with feeling.

The guard pointed his walkie-talkie aerial at Gex. 'I'll be

watching you, son.'

'OK, Dad,' Gex replied, unable to stop himself from inflaming the situation.

'Thanks,' Gex said when the guard had gone. The Andeans had managed to raise the canopy of the damaged tent now, the pan flutes seemed much healthier and the squeaking sound I'd heard was revealed to be a cage full of guinea pigs. Surely they don't shear guinea pigs in the Andes? How many guinea pigs does it take to knit a scarf?

I pulled Gex and Keith over to a quiet corner.

'What the hell were you doing?' I asked.

'It was Keith, he pushed me,' Gex said.

'That's it,' I said. 'I've had enough of you two.'

Gex and Keith looked at each other, like butter wouldn't melt.

'What have we done?' Gex asked.

'Well, let's see. In the last week, you've taken me to a MILF bar and got me into a brawl. You dragged me all the way to Jersey in the middle of the night, to extract you from a card game, you raided the minibar and replaced the Jameson's with urine and now you've nearly wiped out three generations of Andean guinea pigs.'

'Is that all?' Gex asked.

'That's enough to be going on with,' I snarled.

'Yeah?' Gex said. 'Well, well, *you* wore my boxer shorts.'

I took a sharp breath. He knew about that? 'Say what you like about me,' he said. 'But I ain't never done nothing like that.'

'You don't wear another guy's undergarments,' Keith confirmed, looking grave. 'That's crossing a boundary, man.'

'It's a bit gross, sure, but don't act like I snogged your girlfriend, or synched your iPod.'

'That would have been easier to take,' Gex said.

'I cleaned them,' I said, wondering how I'd got onto the back foot here. 'It's no big deal.'

'So why'd you hide it?' Gex asked.

'Hold up. Hold up! Don't try to make this about me,' I said. 'Just get out, go back to the hotel. Stay out of trouble for two more nights. Don't forget I'm on probation, OK?'

Gex shook his head. 'I'm getting out,' he said. 'But I ain't going back to the hotel. And screw your probation.'

He turned away, then back quickly, pulling his phone out of his pocket.

'And you know what else?' he said, thumbing buttons. 'There's gonna be a contact killing.'

'What?' I asked in alarm.

'A contact killing,' he said. 'I'm deleting you from my phone. There, you're gone, man,'

'Contact killing? I asked. 'Is that a thing?'

'Yeah, it's a thing.'

'OK, then, I'm going to kill *your* contact,' I said. 'With prejudice.'

I stabbed buttons furiously. He glowered at me one last time and stalked off. Keith following along behind.

What a couple of babies.

After that I swung by the AKG stand. With Brandi occupied on the other side of the hall, this was the time to strike. As I approached I saw an attractive Chinese girl standing talking

228

to a large man in a floral shirt. I waited for her to finish, then stepped up.

'Melanee?' I said.

'Hi, Ben,' she said. 'I recognise you from the TV.'

'Oh God,' I said. 'That was a car crash.'

'Not at all,' she said. 'You're even cuter in the flesh.'

These PR girls are so good at making people feel good about themselves, I thought. I had to remind myself she didn't mean anything by it. Melanee ushered me over to a little table on the stand.

'So can you do an event with us?' Melanee asked.

'What sort of thing did you have in mind?'

'What we'd really like,' she said, 'is a demonstration of knitting in the European style, from an expert.'

'Is this because you're trying to promote the European style in the US?' I asked.

She nodded. 'It really is a superior method, don't you agree?'

'I like it,' I said, shrugging. 'But it's not the American way. Things are different here.'

'We just want people to have the option,' Melanee said. 'We'd like you to demonstrate just how fast and smooth this style of knitting can be. Then they can decide for themselves.'

Well, put it like that and how could I possibly refuse? Also Melanee was hot. And Brandi would never find out.

'Why not,' I said, nodding.

'Great,' Melanee said. 'Tomorrow at 3pm, OK?'

'Sure,' I said, grinning.

I left the KnitFair with a huge bag of samples. Enough to knit a dozen scarves. I even found some in royal blue, the colours of Hampton FC. It did have a bit of glitter threaded into it, but I thought I might be able to pick that out.

There was no sign of Gex and Keith back at the hotel. Or my parents. I still had a little work to do on the Hoopie. I wasn't sure how I was going to get it to Tony. I couldn't ask Trey to take it, could I? Maybe Jasmine could arrange a courier for me. More money I didn't have.

I stopped outside Madison Square Garden to take a few photos of the building with the BlackBerry, which buzzed just as I'd finished. An email from Mr McGavin.

Hi Ben,

Thanks for your email. You've got a deal! I'll go around this afternoon and see if I can do anything to help.

Hampton lost again last weekend and we're looking at relegation if we can't win the last two. Problem is the final game is against the Milford scum. They're top of the table. Good news is Joe Boyle might be back for the last game. It would be great to have the scarf by then if possible? It might make all the difference.

Best wishes,
Gordon McGavin

Oh, come on, don't put that on me as well, I thought.

'Hello again,' someone said. I looked up to see Melanee standing on the steps before me. She really was very pretty.

'Hi,' I said. 'Are you finished for the day?'

'I escaped,' she said. 'Hey, a few of us are going to a bar on 32nd Street. Wanna come?'

'Well, I've got a jumper to finish,' I began.

'Oh, screw the jumper,' she said. 'Come and have a drink.

'Well, maybe a soft drink,' I said.

I could finish the Hoopie later tonight, or in the morning. It wasn't as if I had any other offers.

We walked half a block to the bar. Melanee's colleagues were already there with a few bottles of wine in front of them. Who knew knitters liked to drink so much? Melanee introduced me to Beth, Rod and Diego.

'Want some?' she asked, waving a wine bottle.

'No thanks,' I said. I could still feel the cerise headache poking its way through the haze of the painkiller and I didn't want to worsen it. 'I'll have a Coke. Diet Coke.'

She poured a glass for herself and waved for the waiter.

'Busy day?' I asked as we sat opposite one another.

'I'm pooped!' she said. 'I'm excited about your demonstration tomorrow!'

'Me too!'

'I think we should drink a toast,' she said as the waiter arrived. 'Are you sure you won't have a proper drink?'

'No. Oh, go on, maybe an Appletise.'

'A what?'

'Fizzy apple juice?'

231

She stared at me for a while then said, 'I'm going to pour you some wine, OK? We're OK here,' she said to the waiter, who rolled his eyes and walked off.

'I don't really like – oh,' I said when I saw she was already pouring. 'Big glasses here.'

'A couple of glasses of wine now and again are good for you,' she said. 'I get so stressed at work it helps me to relax.'

'Have you tried crochet?' I suggested. 'That's relaxing too.'

She flashed me a smile. And while her teeth are only an eight out of ten, compared to Brandi's ten, eight is still pretty spectacular and I have to admit I was utterly dazzled. Like a deer in headlights I froze.

It didn't take her long to finish her glass. I had a couple of sips out of politeness while I listened to her talk about her work. It was a nice place, full of good-looking young people sitting in pairs or groups, laughing and chatting. I chatted to Beth for a while and Melanee talked to Diego. Beth told me she owned a small yarn shop in Yonkers. She had hair so frizzy it made Mum's look like Penelope Cruz. I couldn't relax though. I kept thinking about the unfinished Hoopie. I did not want to disappoint Fat Tony and his goons.

'There's a great cocktail bar with a dance floor,' Melanee said to me after a while. 'Rod and Diego are going. Let's finish our wine and go with them.'

'But the Hoopie . . .'

'Forget the Hoopie. Come to the Highball with us.'

'It's just that Fat Tony said . . . sorry, did you just say the Highball?'

'Yeah. The Highball Lounge, midtown.'

'I suppose they must . . . do they make highballs?' I asked.

'The best highballs in New York,' she said.

'Well, maybe just one,' I said, swallowing nervously.

Sometime. Someday. Somewhere

I woke with a mouthful of sand. Or a tongue made of sandpaper. Or perhaps I was buried in sand with my mouth open. There was a sandy demon in my skull pressing hard on the back of my brain with something sharp. I opened one eye and a second demon jabbed a sharp spear of sunlight into the back of my eye socket.

I heard a groan. It took me a while before I realised it was coming from me. My open eye gradually focused. I saw white sheets and a bright thing that might have been a window.

I could hear traffic cheerfully honking in the street below. New York. I was in New York. I was at the hotel, rather than some gutter. Thank God for that at least. But what had happened last night? I lay, puzzling. Trying to remember.

It was no good. I'd need to raise my head and try opening my other eye. That's if I still had another eye. Had I definitely had two to start with? I couldn't be sure of anything. I suddenly remembered an urban myth I'd heard about a man who wakes in a hotel room, holding a mobile phone, with his stomach cut open and his liver missing. Maybe it wasn't an urban myth. Maybe body-part traffickers had taken my eye, my liver, my spleen! How would I get by without a spleen? I took a deep breath and pushed up with my arms. I managed to lift my head a few inches and opened my other eye. The relief I felt that the eye was still there was somewhat tempered by the fact that the demon was waiting for this and quickly jabbed another spear into that eye too.

I sat up and looked around, blearily. No Gex. I was pleased about that. After our row yesterday I was in no mood to talk to him just now. I peered under the covers. I was wearing Gex's boxers. Usually a thought to terrify, but today actually quite comforting. I was otherwise undressed. I saw my Bloomingdale's bag on a chair and heaved a sigh of relief. I still had Fat Tony's Hoopie. I lay and tried to remember. What had happened? How had I got back? Who had undressed me? Did I have any Canadian paracetamol?

Saturday 18th May

10.15am
I took some pills, called room service and ordered a cup of tea. Rock and roll. While I waited, holding my head, the phone rang. Melanee.

'Hey, Ben,' she said. 'I'm just phoning to see if you're OK. You seemed a little . . . tired last night.'

'You brought me back here?' I asked.

'Yeah.'

'How many highballs did I drink?' I asked.

'One,' she said.

'One!'

'And you didn't finish it,' she said.

I furrowed my brow, trying to remember. 'Why do I feel so bad?' I asked.

She laughed. 'You're not much of a drinker, are you?'

'So what . . .' I began.

'Yes?'

'What happened last night?'

'I got drunk,' she said. 'You had like a glass of wine, then a highball and then we danced for a while until you fell down and knocked over a table, so I took you back to your hotel to sleep it off.'

'Dancing?' I asked, hit with a vivid flash of memory. A crowded dance floor. Lithe figures. Thumping bass. Melanee and I dancing close together. My hands on her hips. Then it was gone.

'I didn't do anything . . . er?'

'Anything what?' she asked.

'Anything I shouldn't have done?'

'Well, it was pretty crazy in that bar.'

'But did I do something inappropriate?'

'No, not at all.'

Phew! 'Oh, that's a relief.'

'Apart from all the twerking,' she added.

'Twerking? I twerked?'

'You sure did,' she said. 'You really like Miley, huh?'

The tea arrived then and I said goodbye to Melanee, promising her I'd see her later at KnitFair. I tipped the waiter $2 which he didn't comment on. I poured myself a cup and sat back, closing my eyes.

Then my phone vibrated again. It was Mum calling.

'Oh, you're back,' she said. 'You were out late.'

'We went dancing.'

'Who's we?' she asked sharply.

'Um. Me and Melanee. She does the PR for the American Knitting Guild.'

'I thought her name was Brandi?' Mum said.

'No, Brandi's with the Knitting Guild Association of America,' I explained.

Mum was quiet for a moment. 'Ben,' she said, 'have you been taking some unscheduled flights?'

'What? No! Of course not!' I said. 'Unless you count twerking, that is.'

Poor Megan is at home nursing her dying grandmother,' Mum said tartly. 'And here you are, swanning around New York with a series of attractive PR girls.'

'It's not like that,' I said. 'It's entirely professional.'

'And aren't you supposed to be at KnitFair in half an hour?'

I checked my watch. She was right. I had an appointment with Mid-West Knitwear at 10.45.

'Oh God,' I said. 'You're right. I gotta go.'

'Be careful, Ben,' Mum said. As I hung up, Dermot O'Leary's voice-over popped up again.

'It's crunch time for Ben. Is he going off the rails? Partially drunk highballs and Canadian paracetamol are a dangerous cocktail. Will his self-destructive lifestyle be his undoing? Or will he be able to hold it together for the crucial series of meetings today? Join us after the break to find out.'

'Shut up, Dermot,' I muttered. What was I going to do? I

picked up my tea cup only to be interrupted again. This time it was Claudia Gunter. Oh God, I was in no fit state to talk to her. I rejected the call, I then noticed I had about fifteen missed calls. I'd had it on vibrate all night, but I suppose I mustn't have noticed with all the dancing.

As it happened, I got my act together well enough. I was showered, fed and down at the Priapia stand at KnitFair with ten minutes to spare. I felt a pang of anxiety as I saw Brandi standing there, chatting to Trey, but Melanee just squeezed my hand quickly and slipped away before Brandi saw us. The paracetamol had wiped my headache and I was starting to feel capable of anything, just like I had in the TV studio.

'Ben, there you are,' Brandi said. 'I called you, like, twelve times.'

I'd have to come clean with her, I knew. About the texts from G, about twerking with Melanee, and flirting with the American Knitting Guild. I can't live with all this guilt.

But not just yet. I was in no fit state. So I said nothing. Then Brandi had to go back to her stand and Mr D'Angelo told me where to sit and got me a glass of water. Someone at Priapia had made up some display cards with pencil and ink drawings of the Hoopie. They looked amazing. Whoever the designer was I could tell they really understood what I was trying to do.

The morning round of meetings went surprisingly well. Or at least that's the feeling I was left with. The display cards and the paracetamol had done the trick and I was either talkative and charming, or smug and full of rubbish depending on your viewpoint. I saw so many plump, middle-aged Americans they

237

all blended in with one another after a while, and they all said pretty much the same thing. That they loved the Hoopie design, and would definitely take a test quantity once I was set up to mass-produce the garment. I made sure I got a business card from everyone and wrote on the back what quantity they would take and what they would pay. It was all extremely promising, assuming I could get my hands on enough funding for a few machines. Or else get Mr D'Angelo to produce the garments for me.

The pills started to wear off after a while and I could feel the headache coming back. I struggled through until midday when Mr D'Angelo came over to see me. I showed him the cards. He nodded.

'That's great, Ben, but you need to increase those numbers,' he said. 'It costs a lot to set up production. We need to produce thousands to make the costs work, not hundreds.'

The BlackBerry buzzed almost as soon as he'd walked away. An unknown number. I blinked at the screen. My head pounding.

Where are you? We need to talk. Gx

I was puzzled for a moment. Something about the text seemed odd. Why was Gex texting from an unknown number? Then I remembered we'd murdered one another's contacts. After a moment's thought I texted back.

At the KnitFair. Stand 102.5

There was still something though about his text that was worrying me. Was it the full spelling? Usually he'd write *Wher RU?* Or even just *Wr U*. And *We need to talk?* Despite the argument we'd had, this sounded serious. As I headed back to the stand, I pulled out the BlackBerry for another look. What I saw made me stop in my tracks. A party of full-size knitters streamed around me, static electricity crackling gently in the air. I felt my hair stand on end as I read the text again.

Where are you? We need to talk. Gx

Gx! Not Gex! Oh my God! And I'd told him where I was. He thought I was Brandi. The horror dawned on me. G was coming! He'd run into Brandi. She'd find out I'd been texting him. He probably thought I/Brandi wanted to renew the relationship. When he got here and found out it was all a terrible misunderstanding, he might go mental. He might kill himself, or Brandi. Or worst of all, me!

Back at the stand I couldn't concentrate. My mind was whirring. I now had a list of things to worry about as long as my arm. I made a list on the back of a Hoopie pattern sheet.

- I was about to be owned by a knitting machine.
- I had a constant, low-level cerise headache.
- G was coming, with all the trouble that entailed.
- I was becoming dependant on Canadian paracetamol.
- My relationship with Megan was clearly over. And her mum was mad at me too. That was the last I'd see of her Tupperware.

239

I sidled over to the American Knitting Guild stand straight after lunch for the European Knitting demonstration. I'd lied again and told Brandi I was going to a symposium on Azkabani Finger-Stitching. My headache was gone, thanks to one of Brandi's magic pills. I didn't feel quite so light-headed as I did in the TV studio, but I wasn't quite myself either. I've decided to knit a Hampton scarf to keep things simple. I'm not sure whether it was the pills or what, but I was smoking. I did twelve rows in a quarter of an hour and with no mistakes. People were gathering to watch me. If I perform like that at the DeathMatch tomorrow then it will be pretty special. If I perform like this at the DeathMatch, then maybe I *can* beat that machine!

After the demonstration Melanee brought me a cup of coffee. I really wanted tea of course but didn't want to make a fuss.

'That was amazing,' Melanee said. 'Thanks so much for doing this, Ben.'

'No problem,' I replied. I was just pleased Brandi hadn't walked by and seen me. Maybe I could keep this under my beanie.

'Excuse me,' a man's voice said from behind me. 'I'm looking for Brandi DeLacourt.'

'Wrong stand,' Melanee said. 'You want the Knitting Guild Association of America.'

'Are you sure?' the man asked. 'I got a text from her telling me to meet her here.'

Uh-oh. The hairs on the back of my neck stood and I turned to look. It had to be him. G.

'I'm sure,' Melanee said. 'You need stand 101.2.'

The man sniffed and turned to leave.

'Sorry, Melanee,' I said. 'I have to go.'

If I was quick, I could make it to the KGAA stand before G got there. I knew a short cut, through the South Carolina Loom-makers' Association. I raced all the way, knocking over a rack of chunky yarns and a display of crochet hooks outside the Puerto Rican Crafting Society stand.

'*Ay caramba!*' someone shouted.

'Sorry,' I yelled back over my shoulder. 'Knitting emergency!'

'Hi, Ben, how was the symposium?' Brandi asked as I ran up to the KGAA stand, puffing.

'Inspirational,' I said. Why does lying come so easily to me?

As I looked around, checking for the approach of G, Brandi pulled something out of her handbag.

'Hobnobs!' I cried. 'Where did you get these?'

'I went to the English store.'

'You went all the way to Brooklyn for me?'

She nodded.

Suddenly the guilt was all too much to bear. The lies had to stop. 'Look, Brandi, there's something I have to tell you,' I said.

'OK,' she said, leaning towards me, her big eyes burning into my soul. She was just about to see what a loser I was.

'I've let you down,' I began. I went on to tell her what I'd done. How I'd texted G to try and let him down gently, to try and get rid of him. I watched her face turn from open trust through surprise, disbelief and finally anger.

Brandi wasn't just angry though. She was furious. I'd never

seen her even remotely cross before. And she put a proper face on, let me tell you.

'I can't believe you texted my ex-boyfriend!' she said.

'He started it,' I protested. 'And you didn't want to know about it. I was just trying to let him down easy.'

'Maybe I don't want to let him down easy,' she said.

'You want to make him suffer?' I said. 'That's doesn't seem like you.'

'Maybe I don't want to let him down at ALL,' she said, before turning and stomping off, her hair bouncing furiously. I watched her go, wondering if I should run after her and apologise properly. I was a little shocked by her last comment to be honest. She still had feelings for this guy? How could I have known that? I will never understand women.

Then I realised she'd stopped and turned, a dozen feet away, her face flushed.

'And for your information, Ben Fletcher,' she shouted. 'It was Bobby *McFerrin* who sang "Don't Worry be Happy", not Bobby *Fisher*.'

I stared at her in astonishment.

'So, you're not so smart,' she fired before turning again and disappearing into the crowds of people, some of whom had stopped to watch the show.

'Bobby Fisher?' a passing man said, looking at me and shaking his head. 'He played *chess*, you dummy.'

3.21pm
Gex has really done it this time. After my confession I went off to the café to drown my sorrows with a disgusting cup of

242

tea. My difficult day wasn't over yet, though. I got a phone call from Keith, who informed me that Gex was in trouble. 'What sort of trouble,' I asked?

Now. What's the one thing I told him not to do? What's the one, specific thing I warned him against?

That's right. It turns out Gex had been shoplifting from Bloomingdale's. From *Bloomingdale's*!

'He was seen by a security guard shoving something into his pants,' the panicked Keith said.

'Has he been arrested?'

'No, he ran and hid. He's holed up in the ladies' fitting rooms.'

'What? What's he doing there?'

'The store is crawling with security guards on the lookout for him,' Keith said. 'He figured that's the only place they wouldn't search.'

It had a certain logic.

'But how's he going to escape?' I had this sudden vision of Gex staying there forever. Living in the ladies' changing rooms at Bloomingdale's. Only coming out at night when the shop had closed, to steal Mars bars from the vending machines. He'd probably be all right, knowing Gex.

'He needs you to go rescue him,' Keith said.

'Why can't *you* rescue him?' I protested.

'They saw me too, man,' Keith said. 'I can't go back. My mom will kill me if I get arrested.'

'Pathetic. Some gangster you are,' I said.

'So are you going to help him?'

'I'll think about it,' I said, and hung up.

It was time to call Ms Gunter in any case, so I skyped her

straight away and told her what had happened.

'You have to drop him, Ben,' she said. 'You can't get caught up in this.'

'But he'll be arrested. We're supposed to be flying home in thirty-six hours. What if they take his passport?'

'That's his problem,' Ms Gunter said. 'I know he's your friend, but he's let you down here. You are not being disloyal, you are being smart.'

'But he needs help,' I pointed out.

'Ben,' she said, her face looming large on the BlackBerry screen. 'It's not just your future at stake. You know what a risk I took in arranging for you to leave the country.'

'I know, I know,' I said.

'And if you are arrested, they might take your passport too. As you are already on probation they might decide to detain you and put you on trial in the States.'

That didn't bear thinking about.

'OK,' I said. 'I understand.'

'Thanks, Ben,' Ms Gunter said. 'I know you'll do the right thing.'

I had no stomach to stay longer at the KnitFair after that. I didn't have any more appointments. Mr D'Angelo had said I could hang around, trying to sell to random people walking by, but my heart wasn't in it. Also, there were the finishing touches to make to the cerise Hoopie for Fat Tony. I could afford to be late with that. I wandered down to the subway and checked the board. The A train would take me back to 38th Street. The B train would take me to 59th and Lexington. To Bloomingdale's.

A familiar tinkle of laughter got my attention and I turned my head to see Brandi standing on the platform, face to face with G. As I watched, open-mouthed, he leaned forward and kissed her. I made to step forward, to pull the cad away, before I realised that Brandi was kissing him back. A train pulled up and they hopped on, giggling.

I really do not understand women. They're full of contradictions, the whole world over.

I shook my head and went to stand on the platform for the A train, remembering all the good times with Gex. It didn't take long. There was the time he'd stood up for me against Lloyd Manning. The time he took the rap for me when I accidentally broke the window of the sponsored toilets. Then there was New Year's Eve just gone, when Gex and I and Freddie and Joz had danced and drank and laughed and laughed.

Up against that were all the times he'd let me down. When he'd insulted me, or borrowed money and not paid it back. When he'd not turned up after we'd arranged to meet. Or even worse, turned up unexpected. The time he'd lit up a cigarette in my room, the time he'd hidden a case of lager in our garage without telling me, getting me in trouble. And of course the infamous Martini Rosso incident.

An A train arrived. I stood and watched the doors open.

I stood and watched the doors close.

Behind me I heard the rattle of the B train. The screech of brakes as it stopped. The hiss of the doors as they opened.

Heaving a large sigh, I turned.

I took the B train.

* * *

245

Like the bellend I am, I'd forgotten to ask Keith to let me have Gex's number. I'd deleted it from my phone. And now Keith wasn't answering, he was probably on the subway to Jersey, running like a little girl. I'm like the cleaner in *Pulp Fiction*. Called in to sort everything out when the regular gangsters have screwed up.

So when I arrived at Bloomingdale's I wasn't really sure where to go. According to the store map there were ladies' fitting rooms on three floors. I could hardly stand outside each one yelling, 'Gex!' I'd definitely attract attention. I thought furiously. I had to use my knowledge of Gex's character to work out which one he was in. The ground-floor changing rooms were near the accessories. The top-floor fitting rooms were near the maternity wear. The fitting rooms on the first floor however were right slap bang in the middle of the lingerie section. Of course.

I made my way there and approached nervously. The coast seemed clear, so I tried a whispered, 'Gex!'

No answer.

I tried again.

'Gex!'

'Ben?'

'Yeah, it's me.'

'You came?' he sounded really surprised.

'Stay there,' I hissed. 'I have a plan.'

A large lady pushed past me at that point; she was carrying some underwear that didn't look like it was going to fit. Her husband stood to one side holding a hundred shopping bags. He smiled and gave me a 'what are they like?' look. I smiled back weakly.

246

'I'm going to go and choose something for you . . . honey,'
I called out.

'Eh?' Gex called back.

'Ahem!' I said, hoping he'd get the message. 'I'm going to
go and choose you some ladies' clothes. Because you said you
wanted to look more *feminine.*'

A pause.

'*Oh, yes, that's right,*' Gex replied in a falsetto.

The waiting man rolled his eyes at me conspiratorially.

I hurried over to the knitwear section knowing exactly what
I needed. There. The cowled dress I'd seen on Monday. Now
what size? Gex was thin, but tall and quite broad across the
shoulder. It would have to be XXX large. Thank God for the
larger American lady, I thought, grabbing the biggest one they
had, taking a second to appreciate the sublime quality of the
lambswool.

I brought it back to the fitting rooms. The waiting man
nodded appreciatively. He knew fashion. I threw it over the
top of Gex's cubicle and waited a couple of seconds.

'*I ain't wearing this,*' he sang.

'Just try it, darling,' I said.

Muffled grunts, thumps and curses emerged from within
the cubicle. Then silence. Presumably as Gex admired himself.

'You can come out now,' I said. 'Let me have a look.'

'*I don't want to,*' Gex replied, falsetto. The waiting man
nodded understandingly at me. I shrugged.

'I'm sure you'll look beautiful, darling,' I said.

Gex slowly pulled back the curtain. With the cowl-hood up
his face was only partly visible, even so I sensed the waiting

man leap back in alarm.

'*How do I look?*' Gex asked.

I paused. His chicken legs were hideously visible where the dress ended at mid-calf length. Part of me really wanted to take a picture there and then. This was gold dust.

But the honourable friend in me, plus the fact that time was running out, won out for the moment.

'Divine,' I replied. 'Come on.' I grabbed him by the arm and led him towards the cash desk. The waiting man gave me a pitying look as I passed.

Unfortunately, with Gex having pulled the cowl so far forward, he couldn't now see where he was going and kept bumping into things.

'Ouch,' he said as he bruised his shins on a rack of suspenders. 'I mean, *ouch*.'

I was worried this would attract even more attention, so I asked him to pull his cowl back just a little. Unfortunately, as I did, a security guard appeared from nowhere and walked straight towards us. Before I knew what was happening, Gex had grabbed me in a great bear hug, his cheek pressed against mine. I froze in horror.

'What are you doing?' I hissed.

'Gotta make it look convincing,' he said.

'That's convincing enough,' I warned as I felt him shift his cheek slightly, practically taking a layer of skin off with his stubble. Surely he wouldn't try and kiss me?

Mercifully that wasn't necessary though. The guard moved along, his eyes darting back and forth as he searched for a blond teenager in a black tracksuit. We made it to the cash

248

desk, shuddering over what we'd just had to do.

To her credit, the shop assistant didn't bat an eyelid when she saw Gex. This is New York, after all. Six-foot, teenage trannies must be ten-a-penny here.

'Do you want that in a bag?' she asked as Gex held out his wrist so she could scan the bar code.

'No, she'll wear it home,' I said.

'OK,' the girl said, smiling.

'But could I have a bag anyway?' I asked.

'Sure,' she said, handing me a brand-new Bloomingdale's bag. My old one was getting a bit battered. At least I'd leave with something for the £95 I'd just stumped up for something I could have knitted in my sleep. I was now overdrawn. I'd never been overdrawn before. The thought made my skin crawl.

We made our way hurriedly to the nearest exit, walking straight past two guards, who didn't look twice at me or Gex. As soon as we were out on the street Gex started to take off the dress.

'No, honey,' I said. 'Keep it on till we get back to the hotel.'

'You're kidding!' Gex said.

'And talk like a lady,' I reminded him.

'*We is clear now*,' Gex said.

'You can't be too careful,' I told him. Well, after what he'd put me through, I wasn't going to let him have an easy ride. 'We'd better walk, the cops might be staking out the subway.'

Of course they weren't, but in Gex's paranoid condition he accepted anything I said. So I made him walk five blocks in a lady's hooded cowl. Just as we reached the hotel I held back. Gex turned to see what I was up to and, timing it just right, I held up the BlackBerry and took a happy snap.

'You . . . *bellend*,' he said.

'Thanks for getting me out,' Gex said when we were safely back in the room.

'What were you thinking?' I asked him. I was full of adrenalin and building up a big head of steam, ready to let rip. I was not going to let him get away with it this time.

'I wanted to get these for you,' he replied. He reached into his tracksuit bottoms, pulled out a long cardboard box and handed it to me.

I opened the box, though I knew what was inside. The Spry needles I'd been slobbering over that time he'd come with me to the store. He'd noticed. He'd remembered. I stroked one with my forefinger. It was soft and silky smooth. I lifted it out and spun it carefully. The balance was perfect. I could knit like a dream with these. I felt that with these needles, maybe I could beat that damn machine.

'They're the right ones, yeah?' he said.

I nodded. 'Yeah. These are the right ones.'

He waited, clearly expecting me to say thank you.

And maybe he was right to. He'd done this for me. He'd taken a big risk for me. Because he was sorry about the row we'd had and he didn't know how to say it in words.

I felt a bit emotional.

'Thanks,' I said. I looked up at him. 'But no more stealing, OK?'

'Never again,' Gex said, with feeling.

The fun wasn't over just yet though. We were startled by a phone call. It was Jasmine on reception telling me Keith was downstairs. I asked her to send him up, intending to have a few words. Gex got changed and a couple of minutes later there was a knock at the door. Assuming it was Keith, I just went ahead and opened it. A big man swept into the room, I had to walk backwards double-quick to keep from being steamrollered. Behind him came another man. One I recognised, the man with the bulge from Fat Tony's restaurant. I swallowed nervously as the two men quickly checked the room.

They ignored me and Gex. Then Keith walked in, looking scared. Finally, into the room, closing the door behind him, walked Fat Tony himself. Suddenly I was in that scene in *Pulp Fiction* where Samuel Jackson and John Travolta bust into a hotel room and taunt the boys before shooting them.

'Hi, Ben,' Tony said brightly.

'H-hello, Tony,' I said. Keith sat down on the sofa, looking green.

'Would you like a drink?' I asked.

'Sure, you got any Scotch?' he asked, moving towards the minibar.

'No,' I cried, leaping in front of the little fridge. 'Just soft drinks.'

'Oh, nothing for me, then,' he said.

Phew.

'I have your sweater,' I said, pulling it carefully out of the Bloomingdale's bag. 'I was just going to neaten up some of the edges . . .'

He took it and held it up admiringly. 'Don't worry about

251

that, Ben,' he said. 'It's beautiful. Perfect. Thank you.'

'No problem.'

'Great colour. My girl will love it.'

'I hope so,' I said, squinting.

'Problem is, my wife might see my mistress wearing it. And then she'll want one too.' With that, he laughed. Mr Bulge and the other guy laughed along with him and after a brief hesitation I joined in.

'I'd be happy to knit another,' I said quickly. I was buying time. Perhaps he'd agree not to kill me as long as I kept working for him. Like the princess in *Rumpelstiltskin*, except knitting thread into Hoopies rather than spinning straw into gold.

'Sure,' Fat Tony said. 'I know where to find you.'

I swallowed.

'His mom gave me a call,' Tony said.

'Whose mom?' I asked, confused.

'His,' Tony said, nodding towards Keith. 'My sister.'

It took me a moment to work out what he was saying.

'Keith is your nephew?'

'Yeah, didn't he tell you?'

'No, he didn't,' I said, looking over at Keith. 'I thought he was a member of . . . I thought he was in . . .'

Tony waited. 'You thought he was in . . . ?'

'I thought he was an associate of yours,' I said. 'In your . . . business.'

Tony watched me for a moment, then he let rip with a huge belly laugh. Bulge man and the other guy laughed right along. Suddenly the tension was broken and I started laughing too. Gex joined in, half-heartedly. Only Keith remained poker-faced.

'Don't get me wrong,' Tony said eventually, wiping his eyes. 'I love the guy. He's my sister's kid. But I wouldn't employ him in my . . . business.'

'I see,' I said. I'd been right to suspect. Keith was no gangster. Gex looked shell-shocked. His world had come crashing down.

'I might employ you, though,' he said, fixing me with an intense look.

'Me?'

'I got a good instinct about people,' he said. 'The night I met you. I knew you were a guy I could trust.'

It was the aftershave, I wanted to say. *Not me.*

'You came all the way out to Jersey when your guys needed you,' Tony said. 'You put your hand in your pocket. And you can knit. Boy, you can knit.'

'Just to be clear,' I said slowly. 'Are you offering me a job?'

'Sure, why not?'

'But I'm from England. I have to go back on Sunday.'

'You don't have to go back,' he said. 'Stay here. Work for me.'

'I don't have a visa.'

'Visas can be arranged,' he said. 'Why don't you come out to Jersey tomorrow, meet some friends of mine.'

I shook my head and explained about the DeathMatch.

'KnitFair, huh?' he said. 'I'd like to see that. I don't suppose you know where I could get a ticket, do you?'

'As a matter of fact I do,' I said, pulling out my wallet. I handed him the extra tickets I had.

'Well, now I owe *you* a favour,' Tony said. 'You're a good guy.'

'It's nothing,' I said.

Tony stood.

'Anyway, I gotta get this kid back home. His mom's been up all night. She's waiting to skin him alive.'

Keith swallowed.

'Bye, Tony,' I said as he headed for the door, his two henchmen preceding. 'Thanks for stopping by.'

6.48pm

Mum and Dad just called to see if we wanted to join them for dinner. As neither Gex or I has any money we agreed and arranged to meet them in the lobby bar. Gex, though, had one of his IBS 'episodes' in the bathroom so I yelled that I'd meet him downstairs and to use the air freshener once he'd finished. As I walked into the bar I heard Dad speaking.

'It's certainly very stiff when I wake up first thing in the morning.'

'For Christ's sake,' I said, sitting down. 'Don't you two ever talk about anything else?'

'What? I'm talking about my knee,' Dad said.

'Oh. OK. But you can see why I might have jumped to the wrong conclusion,' I said. 'The way you two have been mooning about like lovesick teenagers.'

'Look, we're just making up for lost time,' Dad said. 'I told you, we didn't have much of a honeymoon.'

'Yes,' I said. 'Which reminds me. Who's this person you were talking about that ruined your first honeymoon?'

'It doesn't matter,' Mum said, giving Dad a furious look.

I wasn't going to let it lie though. I had to know.

'Is this to do with Diablo?' I persisted. 'Mum, did you have an affair with Diablo?'

They both looked at me, wide-eyed. Then they both laughed out loud.

'No!' Mum cried. 'Of course not.'

'So who was this other person?' I asked, feeling myself blushing.

'It was you, you idiot,' Dad said.

'Eh?'

'I was pregnant with you,' Mum said. 'I was three months gone and still vomiting buckets.'

'I thought she was going to sick you up,' Dad said.

I was outraged. 'I was conceived . . . out of wedlock?'

'Let's just say we'd taken one or two long-haul flights by then,' Mum said.

'We'd built up a few air miles,' Dad added.

'Oh, stop it,' I said as Gex arrived. I have never been more pleased to see him.

They offered to buy us a drink in the hotel bar when we got back from the restaurant, but I really didn't feel like it. I was worried about the DeathMatch tomorrow and I still had a bit of a headache. I left my parents with Gex, playing Semi-Rude Scrabble in a banquette.

As I got back to the room the BlackBerry buzzed. It was Brandi.

Just wanted to say sorry I yelled at you before. And thanks for everything you did to bring me and Gavin back together. See you tomorrow! Bx

Gavin? G is Gavin? I wasn't expecting that. Well, that was something resolved, I suppose. I had a long bath and tossed and turned in bed before dropping off. I must have slept deeply because Gex didn't wake me when he came in, for once.

Sunday 19th May

9.56am
I felt OK when I got to the KnitFair. My headache was gone for a start and I was glad of the early night. Whatever else had been going on, the meetings had gone well yesterday and if I got a few more today, I might get up into the thousands that Mr D'Angelo wanted. I was positive, I was hopeful, I was New York.

All that soon came crashing to a halt when I saw Mr D'Angelo.

He was wearing a cerise suit.

'Morning, Ben,' he said brightly.

'Morning, Mr D'Angelo,' I said. 'That's an interesting suit.'

'I know! Great colour, huh?'

'Very . . . vibrant,' I replied, the first stab of pain jabbing me in the temple.

'So, you gonna get those orders today?' he asked.

'I hope so,' I said but that clearly wasn't the answer he wanted. 'I sure am!' I said.

'That's my boy,' he said, then walked off.

So I had to spend the morning trying not to look at him. The meetings went OK, though I was distracted by the headache building gradually, and the growing anxiety about the DeathMatch. I'm not sure how many orders I wrote in the book. I didn't want to see. Either I had enough to make Mr D'Angelo want to invest in the Hoopie, or I hadn't. Either way, it all depended on how the DeathMatch itself went.

Brandi turned up at lunchtime and took me for a bite in the Fair Isle lounge bar. She ordered a 3-ply burger for me and a couple of bottles of mineral water for herself. I'd told Mum and Dad to come along just before 4pm. I wanted some time alone to prepare myself, mentally.

'Are you OK?' Brandi asked. 'You look terrible?'

'Thanks. I have a headache.'

Brandi reached into her bag and rummaged for a bit. 'I'm all out of pills,' she said.

'OK, well, don't worry,' I said. 'Maybe it's time I went cold turkey.'

'It's just paracetamol,' she reminded me.

'Canadian paracetamol,' I reminded her. 'That's how Lance Armstrong got started.'

'Well, I got to stop by the office anyway,' she said. 'I have some more there. I'll bring them back before the event. We can't have you competing with a headache.'

'So,' I said. 'You and Gavin, back on.'

She grinned sheepishly.

'How does that work?' I asked. 'It's just that you seemed so certain you never wanted to see him again.'

She shrugged. 'A girl can change her mind.'

'I suppose so,' I said.

'I was upset. I was angry with you. I rushed off and suddenly, there he was. All concerned and handsome and I kind of just found myself in his arms.'

'Are you doing this for the right reasons?' I asked. 'I'd hate to think my stupidity has pushed you back into an unhappy relationship.'

'Definitely not,' she said firmly. 'This is right. I should be thanking you.'

'All part of the service,' I said. How is it that I'm so good at solving other people's problems, even without trying, when I have so many unresolved problems of my own?

After lunch Brandi went to the loo. You can't drink two pints of mineral water without consequences. I took the opportunity to skype Ms Gunter.

'Christ, Ben,' she said. 'You look awful.'

I'd run out of excuses. It wasn't the screen, or jet lag, or GM food. I was putting on weight, I wasn't sleeping well, I was suffering from headaches. I'd been drinking alcohol, popping pills and hanging out with organised crime figures. Most of all, I was tired.

'I'm looking forward to coming home,' I said. 'I miss Hampton.'

'Are you OK? Are you going to cry.'

'No,' I retorted. 'I'm not going to cry.'

'Ben,' she said. 'Did I make a mistake, letting you go to New York?'

258

'No,' I said. 'I'm fine.'

'OK,' she said. 'You need to hold it together, OK? I can't have you going off the rails over there.'

'Don't worry,' I said. 'I can do this.'

I stumbled and stammered my way through a few more meetings, keeping an eye out for Brandi. But the fair was running down. Stands had started to empty, or else people were breaking out the Buck's Fizz and talking loudly about great deals. Someone set down a plastic cup of orange juice in front of me.

I looked up and was immensely relieved to see Mum.

'No Buck's Fizz for you,' she said. 'You need to be in peak physical condition.'

'I'm never touching alcohol again,' I said, sipping the OJ.

'Your father says that every Saturday morning,' she replied. 'You excited?'

'I'm dreading it.'

'Oh, Ben,' she said. 'It's just a bit of fun.'

'It's not, Mum,' I said. 'Nothing's just a bit of fun. The meeting with Priapia wasn't just a casual chat. The media interviews weren't just a bit of a laugh, this last week wasn't just a holiday in New York, my evening with Melanee wasn't just a quick drink and those pills aren't just paracetamol.'

'Actually, they *are* just paracetamol,' Mum said, reading the ingredients on the packet.

'You know what I mean,' I said.

'So don't do the DeathMatch,' she said.

'It's too late now,' I said. 'Everyone's counting on me. I can't let them down.'

'No,' she said. 'You don't like letting people down, do you?'

'No, I don't.'

'Just remember, Ben,' she said, 'you can only do what you can do. You can't take the world on your shoulders.'

'I seem to remember you telling me this once before,' I said.

'And I'll keep on telling you until you start listening to me,' she said. 'Now I'm going to go and find your father. He saw a bike shop just outside the venue and said he'd catch me up in five minutes. That was an hour ago.'

Brandi came bustling up. 'Hi, Mrs Fletcher,' she said, smiling brightly. As she sat, the BlackBerry alarm went off. I looked at the phone rattling on the table.

It was time. The KnitMaster 3000 was waiting. My nemesis. I stood.

Of course I was going to lose. The only thing I could do was try and minimise the damage. Try not to lose by so much. If I got pulverised then it would be all over. The media people would either laugh at me or, more probably, just ignore me altogether. That wouldn't be so bad but without any publicity, Mr D'Angelo from Priapia would drop me like a stone. Mr Hollis from Virilia would probably do the same. Mrs Tyler would tell me I'd let the school down. Brandi would get fired because of the negative publicity, Tony the Mob boss would cap me for giving his mistress a Hoopie with three dropped stitches. There'd be earthquakes, fire would rain from the skies and New York would be plagued with locusts.

Maybe I'm exaggerating a bit, but I'd certainly be going back to Hampton with my tail between my legs.

If, on the other hand, I could get an honourable defeat then things might be salvageable. What I didn't want was for the machine to finish in fifteen minutes while I was still on row three. Even for hardened knitting enthusiasts that wouldn't be much of a spectacle. That would be an embarrassment for everyone concerned. I had to maximise my own performance while trying to slow the machine down as much as I could. I knew how to do the latter, but was there a way of improving my own speed? I looked down at the Bloomingdale's bag and reached to pick it up. I pushed my hand down, through all the wool and needles right to the bottom, where my fingertips felt a cardboard box. I pulled it out and laid it on the table. The stolen needles. I watched the box. It watched me back. Then I looked at the other box. The paracetamol.

'You gonna take a couple?' Brandi asked, looking at her watch. 'The contest is *going* to start soon.'

'No,' I said, after a moment. 'I'm good. They mess with my head.'

Brandi picked up the stolen needles. 'Don't forget these.'

'They're not mine,' I said. 'Could you hang on to them? We need to return them to Bloomingdale's.'

'OK,' she said, slipping the long box into her handbag.

I didn't want drugs. I didn't want stolen needles. If I was going to do this, I was going to do it English-style.

I was going to lose fair and square.

And I marched off to do battle with a machine, armed with my cheap 10.5 acrylic needles. My head was throbbing, but I felt calm and relaxed for the first time in I don't know how long.

I could hear the buzz as I approached the KnitDome. The

261

organisers had been busy and had cleared out the demonstration ring at the centre of the hall. The ring was draped in a dome-shaped canopy made of thick strands of rope, woven to look like an oversize woolly hat. They'd erected temporary seating which was already full. People stood in the aisles between the stands jostling for a glimpse. I stopped and stood for a moment, taking deep breaths, preparing myself.

'This is brilliant,' Brandi said, hopping up and down next to me. Mum walked up and put a hand on my shoulder.

'Are you OK?' she asked. 'You don't have to do this.'

I smiled at her. 'I'm fine, Mum,' I said. 'I'm glad you're here.'

And then I stepped forward, slipped through the crowd and out into the dimmed KnitDome. As I walked out into plain view, a bank of overhead floodlights suddenly flicked on and a huge cheer rose up from the crowd. One of the spotlights shone right on a chair with a small table beside it. There was a box of wools of all different varieties. A sign over the box read, *Wool provided by the Idaho Yarn Company*.

My nemesis lurked at the far end. It was large and white, all smooth, straight lines and hidden joints. A team of white-coated technicians bobbed and weaved around it, adjusting this lever, polishing that knob. I saw Dr Kovac waiting to one side. He was watching me, a half-sneer on his face. As I approached he walked forward to meet me directly in the middle of the Dome.

'Ben,' he said.

'Dr Kevorkian,' I replied, unable to stop myself. He gave me a long look.

'Do you know, Ben,' he said eventually. 'At first I felt sorry for you. Some dumb kid from a backward country, no idea what he was up against. Standing in the way of advancement. A futile, misguided effort to stop the tide of progress.'

As he spoke he carried on smiling. A fake smile. He was such a phoney.

'But not any more,' he said, still smiling. 'We're going to humiliate you today. Smash you. And it's important we do, because people need to understand something about the clothes they wear and the fashions they follow. None of that is possible without one of those machines.' He stuck a thumb over his shoulder, indicating the 3000.

'Well, that's a nice speech,' I said. 'But I happen to think there are a lot of people out there who don't agree with you. People who understand the importance of individuality and creativity. People who aren't looking for quick and cheap, but are looking for quality garments, crafted with heart and . . .' I tapped my chest, '. . . love.'

'Well, let's just see how your English heart goes against the very latest US technology,' he said.

'Ladies and gentleman,' a familiar voice said over the PA. I turned to see Craig something from the radio. My heart sank.

'Welcome to . . . the KnitDome,' Craig went on. There was a huge round of applause and cheering. I squinted against the spotlights to see Mum and Dad, Gex, Trey and Keith in a row. They were standing and whooping. Behind them were the *Knitwits!* girls, then Tony and the man with the bulge. Tony waved. The man with the bulge looked bored. Standing in the aisle, with Gavin by her side, was Brandi, giving me the thumbs up. I even thought I saw Melanee in the shadows, standing well away from Brandi and clapping her hands over her head.

It felt good to know I had so much support.

'This afternoon. For one time only,' Craig cried. 'It's the ultimate yarn-based smackdown.'

More cheers. New Yorkers tend to make for very appreciative audiences.

'In the blue corner. We have the KnitMaster 3000. Designed and built by Dr Gregory Kovac of KnitCorp. It is the fastest, the newest, the smoothest knitting machine ever made. And it was designed and built right here in the United. States. Of. America!

The cheers turned to howls and hit the roof. That was a cheap trick, I thought. Playing the US-made card.

'And in the red corner,' Craig went on. He paused briefly. '. . . we have Ben from England'

Was that it? The crowd seemed to be wondering the same thing and seemed unsure as to whether they should cheer at this point. I heard Mum whooping and a smattering of applause but that was about it. Damn him! This whole thing was his fault.

'Ben,' Craig called. 'As the challenger, you have the right to choose what wool to use. Our wool tonight is kindly provided by the Idaho Yarn Company. Finest wools and yarns for home, shop and industry. So, Ben, take a look through the wools in the box there and tell us what's your choice?'

'I don't need to look,' I called back. 'I'd like a nice, chunky wool. A 4-ply alpaca. Untreated.'

Now this caused no small amount of consternation among the KnitCorp technicians and they began adjusting the machine's settings. Kevorkian glared at me.

I walked to my seat, pulling out my trusty old freebie needles.

An assistant brought me over a bagful of 4-ply and I thanked her.

'Good luck,' she whispered. 'I hope you win.'

'Ben will be knitting his own design. The . . . Hoopie. The KnitMaster 3000 will be knitting the latest design from Fabrice Gentile. The knitting will proceed for half an hour,' Craig said. 'Then there will be a short comfort break for Ben. The KnitMaster 3000 needs no rest of course and can operate non-stop 24/7 with minimal maintenance.'

I frowned at him. Did he have shares in the company or something? Things were set against me, that was for sure, but I felt OK. I had my support team behind me and I was ready. The assistants and technicians cleared the area. I looked across at the KnitMaster 3000, a blinking green light telling us it was ready. I took a deep breath. Despite the situation, despite the weight of expectation hanging over me, at that moment, I felt calm. I felt content. I felt ready. I realised my headache was gone. I hadn't needed the drugs. The free needles felt good in my hands. I hadn't needed the stolen Sprys.

'KnitMaster 3000. Ben Fletcher,' Craig said solemnly. 'You may begin knitting.'

The KnitMaster hummed into life and began vibrating gently. Before I'd even moved, the first row of its jumper began feeding out of the slot at its front.

I closed my eyes and visualised my Hoopie. I knew it so well this stage wasn't really necessary any more. But I wanted to be in the zone. Sherlock's Mind Palace. The semi-conscious state I needed to achieve in order to perform my superhuman needle speed.

It took a few seconds but then I was there. I began to knit.

I was fast. I was very fast. The wool was good quality. It flowed like liquid gold through my fingers. The needles felt comfortable, I kept the stitches loose, allowing me to complete rows quickly. I knew the KnitMaster's jumper was a far tighter weave, not really suited to such thick wool.

The background hum of the crowd and KnitFair USA faded away to white noise. I lost myself.

After fifteen minutes or so I allowed myself a quick glance up at the machine and was shocked to see how much of the jumper it had completed. I was already well behind. The crowd sat still, apparently engrossed. Watching me lose.

But at around twenty minutes the KnitMaster suddenly beeped harshly and a red light appeared on the console. The cluster of technicians sprang into action like a Formula 1 pit crew. I tried to ignore them and redoubled my efforts. This was my chance to catch up. I couldn't help but take a sideways glance at Kevorkian though. He looked furious. My wool choice had made his machine seem unreliable. I winked at him and carried on.

I was knitting smoothly, trying not to go too fast for fear of making mistakes. There was no point completing the garment quickly only to find it riddled with holes. Even with care, though, I dropped a couple of stitches.

I was dimly aware of the technicians getting the machine going again but I was almost totally immersed in the job. It seemed just an instant later that the buzzer sounded and the floodlights flicked on again. I looked up, dazed, realising this was the half-time break. I would have preferred to just carry on but I didn't have much choice. The crowd stood to stretch their legs, buzzing with excitement. The pit crew surrounded the KnitMaster, tinkering, cleaning out stray strands of wool. Brandi scuttled over to me, Gavin following.

'Ben,' she said, the pile of hair on her head backlit by the floodlights and wobbling a little. 'You were amazing.'

'Thanks,' I said. 'But the machine's well ahead of me, even with the breakdown.'

'You gotta keep going,' she said. 'Don't give up.'

I peered over her shoulder at Gavin, who stood there watching me back. Seizing his opportunity he leaned forward and stuck out a hand.

'Gavin Rogers,' he said, crushing my hand.

'Ben Fletcher,' I said.

'I like your design,' he said. 'You're a great knitter.'

'Thanks,' I said. He seemed really nice. Not quite the axe murderer I'd expected. Anyone who appreciates the simple beauty of the Hoopie must have his head on straight.

We walked over to a trestle table with drinks and biscuits and Brandi got a Hobnob for me out of her bag. Mum came over to offer her support. Then I noticed Fat Tony standing behind her.

'Hello, Tony,' I said.

'Hi, Ben,' he said. 'Can I have a word?'

'Sure,' I said, checking my watch.

We walked off to one side, the bulge man following a few paces behind. The fair was being packed up. The clanking of chairs being stacked was mingled with the popping of corks. It was all nearly over. Just another half an hour then I could go home, beaten, but having done my best.

'Ben,' he said. 'I know a couple of guys who work here at the Garden.'

'OK,' I said, wondering where this was heading.

He looked around. 'Guys who owe me, you know what I mean?'

'I think I can guess,' I said, remembering Keith's story about the man dangling from the window.

'Guys who know where things get plugged in,' he said.

Plugged in? I tried to translate this. Some kind of gangland slang? Tony must have noticed my confusion.

'I mean I know some people who have access to the electricity supply for that machine,' he said slowly. 'You understand what I'm saying?'

'Oh,' I said. 'Oh! You mean you could ask them to turn it off?'

'Now you've got it,' Tony said.

I did get it. I got what he was offering me. The chance to beat the evil Kevorkian. Imagine what would happen if I actually won today. Fame, publicity for the Hoopie. Financial security for me and my family. I'd return to England a hero, having conquered America. In fact, maybe I could stay here. Take that job with Priapia. Take the job with Fat Tony himself! Move my family to Long Island and drink highballs with Leo DiCaprio. Go see a Miley gig with Melanee Chang.

All I had to do was nod.

But what else? I'd be indebted to the Mob. I'd damage KnitCorp. And maybe Priapia. Kevorkian would survive, but think of all the orders that would be cancelled, all the jobs that would be lost. And I'd have to live with the fact that I'd cheated. No. I wouldn't take the paracetamol, I wouldn't use stolen needles, and I wouldn't call in a favour from the Secondi crime family.

I shook my head. 'I'm very grateful for the offer, Tony,' I said. 'And I'm tempted. But I want to play this fair and square.'

'You sure?'

I nodded.

'You know what you're turning down here?' he asked.

'I do.'

'Cos you're getting your ass handed to you in there, you know?'

'I know.'

Tony nodded. 'You're a good guy, Ben.'

'Thanks.'

'An idiot. But a good guy.'

'Well, thanks again.'

He pointed a fat finger at my chest. 'You got a talent. And you work hard. You're gonna be a success even if you don't win in there today.'

'Ben,' Brandi said, rushing up. 'It's time.'

I shook Tony by the hand.

'Kill 'em,' he said.

'I'll do my best,' I replied before walking back out onto the stage.

Craig called out my name again as I entered the KnitDome and this time the cheers went to the rafters. The crowd wasn't going to miss the opportunity this time. My spirits surged and the hackles on the back of my neck crackled with electricity. I ignored Kevorkian and the pit crew and sat, picking up my Hoopie and my needles.

I looked up into the stands to check everyone was there. Brandi and Gavin had moved up to sit with my parents, Gex, Keith and Trey. Alanna and Marie, Fat Tony and the bulge man sat in the bottom tier now. Tony gave me the thumbs up. Bulge man yawned, he reached into his jacket, to where the bulge was and pulled out . . .

. . . a Kindle. He began to read.

I smiled. I was ready.

'You may knit,' said Craig.

And boy, did I knit.

For the next half-hour I wasn't just in the zone, I was the President of the zone. They named the zone after me. I don't know if anyone filmed it, but I just knew I was even faster than I had been at the AUKKC. The needles were a blur, the wool a molten stream. I knew the Hoopie so well, had knitted so many before, I hardly even needed to visualise. Every stitch just sprang into place, as if pre-formed. I felt good, I felt strong, I felt relaxed.

I even found time for the occasional check on the machine. I was interested to see two technicians were hovering about it, picking out clogged-up bits of wool, trying to keep the machine going. Dr Kevorkian stood in the background like an evil overlord.

Like I said, I was fast. But I wasn't fast enough.

The machine disgorged the completed cardigan a good ten minutes before the hour was up. The KnitCorp boffins carried it over to a display table and laid it out triumphantly. I carried on knitting, I only had a few rows to go and I was determined to complete the Hoopie within the hour.

As the seconds ticked down, the crowd had gone quiet. I stood and carried the Hoopie over to the table to a moderate round of applause. I heard Mum give a lone whoop but it was all a bit of an anti-climax. It was a fine Hoopie. Not my best, but it was fine.

Suddenly I felt exhausted. It was over. The adrenalin drained from my system and I was left with the knowledge that I'd lost. That I'd let everyone down. That it was over between me and Megan. That the rise of the knitting machine was unstoppable.

Craig something was cock-a-hoop as he presented the big cheque to smug Kervorkian. I shook the hand of my nemesis but he didn't even look me in the eye.

I felt a little better as I came off stage though and my friends and family gathered around to clap me on the shoulder.

'They cheated,' Dad said. 'That ref needs a white stick.'

'You were amazing!' Melanee said, giving me a hug and a kiss which made me blush to my roots. I saw Brandi watching with pursed lips. 'This will be such a boost for the European style.'

'Please tell me you'll do another interview for *Knitwits!*,' Alanna said. 'You are an inspiration, Ben Fletcher.'

'Anytime you need a job, look me up,' Fat Tony said.

Mum just gave me a squeezy hug and that was best of all.

As we left the KnitDome, I saw a team of technicians stripping the KnitMaster 3000 and pulling out clumps of tangled yarn. They looked thoroughly miserable.

Maybe, in a way, I did win after all.

After leaving Madison Square Garden for the last time, we said goodbye to Alanna, Marie and Keith, who seemed to be getting on quite well with Marie. I watched them walk off down 33rd Street, Keith carrying Marie's sample bag while she talked at him animatedly about crocheted owl cushion covers. Some of us went to a restaurant on 32nd Street. Gavin knew the owner and we got a private room.

'Do they do Philly cheesesteak here?' I asked him.

'The best Philly cheesesteak in the country,' Gavin said.

I've noticed everything here has to be the best something in somewhere. 'These are the best highballs in Manhattan. That place does the best cheeseburgers in the Tri-State Area. This is the best loose-meat sandwich on the Atlantic Seaboard.'

'Well,' I replied. 'One more time can't hurt.'

Trey was there, Mum and Dad, Gex of course. Brandi and Gavin. Not Melanee. She'd slipped off straight after the contest with a smile and a wink. Fat Tony and Mr Kindle had also made their exits.

'You was bricking it in there,' Gex said.

'No I wasn't,' I replied. 'That was one of the only times in my life when I was feeling completely relaxed.'

'You looked like you was bricking it,' he said.

'Well, I wasn't!' I snapped. Trust him to ruin the moment.

'OK, OK,' he said. 'You know what?'

'What?'

He leaned in closer and whispered so as not to be overheard.

'I was proud. Like that you're my mate.'

Then he looked away and asked Gavin if he was allowed a beer. I was glad he had because at that moment I found I had something in my eye.

Then Brandi was there, giving me a huge hug. I hadn't had much of a chance to talk to her immediately after the DeathMatch.

'I'm so proud of you,' she said. 'I can't believe you're going home tomorrow.'

'I'm really going to miss you,' I said.

'You'll be back,' she said.

'Definitely,' I replied.

It was time to sit then as the waiter came around for our orders.

'Beer, Ben?' Gavin asked.

'No thanks. No alcohol for me,' I replied.

'Really? We're celebrating. What about a cocktail? They do good cocktails here.'

I hesitated. 'Actually,' I looked at the waiter. 'I don't suppose you do . . . tea?'

'Long Island iced tea?' the waiter asked.

'No. A nice cup of tea. English breakfast, ideally?'

He blinked. Then shrugged. 'Sure, no problem,' he said.

Trey came to sit next to me over dessert. Gex had needed to visit the 'can' as he's taken to calling it. 'So maybe she wasn't into you after all,' Trey said, nodding towards Brandi, who was all over Gavin.

'Of course she wasn't into me,' I said. 'She's gorgeous. Out of my league.'

'What about your girlfriend back home,' he said. 'Ain't she gorgeous?'

'Yes, but . . .'

273

'Yeah but what?'

'Megan's not into me either,' I said. I filled him in on the incident with the BlackBerry and Brandi's knickers.

He laughed for a long time.

'I'm glad the end of my relationship is amusing you,' I said.

'If I were you,' he said, wiping away a tear. 'I would stop assuming I know what girls think. They like to keep you guessing.'

I watched Brandi laugh at something Gavin had said. She touched him on the arm. Trey was right. Girls were hard to read. But some were worse than others. Maybe I didn't always know why Megan did what she did, or said what she said. But I had a suspicion that had less to do with her being contradictory and more to do with me being a total idiot. If only I'd realised how lucky I was to have someone like Megan. Now I'd gone and messed it up.

Gex came back from the loo, walking gingerly.

'I need to get back to Hampton, innit?' he said. 'The food here don't agree with me.'

'Eat some vegetables!' I said, exasperated.

'No chance,' he said.

After the meal, we walked slowly back to the hotel. Brandi and Gavin fell into step on either side of me.

'So what are your plans, Ben?' Gavin asked. 'What's next?'

I shrugged. 'I'll go home. I'll take my AS exams. I'll knit scarves, I'll knit Hoopies.'

'But what about what Mr D'Angelo said?' Brandi asked. 'What about your business plan?'

'No point having a business plan without investment,' I said.

'You need to think big,' Brandi said.

'Brandi,' I said. 'Were you not there today? I lost. The machine won.'

'So what?'

'So Mr D'Angelo doesn't want the Hoopie now. No one wants the Hoopie.'

'I want the Hoopie,' Gavin said.

'You want the Hoopie?' Brandi asked.

'I want the Hoopie.'

I peered at him in the bright street lights. Jolly taxis whizzed by a few metres away. Gavin seemed perfectly serious.

'I'll buy the Hoopie,' he said. 'Give you some start-up cash. You can get some machines, start a production line.'

'And what cut would you take?' I asked, the *Dragon's Den* having rubbed off on me a little, it seemed.

'Fifty per cent of profits,' he said.

'Net or gross?'

'Net.'

I stood and thought this over. Is this what I wanted? Is this what I'd been fighting for? Handed to me on a plate.

'Think it over,' Gavin said. And we kept on walking.

10.42pm

I stood in the doorway of the hotel room, staring, trying to comprehend what this thing was that had appeared in my room.

'Come on, Ben,' Gex said, pushing past me. 'What's the hold-up? I'm touching cloth.'

I let him in and he rushed into the bathroom, ignoring the

alien object that had somehow transported itself into our hotel room. On the outside, it looked very much like a suitcase. One with two wheels and an extendible handle. I used to have a suitcase just like it, I thought to myself. Aeons ago. Before a warp portal had opened up at Heathrow Terminal 5, and sucked it into another dimension, never to return.

And yet here it was. Or more likely an alien shape-shifter which had taken on its form. The chances of BA having found the actual suitcase and brought it here to my hotel room were too remote to be seriously considered.

I approached the being.

'Do you speak English?' I asked it.

It didn't respond, so I slung it on the bed and opened it.

My clothes! My Stiletto! My knitting!

Throwing caution to the wind, I took out the half-finished Hampton FC scarf and fondled the weave affectionately. My phone was low on battery but turned on OK. I had a few messages, and a text from Freddie saying Mr McGavin and his dad both wanted a Hampton FC scarf just like Dad's. There was a text from Megan too, sent before I'd destroyed her family.

Just to let you know that I'll be thinking of you every day. And every night. I wish things had been different. I would have loved to have eaten Oreos with you up the Eiffel tower and drunk thunderballs in St Peter's Square and seen a drag show on the Sunset Strip and all the other things you wanted to do. Can we do it next time? That's if you'll still want me to by then. You'll probably meet some gorgeous American blonde and never come

*back. P.S. Sorry for all the dumb jokes. It's just my way
of coping. Me xx*

I'm such a bellend.

Monday 20ᵗʰ May

6.56am
We went to Dino's for one last stack of waffles the next
morning. Gex was very unhappy about being awake so early.
Trey and Brandi were coming around at 7.30 to collect us in
a big car to take us to the airport.

'So are you going to take the money?' Mum asked.

'That's the smart thing to do, I suppose,' I said.

'But?'

'What makes you think there's a but?'

'I can hear it in your voice.'

'The but is this,' I began. 'I hadn't meant to get into this Boy
vs Machine DeathMatch. It wasn't my idea. But all that stuff
I said about wanting to reclaim knitting. You know, reclaim
hand-made and take back knitting from the machines? It all
made real sense to me. I actually do believe that.'

'You feel you'd be a hypocrite to go and buy a knitting
machine now?'

'It's more than that,' I said. 'I don't want the Hoopie to be
knitted by a machine. I want it to be knitted by hand.'

'You like the imperfections.'

'I like imperfections,' I agreed. 'I like flaws.'

I thought of Jessica Swallow's wonky teeth, compared to Brandi's magnificent dental showpiece. I thought of Hampton FC trudging around a muddy pitch, compared to the glamorous professionalism of the Mets. I thought of dusty old Pullinger's on the high street, compared to the retail heaven that is Bloomingdale's.

'I love it here, Mum,' I said. 'Don't get me wrong. But it's time to go home.'

We met up with Trey, Brandi and Gavin in the lobby of the hotel. While Gex and Dad went up to get the bags and Mum chatted to Brandi and Gavin, Trey came over to talk to me.

'It's been good to know you, Ben,' Trey said. 'I had a lot of fun.'

'Me too,' I said. And the thing was, despite everything, I meant it. It had been an amazing week.

'Could I have a word, Ben?' Gavin asked, coming over. We retired to a quiet couch.

'Have you thought any more about my offer?' he asked. 'I'm totally serious.'

'The thing is –' I began.

'Sell me the US rights to the Hoopie,' Gavin cut in. 'I can't pay as much upfront, but you'll still get a cut.'

'Go on,' I said.

'Here's the deal,' Gavin said. 'I'll give you a thousand dollars, in cash right now, for the US rights to the Hoopie design. If it goes into production. If we can firm up those orders you got. If we can make a profit, then you get five per cent of that.'

'Gross profit, or net profit?'

'Net, of course.'

'Ten per cent,' I said.

'Deal,' he said, holding out his hand.

'Ah,' I said to Jasmine as I checked out. 'I thought the extra charges were being picked up by the Knitting Guild Association of America.' The others were stuffing themselves and our luggage into Trey's car out in front of the hotel.

'I don't think so, Ben,' she said apologetically.

'And how much are they?'

'The minibar bill comes to $492.65 including deep-cleaning the fridge. The room-service tab is $389.25.'

That only left me $118.10. I'd gone overdrawn by $95.00 at Bloomingdale's on Saturday rescuing Gex, so only had $23.10 left.

I sighed and counted out the notes. It had been nice for the twelve seconds it had lasted. Jasmine gave me the change and I jingled the thin coins in my hand.

'Come on, Ben,' Mum shouted from the kerb. 'All the bulkheads will be gone.'

I said goodbye to Jasmine for the last time and walked out of the hotel.

'Want some ADVICE?'

'Hello,' I said, holding my breath. I regarded my homeless guy, clutching his cup. A knitted rabbit poked out of his filthy coat pocket. 'Tell you what,' I said. 'I'll give you some money. But I don't want any advice.'

'You don't?'

'No. Instead. I want to give *you* some advice.'

'OK,' he said agreeably, rattling the cup at me.

I dropped the coins into the cup, then after a moment's hesitation, I stuffed the notes in too.

'What's the advice?' the man asked, his eyes lighting up.

'Please have a bath,' I said.

He stared at me in puzzlement.

'Take a *goddam bath*,' I said in my best New York accent. 'You stink worse than a Costa Rican love toad.'

I left him sniffing his armpits and got into the car. Maybe I was a little bit New York after all.

Got a text from Joz on the way to the airport.

> *Electricity fixed! Mr McGavin came around to sort it.*
> *Thanks Ben!*

Oh well, at least I'd accomplished one thing on this trip. It did mean I had to knit a scarf on the flight back home.

3.12pm – Somewhere over the Atlantic

Mum's asleep. We just had an interesting conversation.

At JFK I told her that she should sit with Dad up in Executive Club. I was relieved they seemed to have got through the Diablo issue.

'No, I'm OK,' she said. 'I'm happy to sit with you. If you don't mind?'

'No, I don't mind,' I said. I'd had enough of Gex for a while. 'I'm surprised though,' I said. 'I thought you and Dad were having a second honeymoon. There was certainly a lot of . . . innuendo.'

'Oh, don't get me wrong, Ben,' she said. 'I had a lovely time. It's just your father . . .'

'Yes?'

'Well, I think perhaps he was trying a little hard?'

'He was a little jealous of Diablo?'

'He was,' she said. 'And he overcompensated. Flowers, dancing, romantic meals. Frankly, I'm looking forward to getting away from him for a few hours.'

7.43pm – Hampton

OK. There have been events.

As the plane taxied to the landing gate, I turned on the Stiletto and checked my messages wondering if Megan might have sent something welcoming me back home. OK, so it wasn't very likely, and I wasn't surprised to see I had no texts apart from one from Freddie asking me if he could copy my geography homework. He seemed to have forgotten I'd been in America. I checked my emails. Nothing. But just as I went to turn off the phone in disgust, I saw a little red phone on the Skype logo. A missed call.

I opened Skype. Had Megan tried to get in contact? The plane had now reached the terminal and I heard the *clunk-hiss* of the doors being opened.

But no. It wasn't Megan. It was Mrs Frensham, of all people.

Mrs Frensham had tried to skype me? I clicked on the call button as people started to shuffle past. Mum reached up to get her bag out of the overhead locker. Mrs Frensham's phone rang, and rang, and rang.

'Come on Ben,' Mum said. 'I want to get home.'

'Sorry,' I said, turning the phone to silent. 'Let's go.'

But in the queue for passport control I felt the phone vibrate. I whipped it out. There, on the wide screen, in digital immensity, was Mrs Frensham.

Suddenly her face loomed as she brought the phone to her mouth, giving me an excellent view of her gold fillings.

'Hello? Hello?' she said, deafening me. 'I want to speak to Ben!'

'Hello, Mrs Frensham,' I said. 'Pull back a bit, I can see your lunch.'

'Sorry.'

'That's better,' I said as she sat back. 'I can't believe you've worked out how to use Skype.'

'It's an emergency,' she said. 'Lottie's dying.'

'Megan's gran?' I asked after a pause. 'Is she genuinely dying?'

Mum and I exchanged a quick look.

Mrs Frensham nodded. 'Yes, she is. She's in St Andrew's Respite home. I went and visited today.'

'Oh, I hadn't realised it was that serious,' I said.

'Megan's very upset,' Mrs Frensham went on. 'She was close to Lottie.'

'Right.'

'I thought you'd want to know,' Mrs Frensham said.

'Thank you,' I said. A man behind me in the queue coughed meaningfully and I realised the family in front had moved on. I shuffled forward.

282

'She's been getting worse over the last couple of weeks,' Mrs Frensham said.

'Megan didn't tell me,' I said. No wonder the Hoopers were so cross I'd told Marcus that his gran was in hospital.

'She didn't want to spoil your trip,' Mrs Frensham said. 'She's always been thoughtful, that girl.'

I am such a complete idiot. While poor Megan had been sitting by her gran's bedside, worried sick, I'd been flirting with waitresses and PR girls in New York, accusing her of being unfaithful. No wonder she was cross with me. No wonder she'd spent time with Sean. No wonder she'd forgotten to draw her curtains properly.

'What should I do?' I asked Mrs Frensham desperately.

She shook her head at my idiocy.

'You could start with some flowers,' she said simply.

'Yes,' I said, 'flowers. Of course.'

Then I had to hang up because we were at passport control. The bearded immigration officer waved us through and Mum and I rushed down the corridor to the baggage collection area. Dad and Gex were standing there, looking glum.

'That's the problem with Executive Club,' Mum said. 'You might get off the plane quicker, but that just means you have even longer to wait for your bags.'

I looked up at the monitor anxiously. Our carousel hadn't been identified yet.

'Don't wait,' Mum said, resting a hand on my arm. 'We'll bring your bags back.'

'Really?' I asked.

'Yeah,' she said, smiling. 'Go and see Megan.'

It took me a little over an hour to get to the respite home. I was lucky with the coach and the train from Woking. I stopped at Sainsbury's for the flowers because it was on the way and because the security guard always follows me very closely when I go into Waitrose these days. A nice lady at the respite home reception told me which way to go. I stood and took a deep breath, trying to calm my anxiety. Sometimes I wish I was asthmatic. It would be nice to have an inhaler to suck on in times like this. Maybe I need a Canadian inhaler.

I pushed open the door and went into a small waiting room. Mrs Hooper was in there talking to a man I didn't know. He turned and I took a sharp breath as I saw he wore a dog collar. *The priest!*

'Calm down, Ben,' Mrs Hooper said, reading my mind. 'You're not too late.'

'I'm sorry I . . . I mean, well, I'm sorry that . . . oh, you know what? I'm just sorry,' I said.

She nodded. 'It's OK, you can go through. Megan's in there with her.'

'Are you sure?' I asked, suddenly even more anxious. I'd never seen someone dying before. Mrs Hooper raised an eyebrow and I reminded myself I wasn't there for myself, or even for Megan. I was there to bring flowers to someone who was very ill.

I pushed open the door and went in. The first person I saw was Megan, who was sitting in an armchair by the bed, reading a book. She looked tired, her hair a little flat and tied roughly back. She was beautiful. Megan looked up as I came in. Very briefly she smiled but then just as quickly fixed her expression into one of tight-lipped disapproval. But it had definitely been there. A little flash of happiness that made me think I'd made the right call in rushing here. Despite everything, she was pleased to see me.

Her gran lay in the bed under a chintz cover. Tiny and grey, she slept. Flowers and cards occupied every available space. I looked around for somewhere to put my flowers. I knocked a vase over and had to snatch at it to stop it smashing on the floor. In doing so, I knocked about thirty *Thinking-of-You* cards over. I dropped my flowers as I tried to pick the cards up. Megan watched me, clearly exasperated at my ineptitude.

Eventually she told me to stand to one side while she sorted everything out.

'Sorry,' I said.

'What for?'

'For not being here.'

'You had your thing,' she sighed.

'This was more important.'

She turned to me, looking me in the eye properly.

'No, Ben,' she said. 'I understand how important knitting is to you. And of course you had to go to New York. Don't feel sorry about that.'

'But I should feel sorry about everything else.'

'Yes,' she said. Lottie stirred and Megan moved to straighten the pillows.

'Well, I am sorry,' I said. 'I should have trusted you.'

'Yes.'

'I should have understood why you couldn't come.'

'Yes.'

I just managed to catch myself before saying, 'I shouldn't have twerked with Melanee.'

She smiled at me. 'How was the Empire State Building?'

'I didn't quite make it,' I admitted.

'You went to New York and didn't see the Empire State Building?'

'Well, I *saw* it. Just from a distance. I *did* see a crocheting monkey.'

Lottie stirred again. And Megan put a hand on the old lady's forehead.

'Well, I suppose I should go,' I said. 'I just came to bring the flowers . . .'

Megan turned back to face me. It was a bit cramped in there.

'If you think that's best,' she said. She really was beautiful. She didn't need mounds of hair. She didn't need expensive teeth.

There was quite a long pause. The only sound was the ticking of an old clock on the window ledge.

'I . . .' I said, trailing off.

'You . . . ?'

There was another long pause, finally broken by a voice from the bed.

'Kiss her, Simon,' Lottie said. I looked over to see that Lottie was sitting up in bed and peering at us expectantly.

'Yeah, go on,' Megan said. 'Kiss me, Simon.'

So I did.

T. S. Easton

T. S. Easton is an experienced author of fiction for all ages and has had more than a dozen books published. He has written under a number of different pseudonyms in a variety of genres. Subjects include vampires, pirates, pandemics and teenage agony aunts (not all in the same book). He lives in Surrey with his wife and three children and in his spare time works as a Production Manager for Hachette Children's Books. **BOYS DON'T KNIT** was his first novel for Hot Key Books, and you can find out more about him at www.tomeaston.co.uk or on Twitter: @TomEaston

Thank you for choosing a Hot Key book.

If you want to know more about our authors
and what we publish, you can find us online.

You can start at our website

www.hotkeybooks.com

And you can also find us on:

We hope to see you soon!